FRANCES

THE FLEDG

FRANCES FAVIELL (1905-1959) was the pen name of Olivia Faviell Lucas, painter and author. She studied at the Slade School of Art in London under the aegis of Leon Underwood. In 1930 she married a Hungarian academic and travelled with him to India where she lived for some time at the ashram of Rabindranath Tagore, and visiting Nagaland. She then lived in Japan and China until having to flee from Shanghai during the Japanese invasion. She met her second husband Richard Parker in 1939 and married him in 1940.

She became a Red Cross volunteer in Chelsea during the Phoney War. Due to its proximity to the Royal Hospital and major bridges over the Thames Chelsea was one of the most heavily bombed areas of London. She and other members of the Chelsea artists' community were often in the heart of the action, witnessing or involved in fascinating and horrific events throughout the Blitz. Her experiences of the time were later recounted in the memoir *A Chelsea Concerto* (1959).

After the war, in 1946, she went with her son, John, to Berlin where Richard had been posted as a senior civil servant in the post-war British Administration (the CCG). It was here that she befriended the Altmann Family, which prompted her first book *The Dancing Bear* (1954), a memoir of the Occupation seen through the eyes of both occupier and occupied. She later wrote three novels, *A House on the Rhine* (1955), *Thalia* (1957), and *The Fledgeling* (1958). These are now all available as Furrowed Middlebrow books.

BY FRANCES FAVIELL

FRANCES FAVIELL

THE FLEDGELING

With an Afterword
by John Parker

DEAN STREET PRESS
A Furrowed Middlebrow Book

A Furrowed Middlebrow Book
FM8

Published by Dean Street Press 2016

Cover by DSP
Cover illustration: detail from *Wet Afternoon* (1928) by
Eric Ravilious

First published in 1958 by Cassell & Co. Ltd.

ISBN 978 1 911413 85 1

www.deanstreetpress.co.uk

FOR
HENRY MAXWELL

There grows
No herb of help to heal a coward heart.

from *Bothwell*, Act II, A.C. SWINBURNE

CHAPTER I

'Now', URGED MIKE, 'now. Make your way in that direction, where I'm pointing . . . you'll strike the bleeding road about two miles on . . . you'll easily get a lift to Doncaster and from there you can get others on. Quick! while there's none of the other blighters in sight. Go on! I'll be seeing you. . . .'

The sun blazed down on the shelterless moors, where they had been dropped from army lorries to find their way back to camp as a map-reading exercise. The lad whom Mike was addressing was slight, very fair, and delicate in appearance. His khaki uniform was too large for his shoulders and his fair almost girlish complexion was mottled now with the heat.

'No, Mike, I'm too bloody scared. If they come back this way I'll be spotted. They're always on the look-out for me—they've confiscated my civvies. It's not safe to try it in uniform—it's too risky.'

'Don't tell me what I know already, you yellow bastard! You'll be O.K.—if you do as I say. Get off now. Don't hurry—walk at a steady pace as if you're making for a given point. You're trying to make your way back by the route allotted to our group. *Go on now.* Don't waste time. Get going . . . you miserable little runt. I'll cover for you—and I'll answer for you like I said.'

He stood over the younger lad with an attitude so menacing that the mottled red patches on the boy's hot skin began paling with fear.

'Go on!' urged Mike. 'Everyone knows you're incapable of reading a map or using a compass. I'll fix it for you . . . I've done it before. You get going now and you do what I said. Understand? *Get everything okey doke before I turn up. Don't you let me down.* I'm taking the bleeding risks for you . . . Ninny . . . blast you!'

The boy thus addressed, swallowed, and drew a breath before he answered. Then his words came out with a desperate rush, as if he had forced himself to utter them. 'I don't want to go, Mike. I'll make some blunder. I haven't got the nerve.'

'You don't need any bloody nerve for this. An idiot could get away now. They're all walking about with their bleeding little noses turned towards our home-from-home camp. No other thought in their little minds—but to get back quick and report safely to our Mummy sergeant.'

'I don't want to do it,' repeated the lad wretchedly.

'Listen, Ninny! You're going—and quick. *If you don't you know what'll happen to you.* Now—bugger off—and keep your nose towards your old grandmother and that Tarzan with the lorry . . . Understand?' He gave his reluctant companion a shove in the direction he had indicated. 'Go *on*. There's not a soul in sight. I'll catch up with the other buggers—they're over there by those bushes. . . .'

'Suppose they ask where I am?'

'Oh use your head, you clot. What d'you think I'll say? Ninny's run home to grandma? I'll manage to put 'em off—like I always do. *You get going!*'

The youth whom he called 'Ninny' and whose name was Neil Collins took a last desperate look round, then turned an imploring one on Mike Andersen whose dark eyes, smiling but at the same time threatening, had never left his face.

'All right,' he mumbled, 'I'll do it.'

'You'll not only do it—*you'll do it as I told you. Remember?* Now scarper!'

The boy mumbled something, and turning, began walking in the direction indicated by Mike. He was hot and terrified at what he was about to do. Resentment and anger boiled in him at Mike's power over him. He despised himself for obeying, for falling in through craven fear with this man's plans for his escape. That Mike, who had no home, was using him as a means of effecting his own escape he was perfectly well aware. He had found out long ago that Mike had only cultivated his friendship for that purpose.

Neil had a bad reputation in the draft. He had already twice deserted and served sentences for it. Mike had soon ascertained that Neil had a home in London to which he had on both occasions gone for refuge. He had extracted every detail about the Collins' household from Neil. He knew it as well as if he had been there. He had soon decided that the younger lad should make a fresh attempt at escape—and this time with his help he would not be sent back—they would both get safely away to Ireland where Neil had an old aunt.

The opportunity had come sooner than he had expected. A month ago Neil's elder brother had been killed in Cyprus, and there had been a lot of publicity about it. He had been doing his National Service as he and Neil were now doing theirs, and he had been shot in the back by a guerilla rebel while trying to lift his already badly wounded officer on to his shoulders to carry him to safety. In spite of the shot he had managed to drag the officer—covering him with his own body—to safety before he himself had died.

Mike had urged Neil to ask for compassionate leave, although the lad himself knew that it would be refused him. When it was refused, Mike had worked steadily on the injustice of the whole thing, trying to fan the spark of resentment still burning in the young brother even after two heavy sentences for absence without leave. It had been hard work, for Neil had apparently given his word to his old grandmother to stick his service out to the end without any more desertions. The brother's death—'murder' Mike had called it—had come as a boon. He had not hesitated to use it as a whipping stone for every supposed injustice and every bit of trouble in the camp. He had persuaded Neil to fall in with his plans by sheer persistence and by methods peculiar to his own unpleasant nature. He had established a hold over this weakling which delighted the sadistic side of his character. Lately, he had begun to suspect that others in the camp were noticing it. In fact he had been tackled on the subject by several men whom he described as the 'classy' lot who would soon leave to become officers because of their previous training in their public schools' cadet corps. He had put them off—he was an adept at lying and at wriggling out of every duty and chore; but because he was amusing and could make the sergeant laugh—often at another chap's expense—he was not unpopular. When he had taken up with young Collins the friendship had not gone unnoticed. Mike Andersen was tough—he could knock most people out in a fight—he was afraid of no one—or so it seemed, certainly not of Authority which he regarded as something to be pitied and made fun of but not openly defied.

He watched Neil walking slowly away across the rough heather-covered moor towards the road. 'Make for the telegraph wires!' he shouted after him. Ninny was such a fool that he was quite capable of missing the road and ending up lost on the moor. And yet—he had twice gone off on his own. He must have some guts. Lately he had been displeased to find that Ninny was becoming more obstreperous and he had been forced to use more unpleasant methods to induce obedience. When he was quite sure that the rapidly decreasing stature of Neil's figure meant that the boy was a sufficient distance away, he turned and began hurrying after the other two fellows in their group.

Neil trudged on dispiritedly. He had no heart in what he was doing. He turned over in his mind the possibility of changing his mind and returning to the camp. It wouldn't matter how late he arrived there—they would put that down to his general incompetence. He didn't know how many miles away the camp was. They had all been driven for what seemed a long time in lorries and dropped in separate groups at various desolate spots. He turned round to look at Mike Andersen, but he had disappeared. Far away he could see two groups of khaki-clad figures making their separate ways across the huge expanse of moor, but Mike and the other two belonging to his group had vanished.

He could see what looked like telegraph wires now . . . about a mile ahead. The heat-wave was marked every morning by a thick haze over the moor, and it was difficult to see. He made for the direction which Mike had indicated would bring him on to the main road. He thought that the main road would be dangerous, but Mike had urged him not to be so dumb. If he were seen, all he had to say was that somehow he had got lost during the exercise and that he had been trying to make his own way back to camp. And this was exactly what he was now turning over in his mind. Should he do that? Should he wander about for a time, then get on to the main road and ask for a lift back to the camp from some passing car or lorry? He sat down on a clump of heather to think it out. If only he dared! He did not want to go through with this thing. He had suffered enough in the glass-house. Another desertion would mean, if he were caught—and he had no confidence that he would get away—a whole year's sentence in a civil jail.

Mike had enlarged on the injustice of that, too. Several fellows from their draft were serving sentences now in civil jails. Mike had pointed out that in a country supposed to be famed for its freedom and which invited and received refugees from countries which did not enjoy this privilege, it was a scandal that lads should be thrown into prison with common criminals merely because they had run away from conscription. None of this was new to Neil, whose father had been in the habit of enlarging upon the same subject to his family on the somewhat rare occasions when he visited them. He had enjoined both his sons to refuse to do their National Service—or to leave the country so that they would not be called up. As he had offered no help, either financial or otherwise, to either of them in achieving this, they had taken no notice of his long involved speeches.

Neil, sitting now, a lone small figure in that vast landscape, could not bring himself to go on or to turn back. He simply could not make a decision. He wanted it made for him—and there was no one there to make it. The vision of Mike, and the influence of those strange dark eyes was still strongly with him, and in spite of the heat he shivered. He was terrified of Mike. He knew that now. At first he had liked him, admired him for the ease with which he got out of every difficulty and got over every obstacle. That he did so at the expense of other men did not dawn on Neil for some time, neither did the reason for Mike's friendship with him. When it did, it was too late—he was already too deeply in the older lad's toils.

Should he go on towards the road and get a lift to Doncaster? Or should he sleep a bit in the sun and then make his way back to camp making some excuse for having got separated from the others? What would Mike do if he did this? The prospect was too frightening . . . some of the things which Mike could force him to endure were still vivid in his mind. He remembered the day when he had first discovered that Mike was only making use of him. It had been during a pause in an exercise. The troops had all been lying or sitting about on just such a piece of moor as this. He and Mike had been a little apart from the others near them. It was then that Mike had first put to him the plan for both of them to get away to Ireland. It had been so audacious that Neil had refused immediately. Mike had said nothing at first, but later in the day, during another pause, he had said quietly. 'You just listen to me. You've seen for yourself that I can make people do what I want them to do. Haven't you? Well, how will you like it if I use my power—call it what you will. Suppose I were to use it to encourage the chaps to ridicule you even more than they do now? I *could* you know.'

Neil had been aghast at the vision which this threat conjured up; he stared unbelievingly at Mike. This was his one and only friend. The one person who had stood up for him, fought for him, and in a thousand unobtrusive small ways smoothed his thorny path at the camp and made it easier for him to endure. The very thought of Mike joining the ranks of those whose delight it was to make his life there unbearable was an unthinkable nightmare.

'You're joking, Mike,' he had said feebly. But the tightly-closed lips and the now hard, unsmiling eyes of a new Mike denied anything in the nature of a joke. Mike meant what he said.

It was from that day that he knew suddenly that he was afraid of Mike Andersen—more afraid of him than of any of the petty daily miseries which his so-called friend helped him to endure. 'I don't want to quit again,' he had said stubbornly. 'I did fifty-six days at Colchester the first time. The C.O. talked to me. He made me see how stupid it was. I had to opt whether I'd do the fifty-six days he gave me or go up for court martial. He was decent about it.'

'Why did you do it again then?'

Neil had been silent for some time, and then at last he had said, 'Nona, my twin, was getting married. I was mad. I can't stand the fellow she's married.'

'You got a hundred and twelve days for that?'

'Yes.'

Mike had looked curiously at him. 'Catch me doing a stretch like that—I'd take damned good care they didn't get me.'

'My grandmother gave me away to the police,' said Neil.

'I'd have killed her for it, Old Judas!'

'She has strict ideas on duty and keeping the law and all that.'

'You're a fool, Ninny!'

Neil's heart had sunk. It was the first time that Mike had used the name by which he was generally known to his tormentors. 'The old girl's almost dead, isn't she? And your brother's dead and buried. And for what? A bloody medal which the family can hang up in a case? You know we're due to get shipped to Malaya, don't you? D'you want to get stuck out there? It'll be quite another matter getting away from that dump.'

'I'd like to see Malaya,' Neil had said, obstinately. 'Only I may not go. I've got a bad record here.'

'You're just the sort they send there. Get rid of all the rubbish quickly. Got to have some cannon fodder—time hasn't come yet for guided missiles only. Look at your brother— killed the first few weeks, wasn't he?'

'Yes.'

'Well you don't want to bleed your bloomin' guts out in the bloody jungle, do you?'

'No.'

'Well, then. You listen to me.'

'It's no good, Mike. I don't want to desert again.'

'Not *want*? Not *want*? Who said so? I've got plans for us both my dear Ninny—and they include you. In fact you're indispensable to their success.'

Mike had said no more but he had got to work in various ways, and soon Neil's life became a nightmare. He shivered now as he lay there on the dry heather even at the remembrance of it. Even now, had it not been for this terrible fear of

Mike he would have gone back. He might get some punishment for getting separated from the others—that was all. But it was the thought of what Mike would do to him should he dare turn up again at the camp which prevented him from turning round and going back. Suppose he went to the C.O. and told him about Mike? He had contemplated this on several occasions. But the thought of what would happen to him afterwards if his tormentors and Mike became aware of his treachery had made him desist.

No, there was nothing to be done—but to desert. But he was not going to desert with Mike. A future with him was unthinkable. He would get to London and Nonie would help him to double-cross Mike somehow. She *must*. Len was gone—buried in Cyprus—Nonie would have to help him now. She could influence their grandmother. The old woman was rapidly becoming more and more helpless and was almost bedridden now. She depended on her granddaughter entirely. Nonie would have to persuade her. His decision made, he got up and started walking rapidly in the direction of the telegraph poles. It was surprisingly hot and his battle-dress was horribly thick and irritating to his sensitive skin. He took off the jacket and walked in his shirt. It was further than he thought and he was thirsty and tired. Walking on the clumps of heather and scrub was not easy. At last he reached the road and sat down on the edge to mop his face and neck.

The road stretched winding and treeless like a steel-blue ribbon away among the moors. There was nothing on it at all. It was early afternoon—the time when the long-distance drivers take their afternoon snooze until it is cooler. Neil sat down and looked in each direction. Nothing to be seen. He didn't know in which direction was the camp and which Doncaster. Maps were puzzles to him, and although he had been shown several times how to read one he seldom seemed able to concentrate.

A car was approaching now . . . he stood up and hailed it. It shot past, the driver not even turning his head in the direction of the would-be traveller. After a long wait another car appeared. It scarcely slowed down, as the driver put his head out and shouted, 'Where d'you want to go?' When Neil shouted, 'Doncaster,' the man jerked his thumb in the direction from which he had come. Neil crossed to the opposite side of the road. Nothing was in sight. He was aware that he was shivering again although it was hot. He put his jacket on again after looking all over the horizon to see if there were any signs of his fellow men or of the army lorries which would presently come hunting up the stragglers. Nothing . . . the moor was as empty as the road.

Mike had said that it was easy to get a lift. Maybe it was for Mike. Neil had come to recognise that for himself nothing was easy—because he was in constant fear. If Mike had been here with him he'd have made that motorist stop, turn round, and drive him back the way he had come, to Doncaster. Mike was like that. He scanned the long empty road again. Should he start walking along it? He had better—surely he must be too near the camp here for safety should any of the army lorries come along. He began walking slowly and wretchedly along the road. He had gone about a mile before the van caught up with him and slowed down. A red-faced cheerful man leaned down from the driving seat. 'You're going in the wrong direction for the camp, son,' he said. 'I want to get to Doncaster,' said Neil.

The man's eyes narrowed. He whistled. 'Not on the exercise then?'

'No.'

'Want to get to Doncaster station?'

'Yes.'

'Hop up, then.'

Now this was a contingency Mike had not advised him on. Did one ride outside in the cab with the driver—or did one ask to get in behind under cover? Surely it would be asking for trouble to flaunt his uniform in the driver's cab; but to ask to get under cover might also arouse suspicion.

'Better get in back there,' said the man, pointing to the canvas covering on the lorry. 'You can sleep a bit. There's plenty of sheeting there with the furniture—and some cushions.' 'Thanks, thanks . . .' muttered Neil so gratefully that the man knew his suspicions to be correct. This lad had no travel warrant in his pocket—of that he was certain. His look of relief when he had suggested that he get under cover was sufficient answer to his doubts. The kid was on the run. What should he do?

'Going on leave?' he asked carefully.

'Yes. Unexpectedly. That's why I've got to get a lift to Doncaster.'

'Get in, then. We'll be stopping on the way for a cuppa—that's the only stop. Should make it between five and six. Got far to go from there?'

'London.'

'I may be able to put you on to someone going that way. We'll see. Get in, mate.'

He noticed the delicate flushed face, the almost white blonde hair and the narrow shoulders. Poor little devil . . . I know what it was like back in '43, he thought. Lots of 'em aren't cut out for it—and nor's this one by the look of him. He felt no compunction about helping the lad. It wouldn't be the first time. The kid hadn't asked for a lift. He'd been trudging along the dusty road when he'd overtaken him. The driver's sympathies lay with those who wanted to be free of military service. Let those who wanted war form the bloody army themselves. He hoped his sons would never have to go through what he'd gone through in '43. 'Okay there?' he called, as the lad climbed up and through the canvas flap. 'Fasten it at the top and leave yourself a bit of air. Gets stuffy back there. Got something to lie on?'

The lorry started up again and they were off. It was bumpy—and the furniture none too securely packed. Neil was in constant fear that a large wardrobe would fall on him and when he dared to take his watchful regard off that he saw that a heavy mirror was balanced above him. True, it was tied with rope—but it did not look any too safe. What would be the use of running away if either the wardrobe or the mirror fell on him? He moved as far as he could away from them, so that should they fall they might possibly just miss him. He was dangerously near the flap though and the draught was strong.

He saw a hollow place between two upturned armchairs and, crawling over, pulled two of the seat cushions down with him and, curling himself up, lay there gratefully and exhaustedly. He did not sleep for some time. Waves of fear swept him so that he alternately sweated and shivered. Fear of what he was doing, fear of its consequences, fear of the reception he could expect at the end of his journey, fear of being caught even now, that at any minute the van would be overtaken and he removed ignominiously by the Red Caps. But stronger than these loomed Mike and the urging drive to get away from him. So obsessed and tortured was he by the thought of life under Mike's domination that he had even contemplated death as an escape. But he was afraid of death, too.

He was dead asleep when the van reached a pull-in for lorries and the driver woke him. 'Hi there! Want a cuppa, lad?' Neil awoke with the instinctive terror of the fugitive—his hands out on the defensive.

'Want to oil the throttle and stretch your legs?' he asked, grinning. 'Come on. You'll be okay here. Don't look so scared. No questions asked. Mind their own bloody business in this line—pity other lines can't do the same.'

'Got any money?' he asked later, as the two sat drinking tea and eating great slabs of fruit cake in what had once been a Nyssen hut and was now a popular stop for long-distance drivers. There were several customers there, and their studied disinterest as they relaxed over their tea or lay back after it was soothing to the lad's jagged nerves. Got any cash?' repeated his host.

'Yes. How much do I owe you for the lift?' asked Neil quickly.

'No, no. I don't mean that. You're welcome, lad. How are you fixed for going on further?'

'I've got enough money for my ticket.'

'But you're not going by rail, are you?' The keen blue eyes bored into his and Neil said abruptly, 'No, I hope to get a lift, but everybody isn't as easy as you.'

'I can fix you for London. But it's an old, slow van. Take you some time. But Pat is safe—and he's not inquisitive. He'll drop you somewhere on the outskirts very early in the morning. How'll that suit you?'

Neil considered. Mike was intending to follow-on twenty-four hours later. That would be tomorrow afternoon. It would be easier for Mike because he'd got civvies and he intended to wear them. If he were to be successful in double-crossing Mike and getting away before he arrived to join him then he mustn't arrive in London too late himself. But if it were very early in the morning it would be safer. He could get in his grandmother's window. She slept below street level and her window opened on to a little piece of grass which sloped up to the street. He'd got in that way last time he'd deserted. A lorry was always safer than a train. If one travelled by train there was always the risk of the R.T.O. or the Red Caps at the stations. They could ask to see your warrant, your leave ticket if they liked. A lorry would be safer.

'Thanks. That'll be fine.'

'Why are you going home unexpectedly? Anything wrong at home?'

'My brother's been killed in Cyprus.'

'Sorry about that. Army?'

'Yes.'

'Service or Regular?'

'Service. He'd almost finished it.'

'Bad luck that.' He offered Neil a cigarette, studying his face, his hands, the details of his uniform carefully. Later on he might have to remember them. He hoped he wouldn't have to. If the boy was just running away nothing more would be heard of him. But if, as sometimes happened, he'd done some damned silly thing and was running away from its effects then the details might be needed and given.

'Come on. We'll get along,' he said, when his cigarette was finished, 'or we might miss Pat.'

It was getting dark when they pulled up again, at another similar pull in. And here, sitting at a table playing shove ha'penny, was Pat, a large genial Irishman with a blue peak cap and bright red hair.

'I'll take him. But it's slow. We'll make Putney about five with any luck. That do you, boy?'

'Fine, thanks. How much?'

'Sure! nothing at all. I'll do it for love of the uniform!'

He threw back his head and roared. Neil was frightened. The other customers were regarding their table with interest. But no one questioned him, no one looked in the least curious.

'You don't need to look so frightened, lad.' The driver who had brought him and who was addressed as 'Pug' by his pals said concernedly to him as he was saying good-bye, 'If you look so worried and frightened, people will notice you. Try to behave normally—as if you *really were going on leave*.' These last words, whispered with a chuckle, alarmed Neil more than anything else. *So Pug knew.* Did this Pat know too? *Did they all?* He looked round at the impassive faces drinking tea, smoking, playing shove ha'penny or twitting the two women serving them. Well, and if they did? They were all right. Pug had said so. He had nothing to fear. He tried to arrange his features into a mask of impassiveness like theirs. It was difficult. He showed every emotion on his transparent face. He kept his mouth open when he was frightened. He'd been told that. He shut it firmly and, glancing in the mirror over the counter in which the waitresses prinked, he saw that the firm set lips were most unnatural-looking. He opened his mouth again and accepted a cigarette from Pat.

The van which Pat drove was slow indeed. There was little space to lie down for the load consisted of sacks of some cereal and Neil had to squeeze in between two sacks which he managed to shift. He was quite hidden, but there was not much air and it was far more bumpy than Pug's furniture van had been. Nevertheless he slept again, fitfully, dreaming horribly of the camp, of the exercise, of Mike. It was half-past four when they reached Putney. Pat dropped him near the Underground station by the bridge, refusing to accept anything for the lift. 'Sure, you'll do the same for another lad one day. Good luck to you. . . .' And he was off quickly so as not to arouse suspicion should any cops be on patrol there as he said.

Neil found there was a train very shortly to West Brompton. From there it was only a short walk to his home. He sat down in the deserted station. A negro porter was sweeping the stairs and singing cheerfully. He could not shake off his feeling that he was being followed. He put the exact money in the ticket machine and got a ticket. No one looked at it or clipped it. He sat down on the empty station to wait for a train. He was so frightened that his teeth chattered and his stomach was queasy.

CHAPTER II

ALL OLD Mrs. Collins could see from her position in bed was a small corner of the window with the milk bottle and the two geraniums on the sill. Even to see that she had to strain herself up on her elbow and the effort was painful. She no longer woke at the rattle of the milkman in the street—the drugs prevented that. Now, when she awoke slowly and unwillingly, the empty bottle had already been exchanged for a full one. If she felt able, she would roll herself over to the side of the bed under the window and, after some fumbling ill-directed movements, she would get the window latch undone and pull in the milk bottle. She liked to fling open the pane of glass and feel the air come in, although, in this sudden, unexpectedly early heat-wave there did not seem to be much difference between the air in the room and that which came in.

This morning she awoke with a start, conscious that something unusual had broken her sleep. Her eyes went instinctively to the small aperture of light. She could just make out the milk bottle—and it was empty—so it could not have been the milkman who had woken her. What was it then? She peered again at the greyish pane and realised that it was still early, and that a blurred mass blocked out the view of the piece of waste ground opposite which she could see if she sat up. Pulling herself up, she tried to make out what the mass was. Was it a hand? It was tapping lightly on the glass now—and although from below in the bed it appeared distorted and squat she could make out five separate shapes—like a leaf of some kind. It was a hand, and the mass with dark sockets and a moving black slit below them was a human head magnified and monstrified through the steamy glass. She rolled herself over until she was under the latch and began fumbling with it. She hated having the window shut, but her granddaughter Nona was nervous. The latch was undone at last and she pushed the window wide open letting the fresh air stream in on her. Framed between the two pots of geraniums was the white agitated face of her grandson Neil.

'Neil!' She was startled—and yet not surprised. So he had come twice previously—like a thief in the early hours of the morning. '*You!*'

'Can I come in? Is it all right?' His voice was urgent, defeated somehow.

She stared at him speechlessly for a moment, then slithered over in the bed again so that she had made way for him to enter. He climbed quickly through the small window, his foot kicking the flower pots. 'Mind my geraniums—and mind that milk bottle,' she breathed, 'and don't make a sound. That Mrs. Danvers upstairs has sharp ears. Better shut the window after you.'

He reached his long gangling legs down on to the bed, muddying the covers with his boots. Then, closing the window softly, he collapsed on the bed. While he had been climbing in she had been conscious of his breathing, harsh and loud—as if he had been running. Now, on the bed, he began shuddering violently and the jerks became sobs.

The old woman leaned over from her crouching position and said sharply, 'Quiet now, Neil lad. The walls have ears in this place.' Even as she said this, her eyes went anxiously from his face, now hidden in his hands, to the door and the window. She felt dazed and stupid with sleep still, and began resolutely and determinedly to shake off the cobweb of unreality still enveloping her from the drugs.

'You've run away again?'

He nodded speechlessly.

'I didn't think you'd be back again—not after you'd given me your word to stick it out,' she said quietly.

He lay back suddenly in a childishly helpless way and, removing his hands from his face, she saw two great tears trickling from under his lids. In the cold grey light of the semi-basement his face was grey, his eyes, lips and hair seemed all of a piece with his khaki uniform. As he turned his head away in a sudden gulping sob she saw the nape of his neck showing white and childish, and she saw back through the vista of the years the toddler with those first wisps of baby hair parting at the neck to show that vulnerable little hollow and a terrible compassion flooded her.

'Where's your cap?' she asked, to hide her emotion. 'Not gone and left it somewhere have you?'

Without a word he pulled the beret from his pocket. 'Sit up,' she said, 'and listen. The milkman'll be here soon and he'll look in the window. You can't stay like that on the bed.'

He shifted himself awkwardly until he was on the edge furthest from the window. 'Where'll I go then?'

'What time is it?'

'Dunno. Must be all of seven o'clock.'

'When did you leave?'

'Yesterday afternoon.'

'Hungry?'

He nodded. 'No food since yesterday evening—I got a sandwich then.'

'How did you travel?'

'Hitch-hiked. A lorry—and a delivery van.'

'How far away did the last one drop you?'

'Putney. I came by Underground from there.'

'See anyone coming in here?'

'Not a soul. It was still dark when I arrived. I waited a bit . . . I couldn't wake you, Gran.'

'No. It's the drugs. What happened? Why are you in this state, Neil?' She looked at him with mounting anxiety and apprehension. She had seen him terrified before but never in this sickening state of collapse. When he didn't answer she said, her voice sharp from fear, 'Why have you come *here*? You know they'll be after you in no time—and I'll have to hand you over again. What else can I do?'

He heard in her voice her resentment and reluctance to be again drawn into such a predicament as he had twice placed her already. 'Gran,' he said urgently, Gran. I can't go back. This time it's *finished*.'

At the word 'finished' she was overwhelmed with a new apprehension for him. Looking at him, white, shaken, scarcely coherent she was terrified for him. 'What d'you mean *finished*? You haven't become violent have you? Done something violent, have you?' In her mind were the frequent newspaper reports of violent deeds by youths. Fear is never far from crime, she thought desperately. What has he done? *What?*

He shook his head. 'No! No!'

'Hist! Get down under the bed.'

The rattle of the milk bottles clattered in from the silent street. The boy dropped down and lay flat under the high iron bedstead. The red face of the milkman peered in at the window as he planked down a full bottle on the stone sill and removed the empty one. The woman in the bed lay with her eyes almost closed until he had gone, but she could see the window and the face at it through the dingy pane of glass.

When the man had gone she whispered to Neil to emerge. He scrambled up, his uniform covered with dust. 'Dirty under there,' he observed, brushing himself down, 'Nonie doesn't sweep like I do.'

'She does her best,' his grandmother said indifferently. She felt somehow that it was wrong that what the boy said should be true. He did sweep better than his sister.

'When'll Nonie be here?'

Nonie. Nonie, always Nonie. And so it had been ever since they had been toddlers, thought the old woman. One never thought of them as separate personalities somehow. The twins liked this, liked that. The twins did this, did that. Until they had been torn apart by Neil's military service. Why did twins have to be born as two opposite sexes if they were so amazingly alike and apparently shared only one mind? 'Soon. I heard her getting up some time ago. She'll be here any minute now. Stand over there; I want to look at you.'

The boy, with an impatient deprecatory movement stood away from the bed so that he was in the direct light from the small window. His grandmother looked long and hard at him—at the delicate sensitive face, the light, almost white hair, the big black-ringed hazel eyes. Yes, nature had made one of her double jokes this time. The skin of his face and neck were even more transparent and hid even less than did his sister's the blue veins and the sudden rush of blood at each and every emotion. Nonie, fragile as she looked, was made of fine tempered steel; this boy, her twin, of brittle plastic.

'*Why* have you come back?' She demanded determinedly. 'You haven't told me that.'

'Because of Len.' He gulped nervously and a rush of bright colour flooded his face so that she knew he was lying. 'I asked for compassionate leave when I heard. The C.O. said I couldn't have it because of that last time.'

'You lied then,' said his grandmother accusingly, 'Why should he believe you this time? That's what comes of lying. It's a case of "wolf". When a thing really is true no one believes you.'

'I showed him the bits in the newspapers. He knew it all, but he said he couldn't give me leave. They're paid not to be human, those chaps are. I think *he* was willing to give it me, but he quoted a lot of regulations. They treat a chap as a machine in the Army.'

'What d'you expect when you keep quitting like this?'

'This was different,' he said stubbornly.

'What could you have done if you had been given leave?' she asked dispassionately, 'There was no funeral here; he was buried in Cyprus.'

'I could have been with you and Nonie.'

'But it's all over. Len's been buried a month. What good can you do now? You can only do yourself harm by this running away.'

'I can't go back. I'd rather die—I'd rather be dead.'

'Lots of us would, but you can't have death just for the asking.'

'Len got it.' said Neil, resentfully.

'He didn't want it. It's always those who get it. Len loved life. I heard you promise him that you'd stick out your service to the end. I can see him now—standing here in this room on his last leave. You'd spoiled it for him by quitting again. He was terribly cut up. I can see him now and you over there by the door between two policemen who'd been sent to fetch you to await a military escort. Nonie was clinging to your legs and crying her eyes out. A nice leave for Len that was! I don't mind so much your breaking your word to me . . . but with Len dead . . . how could you break your word to him?'

'Don't keep on about Len's death. It wasn't my fault he was killed.' His nerves broke through his control and he almost screamed at his grandmother. 'Be quiet,' she admonished him sharply. 'Someone'll hear you. There are others in the house.'

Supposing I told her what was really the matter, thought the boy desperately. Supposing I shouted what the truth is. She'd be horrified at even the words I'd have to use to tell her. One doesn't talk about such things—they mustn't be mentioned. She'd tell me to soap out my mouth as they told her in one of her blasted Homes. But he knew even as he considered it that he was too afraid to tell anyone. The old woman was sharp though. She knew when he was lying he'd not taken her in about his reason for deserting again. He tried again. 'I was worried about you now that Len's gone,' he muttered. 'I thought you wouldn't be able to manage without his bit. The C.O. asked if my father was alive. He must have known he was. What was the use of telling him that Dad's about as much use to you as a sick headache? In the Regulations you have a father or you haven't—just as you have a son or you haven't. What's the use of telling them that your son doesn't support you? According to the Army the fact that you've got a son is enough to assume that he supports you.'

'What's the use of talking like that, Neil? I get my bit and your pound helps me. If I don't grumble why should you do it for me? You'll grow bitter and go round like your father achieving nothing. You've got to accept certain things. You're just knocking your head against unbreakable stone, boy. You can't break life; it breaks you, if you let it. Len, now, he took

life between his teeth like a dog does a piece of rag, and just
shook it to his shape.'

'That's what killed him. He shook it once too often.'

'Ssh! lower your voice. I can hear that old busybody from
upstairs coming down for her milk . . . listen.'

The flopping, shuffling sound of someone heavy in soft
shoes was coming down the stairs. After each flop there was
a loud creak of the step and finally the quicker padding of
the slippers along the passage outside the room. Neil, standing
listening with a look of acute fear on his face, dived suddenly
under the bed. The steps had stopped right outside the door.

'Mrs. Collins . . . how are you, dearie?' And almost immediately the handle of the door was tried.

'It's still locked. Nonie's not come yet. I'm not feeling up
to letting anyone in this morning, Mrs. Danvers.'

'Oh, I made sure Nonie was sleeping in with you last night.
I thought I heard her talking to you just now.'

'No, she slept in her own room last night. She'll be here
soon. I'll wait for her to unlock the door. . . .'

'Oh . . . just as you like. I thought maybe you'd like a cup
of tea; just making some and came down for the milk—yesterday's is sour. Doesn't keep in this weather, does it?'

'Thank you, I'm sure, Mrs. Danvers. Nonie'll be here any
minute now. I don't feel up to getting to the door.'

They heard her shuffle off and open the front door to take
the milk bottle from the step; they listened to the ponder-
ous ascent of the stairs. The ceiling creaked ominously as she
moved across the room above. Neil came out from under the
bed again. His agitation had increased.

'You can't stay in this room,' his grandmother said again. '*I
told you.* She hears every sound. I got the milkman to leave my
bottle outside the window because she would bring it in and
chatter when it was left on the step. She heard us talking. She
misses nothing.

'Is my room let?'

'How can it be let when it opens off here? It's just as you
left it. All your things are there. Nonie sleeps there sometimes

when I'm bad. She's been sleeping there a lot lately—she's on bad terms with Charlie.'

'Bad terms with Charlie?' There was such dismay in Neil's question that his grandmother was surprised. There was no love lost between her grandson and Charlie.

'It'll blow over,' she said. Married couples always quarrel these days.'

'And Mary? Do you ever see her?'

'Mary's gone away—you know that.'

'I thought she might have come back now.'

'Well, she hasn't.'

'Where's she gone?'

'She went away with a man . . . I wrote you.' Then, as she saw his disconcerted face, she said consolingly, 'She's not a bad girl. Don't be hard on her. She was older than you in experience, if not in years. She took what was offered her. Who could blame her? I wouldn't.'

But he had turned his face away and she could see the pulse in his thin neck moving as it did when he was upset.

'She wrote me at first,' he said, 'but she didn't answer my last letters.'

'Mary got fed up with you always quitting. She said you'd never finish your service at this rate. You didn't write her you were going to do this?'

'No! I thought she'd have written when Len was killed'.

'She left just after that. She came to say goodbye. I liked Mary.'

'What sort of chap did she go with?'

'How should I know? I never leave this room except to cross the hall. She said he was kind and could look after her. Nonie said he was fat and no beauty. That's all I know. She wanted to get out of here. She took her chance.'

There was the sound of a door opening across the hall, light quick footsteps, and a key was inserted in the lock . . . 'Gran . . . Gran. . . .'

Neil crouched down at the back of the bed as the door opened and his twin sister came in. When she had shut the door he stood up. She gave a quick little gasp, then ran to him crying, 'Neil . . . oh, Neil . . . is it really you? I dreamed about you last night—a terrible dream—and here you are. Were you thinking of me last night?' She flung her arms round his shoulders and asked fondly, 'Why didn't you let us know? Did Gran let you in?' She was searching his face with a love in hers which was maternal and yet not maternal. The old woman did not like it.

'Ssh! Not so loud,' she said.

At her grandmother's tone the girl looked in alarm at her brother. 'What is it?'

'Hang something up over the window,' said the old woman harshly. 'Anyone can see through it.'

Nonie looked from her twin's white strained face to his dusty travel-stained uniform and then back at her grandmother.

'Yes,' said her grandmother. '*Again*; it's the same again.' The girl gave Neil a look of commiseration as she went quickly to a drawer and took from it a piece of blue material. 'No! Not that. That'd arouse suspicion at once. Everyone knows I have no curtain so that I can see out a bit.'

The girl found a piece of thick net curtaining. This she hooked on to two nails at each side of the window frame. Filtered thus the light was even more drab and dead. Nonie turned from it to Neil again. 'Why have you done it? *Why?*' She wound her arms protectively round his narrow shoulders gazing into his face with an anxiety which was demanding and at the same time hopeless.

'I couldn't stick it,' he said tonelessly, defeat in his eyes. 'I thought of Len dead out there. We're due for a draft to Malaya soon. Suppose I get killed too. Why should I go as well as Len? And what'll Gran do with you and Charlie off to Australia?'

'I'm not going until you've finished your service, you know that.'

'I'm not going to finish it.'

'You're doubling it with all these sentences, Neil.'

'I've finished it now. I'm never going back.'

'If you've come home with the idea of helping me you're doing it the wrong way. How can you help me when you're on the run?' said his grandmother sharply.

'There's no need for you to help,' said Nona, 'there's me— and Dad.'

'Him,' said Neil, contemptuously.

'He came,' said his sister defensively, 'he came when he heard about Len.'

'And how long did he stay?'

'Only one evening. But he came.'

'Well, I've come now—and I'm staying.'

'Neil, you *can't* stay here. They'll be here after you. When did you leave?'

'Yesterday—midday.'

'You've taken so long getting here they'll have telephoned the police by now. Did anyone there know you were going to do this?'

'Only Mike Andersen. He's covering for me. They won't have missed me yet the way we fixed it.'

'This Mike Andersen,' said Nonie slowly, 'can you trust him? Mary said she didn't like the sound of him in your letters.'

'Mike's all right. He's all for quitting himself. Nonie! The person who can really help on this is Charlie. *His lorry.*' Neil's eyes were frightened again; his face had the pinched look Nonie knew so well. He had the whole apprehension of the fugitive. 'I *must* get away tonight. Will Charlie help me?'

'I don't know,' said Nonie worriedly, 'Charlie's difficult these days. Get through to that little room there, Neil, and take off your uniform. I'm going to get some breakfast. Are you hungry?'

She went through the small door, papered over, behind her grandmother's bed and called, 'Here, Neil.'

She handed him some jeans, a jersey, a pair of plimsolls, some pink socks and a gay head scarf. 'Put these on,' she said roughly, 'it'll give us a little time to think. I'll come in and fix the head scarf.'

'No! No! I *can't.*' He looked in dismay at the garments she was holding out to him.

'You've no choice,' she said bluntly, 'if you want to stay *here.* Either you wait until they come for you—or you become me, until we can get you away. Don't you see, Neil? You can stay here as *me*. No one but Gran need know. It gives us time to think out something and get you away.'

'It's no good—won't work.'

'But why not? What did you plan to do? You must have had some plan. Why did you come back here at all then?'

'I thought you and Charlie would help me.'

'Neil,' his sister's distress was obvious, 'you know what Charlie's like. It's never been right between us since that last time you came home. He's so jealous; he doesn't understand.'

'Nonie, let's go away together . . . *now*. Charlie's not good enough for you. I can't think why you married him. Let's get away. We could go to Ireland to Great-aunt Liz. . . .'

'And what about Gran? What *are* you thinking of, Neil? You know I can't leave her or Charlie.'

'Then you must make Charlie help me. You *must*. I must get away tonight. I *must*.'

'Listen, Neil. Put the clothes on—just for now, anyhow. It's safer. Anyone can come in with Gran so helpless now. Put them on, *do*. I'll go and work on Gran. She's got to help you, too. She's sure to start on her usual duty talk—you know— how you mustn't turn out like Father. How we owe a duty to the State and all that. It won't be easy, but I'm going to try. Cheer up! . . . we'll fix something. I'm going in to get her breakfast now . . . put on the clothes and wait until I call you.'

She went to the old woman, and as she tidied her up and busied herself about the room while the kettle was boiling, she said violently, 'He's not going back this time. *Neil's* not going back. It'll mean a year in a civil jail! A year! Think of it—and it isn't as if he were a criminal. What's he done? *Nothing . . . nothing*. Just because he isn't cut out for a soldier. It's vile, horrible! Oh, how cruel it all is! There's all these toughs who make this district a menace to us girls, just hanging about doing nothing. Why can't they be put into uniform and be given the guns which Neil loathes? Why not? They want to hurt and kill and have weapons. Neil only wants to be at home with you and me—to do things about the place—just to live as he wants. Why should I be able to live as I like, and Neil, just because he's born a male, have to be ordered about and sent to prison as if he were a criminal, when he can't stand it?'

'Nonie . . . Nonie . . . Quiet now!'

'I *won't* be quiet. I can talk if I want to, and I don't care who hears me. He shan't go back, he *shan't*! I'll make Charlie help him. And *you*, Gran, you've got to help him too.'

'No,' said the old woman flatly. 'No. I know my duty. He goes back. He can have some food and a rest—*and back he goes.*'

The girl came over to the bed and stood menacingly over her grandmother. 'He's *not* going back. If he goes, I leave this house too. You and Charlie can keep each other company, for I shall go with Neil if neither of you will help him. He can go to Ireland to Great-aunt Liz—you *know* he can. I begged you last time—I went on my knees to you and you wouldn't. This time I'm not begging you; I'm *telling* you. You've *got* to help.'

'Nonie,' said the old woman sternly, 'what's come over you? Stop being hysterical like that. It won't help your brother.'

'You're hard—hard and heartless. Len's dead—killed because they sent him to Cyprus—and now you want Neil to be killed, too. His draft is due for Malaya, you know that.'

'If he's deserted again he won't go with the draft anyway. Use your head, girl!'

'You're hard! You're hard! Now Len's gone you're taking it out on Neil . . . that's what you're doing . . . taking out on your grandson the disappointment you've had over Father. You didn't succeed in making Father fight in the war, did you? No, he got himself a nice cushy job and you were ashamed of him and you're determined that Neil shall be different. That's why you sent him back last time and the first time. D'you think I've forgotten that? *It tore me to bits when they came and took him.* I wanted to change places with him and suffer some of his agony myself . . . Neil's all right. If they'd only leave him alone. It's when he's badgered and chivvied and bullied that he gets bewildered and they think he's a clot. I know him . . . I know my twin . . . he's a lovely person if they leave him alone.' She burst into angry tears.

Her grandmother looked steadily at her, 'So that's what you think! You really think that of me?'

'I do . . . you think about what I've said—it's true.'

She rushed into the kitchenette, furious tears streaming down her face. She felt so passionately for her twin that beside his peril nothing else mattered to her. She made the tea blinded by tears. 'Nonie . . . Nonie . . .' the old woman was calling, 'Nonie, if you insist on this, Charlie and you will be further apart than you are now. You are apart, aren't you?' She was ravaged by the girl's distress. 'Things aren't going right with you two are they?'

'It's Neil. He hates Neil. I'm always worried about him. Charlie can't understand. I *must* help Neil . . . he's part of me. When he first went in the Army it was as if I died.'

'If you go against Charlie in this it'll only make things worse—you realise that, don't you?'

'Of course I do. Charlie's tough—he doesn't need me like Neil does. Charlie needs no one—he's self-sufficient and satisfied with himself. Neil needs me; he has no one.'

'He has this new friend up there—this Mike Andersen.'

'That's not what I mean. Gran, you've *got* to help him. All I'm asking you to do is to let him stay here all day. He can sleep in the little room behind here—and eat in here with you. By tonight I'll have got something fixed. Please, Gran, *please.*'

Her grandmother sighed. 'Very well,' she said at last, unwillingly. 'But it's no good, Nonie; they'll get him—they always do. It'd make it easier for him if he went back now.'

'Thousands get away—why shouldn't he?'

'If he goes to Ireland he'll have to stay there. They'll arrest him as soon as he sets foot here again.'

'I realise that.'

'And you still want him to go? Even though you won't be able to see him?'

'I *can't* see him like this. I can't bear it. I'd rather he went away than suffered like this. He'll become a criminal with all this time in jail.'

'All right, Nonie. He can stay here. But no good can come of this. I warn you now. Things are apt to come back on you. It'll end badly. And I won't lie—so don't ask me to.'

'No one's asking you to do anything except allow Neil to hide here all day. . . .'

'All right. Kiss me and don't look like that. You look as if all the cares of the world were on your shoulders.'

'They are . . .' said her granddaughter glumly, as she went in to her brother.

He was sitting on the chair trying to pull on the pink socks she had given him. He had put on her blue jeans and the blue jersey. She tied the scarf pirate-fashion round his head, pulling forward a lock of the fair hair as she wore hers. She attached a pair of gold hoop earrings to his ears, then took them off. 'No. I almost slipped up there. Your ears are much bigger than mine—too big for a girl. The rings accentuate them.' She drew the scarf lower to cover them . . . brushed his face over with a powder puff and drew a lipstick quickly and deftly over his full, rather sensual, mouth. . . . 'Look,'—she surveyed him critically—'you're exactly like me . . . Look at us . . . I wonder why we couldn't both have been boys?'

'Or both girls—that would be more suitable!' said her brother bitterly. 'You must despise me, Nonie, like Gran does. I'm yellow-bellied. I know it. Did you ever know me when I wasn't scared?'

'Everyone's scared—if not of one thing then of another. Some let it get the better of them—that's all.' She put her hands on his shoulders. 'Neil. Tell me the truth. We've never had secrets from one another.'

'You had Charlie. You kept that from me.'

'I was so shattered when you had to go in the Army. It seemed awful to write that I was going to be married . . . I just couldn't bring myself to do it.'

'So you let Len do it for you. . . .' His voice was bitter.

'Neil. Don't be like this.'

'It's a free country—I *don't* think. A free country which takes one brother and kills him, and then forces the other one into the same pattern. There's no war on. I'd fight if the country was attacked—but why shouldn't I choose whether or not I want to be a soldier in peacetime?'

'It's never peacetime. There's always trouble somewhere. You're quoting Father when you talk like that.'

'A lot of what he says has some truth in it—even if he is a shadow Communist.'

'The Commies have conscription, you know that. Come on—let's have some breakfast. You can stay in Gran's room; she's agreed that you may. I've left some food in the kitchen cupboard and I'll bring some in tonight.'

'Nonie . . . *I've got to get away tonight.* You *must* get Charlie to help me. If he'd take me in the lorry—that'd be so much safer than my having to travel by train. *Will* you?' In his urgency he shook her backwards and forwards.

She detached herself gently. 'I'll do my best. Surely you know that. But Charlie's difficult. . . .'

'He doesn't like *me*, I know that.'

'He doesn't like compulsion either.'

'You'll try and persuade him?'

'Of course. Don't talk loudly to Gran. Remember there are others in the house. The old woman upstairs is inquisitive and your voice is deeper than mine. If old Evans comes offering to do Gran's shopping, don't let him in. The only person you must open the door to is the doctor. If Gran were left locked in too often all day he'd insist on her being visited more often by the health officers. You know how she feels about them. I don't think the doctor will come. But let him in if he does.'

'But, Nonie—*like this*? He'll know I'm not a girl.'

'He won't look at you. He's one of the new kind. No time for anything but death—because that means a compulsory certificate—and possible trouble.'

'What's happened to old Penfield?'

'Dead. This one has his practice. You can hear him counting the seconds while he's in the room. It's not Gran's pulse he's counting but the passing of time—his time.'

'Well, why not? What else is a pulse but a clock—same as any other.'

'Here, let me look at you. . . .' She scanned his face very carefully. 'You'll do. You'll pass as me to the casual eye seeing you through the window or crossing the yard to the lavatory. . . .' She suddenly gripped her twin hard. '*I want the truth, Neil*. I know you've been lying. *Why have you quit again?* You've not done something wrong have you?'

'I've told you,' he retorted resentfully, 'that's all there is to it. Why must you and Gran think I'm a criminal just because I can't stick it? Call me a coward—anything you like—but I'm not a criminal.'

'Ssh . . . Don't shout or all my work on you will be wasted. Everyone in the house will know you're here. Come on . . . cheer up . . . and remember that for today you're *me*!' She pulled him protesting through the door into the bedroom. 'Like your new granddaughter, Gran?'

The old woman raised herself up in the bed as Nonie stood there side by side with her twin. She drew in her breath sharply as she looked from one to the other. 'How long d'you think that'll deceive? Granted—it's extraordinary! The likeness is amazing. But everyone knows that Nonie's out at work all day.'

'Surely I can have a couple of days off. I'm entitled to have a headache or a cold without a doctor's certificate. . . .'

'I don't like it. I don't like anything about this business at all,' said the old woman gloomily.

'Have your breakfast,' was all her granddaughter said to this as she busied herself with the tray, placing the teapot and the bowl of porridge within easy reach of her grandmother. 'I've put your coat and slippers on the chair ready for you to go across the hall to the yard.'

'What sort of day is it? Raining? I can't see properly through that double net over the window.'

'Not raining. Just grey and close—a sort of waiting day . . . you know. Neil'll be able to help you get up.'

'No need. I can get myself up. I do it all right—just take my time over it, that's all.'

The girl, so extraordinarily like her twin, with the very fair hair and the dark hazel eyes, the delicate colour which came and went so easily and the curious fawn-like grace, pulled on a coat and picked up a handbag. 'I must be off; I'm late. Don't go out whatever you do, Neil. You'll be safe enough going across the hall—they'll think it's me. But it'd be better if you didn't meet anyone. I'll try and get off early.'

She kissed her grandmother who was already pouring the tea. Her twin, legs astride, was eating bread and marmalade ravenously on the end of the bed. Nonie sighed as she observed this. He looked just a gangling growing boy, and in her blue jeans and jersey terribly defenceless. She closed the door softly behind her as she slipped out.

CHAPTER III

WHEN THE GIRL had gone the two went on eating. The old woman ate as ravenously as her grandson. She was surprised at her appetite this morning. Neil's arrival, after the first shock, had given her the feeling of being part of life again. In the dreary room in which she was now virtually a prisoner because of her illness, the days ran into night and one sleep into another without any noticeable frontiers. The last time he had come home she had not been confined almost continuously to bed; in between the bouts of pain she had been up and sometimes even out for half an hour. Now like the nights and days, the good bouts ran into the bad ones, and in between the pain there were only the dull bearable intervals when the Monster slept—and she gathered her forces together for the next bout. Before these forces could be fully mustered, the Monster, as she had come to think of the pain which gripped her in his crab-like vice, was upon her again. The very nature of the disease which was killing her made it seem a live evil, a veritable creature there to prey and feast upon her as a vulture will follow the last lagging steps of a wounded man, knowing that soon the final meal will be his.

She fought the pain, not as a disease, but as a personal enemy. When the worst was upon her, her limbs twisted in agony, her face contorted with anguish, she would welcome the Monster grimly. . . . 'Well, old friend, here we are again! All set for the next round . . . come on . . . come on! . . . do your worst . . . I can take it. A tough old woman—stronger than any man . . . stronger than my drivelling non-stop-talking

son . . . or my faint-hearted grandson . . . come, try me and
see. . . .' Instead of resisting the onslaught she would welcome
the struggle, taxing her powers of endurance as long as she
could, knowing that when she reached the breaking point
and her reserves were weakening, then, and then only would
she resort to science, and so escape the final fury of the thwarted Monster in oblivion. The little tablets lay there, regularly
replenished. She had only to stretch out her hand to escape
the Monster's worst.

'Neil,' she said now, surprised and delighted at her sudden
hunger, 'see if you can find me some more bread—over there
in the cupboard in the wall.'

He came back with half a loaf.

'Cut me some—not a thin wishy slice like Nonie thinks
an invalid should have—a proper door-step like I used to cut
you after school.'

He cut the bread as she wanted it, and watched her pile it
with marmalade. He liked seeing her enjoy the food. She had
good strong teeth still, and the line of her jaw was sharp and
clear. The illness had fined down every superfluous fold and
line. Her face was a mask stretched tightly over a beautiful-
ly-made skull. Helpless as she was, not one strand of hair was
allowed to escape the relentless knot into which she confined
it, and her granddaughter washed it for her every week-end.

'What day is it?' she asked suddenly, looking up from her
food.

'Must be Wednesday,' replied Neil. 'I left Tuesday—it seems
years . . . and yet it was less than twenty-four hours ago.'

'Twenty-four hours ago! They'll be after you today!' she
said apprehensively. 'Last time it was less than twenty-four
hours that the police were hanging round this door-step.'

'Last time there wasn't Mike to help—or you, Gran.'

'Me!' she laughed harshly. 'I'm an unwilling helper. You
know that, don't you?'

'I'm grateful,' he said humbly. 'I know the trouble I'm causing you.'

'This Mike Andersen you've been writing so much
about—what's he like?'

He looked away from her but she was aware of his sudden agitation again. The mere name of his so-called friend caused a change of colour, a perceptible heightening of his awareness. She pursued it, relentlessly. 'What's he like? What's he look like?'

'He's tall—and large. He's dark—and tough. He's had to be. He's got no parents—he's had to fend for himself.'

'Too many of them are tough now. Can you trust him? Will he do as he said?'

'Yes.' The answer was short and came unwillingly. She knew perfectly well that he did not want to discuss Mike Andersen, that for some reason or other things were not right between them. How much had he lied? Was this Mike really covering up for him? 'And you like him?' she pursued.

'He cottoned on to me right from the start. He came in the draft after mine. He's smart. He knows his way around—knows how to dodge things. He's clever all right. He can make people do as he likes.' He did not look at his grandmother as he told her this.

'You haven't answered my question. I said "Do you like him?" Funny you should have run away again if he's so wonderful. I should have thought that with a friend up there things would be easier—more bearable.'

'Well, they aren't,' he said shortly.

'Funny. I don't like the sound of that young man Mike. You're no good at judging people, Neil, no more than your father is. Len now, and Nonie—they know a good coin from a bad. Strange that you and your father don't.'

'Why do you have to keep harping on Father?' he said resentfully, 'Mike's all right. He suits me.' But there was no conviction in his voice and he would not meet her eyes, and even in his averted face she sensed his tenseness, his guardedness, and her fears grew.

'Take this tray through to the kitchen. The window there looks on to a blank wall so no one will see you. I'm going across the passage. Take care that no one sees you if *you* go out there.' She began heaving, almost rolling her thin body out of the bed until her feet touched the floor. Neil held out

the coat and slippers which his sister had laid out in readiness.
'No,' she said sharply, 'I can manage. Put them down. I can get
them—in my own time—same as I can do everything for myself. When I can't, they'll take me away—but not before. Make
yourself scarce in the kitchen. That old Evans'll be down any
minute now. I'll have to lock the door and take the key while
I'm gone or he'll come in here.'

He picked up the tray, but not before he had seen the horrible struggle she had to bend down to reach the slippers and
still more to get them on her feet, but she accomplished it—
just as she eventually got the coat on and buttoned it up.

He carried the tray into the dark malodorous little hole
that served for cooking and washing-up. A cooker, a sink, a
cupboard, a table and two chairs by the window. That was the
kitchen with barely room to turn. All water had to be heated;
there was only a cold tap. On the first floor there was a tum-
bledown bathroom which served the whole house. The water
there was heated by an unreliable geyser appropriately named
Vesuvius. It took four or five pennies to get a few inches of
hot water and half an hour to clean the bath before it could be
used. In the barracks there had been baths—really hot ones—
and there were hot showers too. Neil liked hot baths. Before his call-up he had looked forward to Saturday afternoons
when Nonie had scrubbed out the bath and he had wallowed
in eightpence-worth of hot water.

He looked round the dreary little kitchen now, noting with
a kind of loving pleasure each well-worn pot, kettle and pan.
It was all small, shabby, homely and familiar. He knew it all—
could find anything in the dark—as could his grandmother.
Up at that dreary place he'd never got over his feeling of being
lost, confused and disorientated. He wasn't like Mike who was
the sort who would find his way around anywhere, in a coal
mine or a jungle. Mike had what he called the nose for things.
Neil had no illusions about himself. Because he was always
scared nothing was simple for him. Fear made him lose his
wits, paralysed him, made him into a clot a stumbling, inartic-
ulate fool. It had always been the same, at school, at the factory
where he'd worked until his call-up, and worst of all in the

Army where it seemed that they could smell his fear and he had quickly become the butt of the sergeant and his draft . . . so that 'Let's take a rise out of Ninny Collins' had become the highlight of the day.

He had never been able to clarify his fear in his own mind or the reasons for it. He didn't know why he was afraid, only that he was afraid. He was scared to death—of himself, of his superiors, of his fellow conscripts, of the rifle with which he had to drill, and of the drill itself, of the filthy obscenities of the latrines, the sleeping huts, of the terrors of the nights there, of the anguish of each waking. He had hated the whole business from the very first day. He wanted to hide, to lose himself in anonymity, to be alone and yet not alone because now he was frightened of himself.

He felt safer here. It was *here* that he wanted to remain. Here, safe with his twin Nonie and his grandmother. She was often crabby and strict, censorious and sharp—but he felt safe with her. If only he could tell her about Mike. Tell her that he didn't want to desert, that if only he could escape Mike he would go back and finish his service. If only Len were here he could talk to him. He had mentioned some of his troubles to Len on his first leave and Len had said that there was nothing to be done but to use one's fists right from the start. But Len was dead; killed out there in Cyprus waging war against the terrorists who were young lads like himself. He had loved Army life, had gone joyfully and excitedly to Cyprus and written vividly of the life there. People liked Len, he made friends easily and had gone into life with all the zest with which he had taken up boxing and cycling. Len was dead. It didn't seem possible; and now that his brother was dead Neil's fears were accentuated. He was frightened of death now. *Death* . . . that was something for the old. Gran, for instance, who wanted it. Why was she alive and Len who loved life, dead?

He put the things in the sink and ran cold water on them dispiritedly before he returned to the room which was formerly the sitting-room and was now his grandmother's prison. She was back there again. Nonie had tidied the whole room before she left. When she came back at night she would put her grandmother in a chair and make the bed properly. Neil watched the determined efforts of the old woman to do her hair and put on a clean woollen wrap. She waived his attempts at help impatiently. Slowly and with horrible deliberation she managed it all, even to the measured calculated movements with which she got herself back into the bed.

'You'd better get some sleep,' she said. 'If Charlie agrees to help you, and I don't think he will, you'll be off again tonight.'

'You don't think he will?'

'If he does, it'll be for Nonie. You can go to my sister in Drogheda—but you'll need money. How much have you got?'

'About eleven pounds.'

'That'll get you there. But I don't know what you're going to do for money once you're there. There's not much work in Ireland.'

'You don't think much of me, do you, Gran?'

'If you don't think much of yourself—how can others? You've always had someone to fight your battles—Nonie and Len. Now both have gone. Nonie to Charlie, and Len—who knows where? But out of this cage we call Life.'

'You've said it. It's a cage all right. Last time I skipped it they gave me a hundred and twelve days for absence without leave. It was *terrible.* You wouldn't believe what it was like. I can't go back. I *can't.'*

'Don't raise your voice. Has Nonie left the blankets on the cot in there?'

'Yes.'

'Then go and get some sleep. You look bad. If you hear anyone knocking or coming in the room, don't move. It'll be someone coming to visit me.'

'Suppose the police come—like last time?'

'You're my granddaughter sick in bed there. Have you ever told anyone up there that you have a twin sister?'

'No.'

'Sure? *No one?'*

'Only Mike.'

'Ah! Now we're talking—Mike, why him?'

'Because he asked me. He's got no family—only an aunt. He wanted to know about mine.'

'And you told him? About Len and Nonie and your father?'

'Yes.'

'And me? Does he know about me?'

'Yes. Mike's got a sort of way with him. Everyone does what he asks them, tells him what he wants to know. . . .'

The old woman felt again that mounting stab of concern, almost fear, which Neil's first mention of this youth had aroused in her. 'You told him too much,' she said shortly. 'You should learn to keep your mouth shut tight. You're no judge of men, I told you that before—I tell it you again.'

'But, Gran—it was you told me to make friends—to try and get away from myself. I was lonely. Mike was the only one who had a decent word for me—the only one who helped me. Why, he's covered up for me often.'

'*Why?* That's the question. *Why?* He doesn't sound the kind who'd do it for nothing. How many times have you done the same for him?'

'Not often—I'm not as clever as he is,' he said reluctantly.

'Then what does he get out of you in exchange?' demanded the old woman watching him closely. At the wave of dark ugly colour which flooded his delicate face she was agitated.

'Well?' she insisted.

'Nothing,' he mumbled unwillingly, his hands clenched.

'Then he's a decent sort. You are lucky to have fallen in with him. Perhaps I've been doing him an injustice. But if you've struck up this friendship, I can't see why you've deserted again; or why he should cover up for you when he's never going to see you again.'

Neil was silent. He *would* see Mike again unless he was clever enough to outwit him. That was just it. He couldn't bring himself to blurt out that Mike of the smiling half-closed eyes and the loathsome hands had become the great looming Fear which blotted out all the other terrors, the punishment cells, the sergeants and every former horror. He could only think now of Mike with a revulsion which amounted to physical nausea. The very mention of his name caused a violent sensation of being trapped, shut in with his own subservience. He put his aching head in his hands.

'Got a headache?' asked his grandmother, noticing the rather small chin—charming in Nona but giving a look of weakness to her brother—the full sensitive mouth and the blue half-moons under the eyes. 'Don't touch those tablets in the aspirin bottle—they're my pain-killers. Nonie put them in the aspirin bottle because the cardboard pill box was broken. If you want an aspirin they're on the mantelpiece.'

'I don't want anything. I'm only tired.'

'Well get some sleep now—and keep that scarf round your head—just in case—remember that someone may come in to visit me.' She said it distastefully. It was abhorrent to her to take part in this deceit. 'All right. Thanks, Gran.' He hesitated, as if he wanted to say something further, then hunching his narrow shoulders he went towards the door in the wall behind the bed. On it hung a large coloured portrait of the Queen mounted on her horse Winston, and dressed in the uniform of the Grenadier Guards. He saw his grandmother's eyes on the picture. It had been Len's. Len had admired the Queen tremendously.

'Put it straight—it's crooked,' she said. He straightened the picture and then went through into what had once been a large clothes cupboard, and was now, with ventilation from a small fanlight, classed as a bedroom.

The old woman lay back wearily. She was suddenly exhausted. The vitality which had so unexpectedly fired her on Neil's arrival had left her as sap leaves a snapped branch. More than exhaustion was the sudden overwhelming premonition of something evil and menacing brooding over them all. What? The boy had not once looked her fair and square in the face. And he had been lying. His face gave him away every time. And she was probably inviting this menace into closer contact with them by her decision to help him in his escape.

But supposing she did fight this unknown thing? How did one fight an unknown terror? What weapons did one use against an unknown evil—except prayer? And that had proved unavailing in the past. This was no ordinary desertion. This was not the same as those last two times when he had run away because he couldn't take it. There was far more beneath it this time. Something stronger than the lad had ability to face up to. He did face up to his fear as far as he was able. He was not one of those cowards who are always hiding behind a façade of boasting and bombast. No, he knew and admitted his deficiencies. Always had. She had tried and tried to put into his frail make-up the seeds of courage; as had Len. Why couldn't the Army find some pills to give strength and courage to boys like Neil if they had to take them against their wills? She had heard that during the war they did use such tablets. Why couldn't they use them now? Neil had neither physical nor moral courage, and she felt instinctively that it was the latter of which he stood most in need now. Why couldn't the Authorities see that he was utterly useless to them. Why must they persist in getting him back each time he deserted adding more and more accumulative time to his service after each savage sentence? The boy must be costing them a thousand times more than his worth to them as a soldier. Yet he had been a satisfactory enough citizen when working in the factory. He had come home on time, brought her his earnings, helped in the home in every way. Why couldn't they see that some lads just weren't cut out for soldiering? Taking lads like him against their will to be trained against possible enemies of the State was only succeeding in making of them real enemies of that State.

Her son, Edward, had ranted on to her about the stupid relentless system, talking of the Military Authorities as criminals who ought to be shot. Len had argued hotly that no State could consider the individual when building its defences. If they exempted one lad they would have to exempt thousands. It was the compulsion itself more than the actual service which went against the grain with most of the conscripts, he had said. Len himself had gone uncomplainingly and cheerfully to do his service and had settled happily into the life there. In the drawer of the small cupboard by the bed where she could lay her hands on them were some letters about her dead grandson. One from his Commanding Officer, and one from the young Lieutenant whose life he had saved. Wonderful letters praising Len.

The old woman looked up at the picture of the Queen. '*He* served you anyway,' she said quietly. 'Maybe that'll make up in some way for this one who's too weak. I've sent him back twice, but Nonie's right, all this prison will only make a criminal of him. I'm sorry—I apologise to you for him and for what I'm going to do. *This time* I'm *going to help him get away.*'

There had been a time when her son Edward, on one of his visits, had wanted to take down the picture of the Queen. It had been during one of his Reddest periods. His mother had been adamant. The picture was Len's. He liked it so much that he'd saved up for a frame for it. She liked it herself. What business was it of Edward's who did not pay a penny towards the rent? What right had he to criticise any one of their possessions or what they did with them? The old woman had been so fierce that her son had subsided and never mentioned the subject again.

She lay in bed now and thought about her son Edward. He had never done a day's service for any Sovereign. He'd got out of it all—just as he'd got out of his responsibilities to his wife and children and left them to her care and provision. A fine strapping man with broad shoulders and a fine head—Len had been like him in looks—he was to her mind utterly shiftless and worthless. All the education they'd given him at great sacrifice had been used to evade his duties and responsibilities as a citizen and father. An education, she thought bitterly, that had been used for doubtful purposes.

Always something new and something ending with an 'ism'. He could talk—and that had been his undoing. Words just flowed from him as rain did from the clouds; he was enchanted, intoxicated, by the sound of his own voice, delighted with his own eloquence. He had that power—for good or evil—of making men listen to him. They listened in spite of themselves—unable to tear themselves from that golden voice.

When he had first discovered this gift of his for oratory, his mother had gone to listen to him. She had been enthralled, dismayed and terrified at the possibilities conjured up by his visible power over his listeners. But her fears had soon evaporated, for he changed in his views, his aims, his sympathies as frequently and as quickly as the winds did. She was intelligent enough to see that in such a variable and uncertain quality he was more of a danger to himself than to others. And yet, that he could and did inflame the vacillating minds of some of them was undeniable. He worked only for some Cause, and that Cause, whatever it was, paid his expenses and on these he lived, content that his wife and children should be left to the care of the State which he constantly abused. Had it not been for his mother, his children might well have been brought up in one of those same Homes in which she herself had been brought up.

She had worked for her grandchildren, and after her daughter-in-law, Connie, had run away with a more steady reliable man, she had adopted them as her own. She hadn't blamed Connie who, delicate after the birth of the twins, had needed some comfort, some love. Both these were unknown to Edward, who, continuously caught up in the fire of some wordy argument or some ethical point, seemed deliberately blind to the physical and spiritual needs of his wife and family. They had become the grandmother's family—they were hers, for Connie hadn't lived to enjoy her new comfort for long. She had died, two years after running away from Edward; but at least she'd had two years' comfort with a man who had loved her and the old woman had not grudged them her.

Edward had come home when Len had been killed. He'd seen the paragraphs in the newspapers. Len's heroism in saving the life of his officer had been made much of—and it seemed that he was going to get a medal. It was going to be given posthumously, and she, his grandmother, would be the one to receive it for him. She was not going to allow Edward to have anything to do with the Investiture—after his Communist tirade about the Monarchy. He had delivered a long oration about murder of the young by the State. He'd even gone on about the medal which the papers had said that Len would certainly be awarded. He'd implied that it would be interesting for him, feeling as he did, to go to the Palace and receive it. She had turned on him then, furiously. *She* was the one who would go and receive it. Len had always given his grandmother as his next-of-kin, his father having often not been seen or heard of by his family for years at a time.

Edward had concluded his oration on Len's death with an outburst about freedom. Of how man had been made before all the rotten man-made laws and religious conventions had bound and enslaved him, and that before long he must wake up to the fact that he had lost his freedom by his own stupidity.

'What d'you want then?' his mother had demanded fiercely. 'D'you want to revert to the Garden of Eden when there was no good or evil?'

'It's not a question of good or evil. It's a question of a lot of laws and conventions which, made by us, now enslave and enmesh us so that we are indeed the prisoners of our own achievements,' he had replied. And from there he had begun another rippling stream of words, which just flowed from him without a break.

Miss Rhodes, the social worker who had been visiting her that afternoon, had been excited and impressed by Edward when he had blown in with his pockets full of newspaper cuttings about Len. 'Seen these? And these?' he had demanded, his eyes blazing. It's nothing but *murder*—plain murder. Murder by the State for its own doubtful ends. . . .'

'Of course I've seen them,' his mother had snapped. '*And* the other side too—the letters from his officers and fellow Servicemen—and his last letter to me. He liked it. He loved the life—read his letter for yourself. He wasn't like you, thank God. He was a fine boy—and you did nothing for him.'

'I did more than a woman like you can realise,' he had retorted coolly, refusing to read the letters. 'If I can make even a few people see that we are all bound—and becoming more and more bound—by chains of our own making—by our own folly and greed, then I shall have done far more for Len than you could ever have done by filling his belly and covering his body.'

Miss Rhodes had been excited—not only at the oratory but at the ideas expressed by Edward.

'What you've been saying is something like Existentialism,' she had declared to Edward. 'Their theory is that man should be absolutely free to decide his own actions; that he should not be influenced at all in his decisions by any psychological or metaphysical contingencies . . . I have been reading Sartre on the subject.'

'And you approve of all that nonsense, Miss Rhodes? My son is a Communist—do you realise that?'

'*Was* . . . was, Mother,' Edward had said coolly. 'I'm not so convinced now. That business of Stalin shook me . . . considerably . . . and now this Hungarian business—not the sort of thing one can ignore. No, I've been shaken, Miss Rhodes—very shaken.'

'Your convictions are so often shaken,' said his mother, drily. 'You're far more shaken by the exposure of a mass murderer than you are by the fate of the victims, or by the death of your own son in a brave action under great danger.'

'It's only a small mind which can't admit it can be shaken,' he had retorted. 'The fact of a son being a son is physical not spiritual. The tenets to which I have been adhering are spiritual. They must affect millions—Len's death affects only a few—those closely related to him.'

His mother had been indignantly silent. What was the use of arguing with Edward? She had left it to Miss Rhodes, and the two of them had carried it on spiritedly and at length. She'd heard Len and Nonie arguing for hours with their father. He loved argument—glorying in words with which he vanquished all their protests and theories. Miss Rhodes had not been vanquished so easily, and the old woman had noted with amusement the effect of Edward's fine head and noble brow, his dark flashing eyes and the great plume of almost white hair which he swept back with a gesture both practised and calculated. Miss Rhodes had been impressed by everything about him. When he had talked like that about his own son's death his mother had been furious.

'You're inhuman,' she said angrily, 'devoid of any normal natural feeling and of any affection. You never had any as a child.'

'That's where you're wrong, Mother,' Edward had said patiently, as if to a child. 'It's because I have so much feeling for humanity that I can accept Len's death as I do. As a sacrifice to our crass stupidity and blindness; to the chains in which we have allowed ourselves to be fettered.'

After he had gone, Miss Rhodes had said excitedly. 'Your son is very intelligent, Mrs. Collins.' 'Think so?' the old woman had said smiling. 'You're surprised to hear such words and expressions and opinions uttered in such a place—isn't it that?'

Miss Rhodes had looked hot and uncomfortable, but her eyes had gone round the damp-marked walls, the thin threadbare piece of carpet, the cheap bits of furniture, and then to the large portrait of the Queen. The old woman could devise what was passing through her mind. Mrs. Collins drew the Old Age Pension plus that bit extra which the Assistance Board allowed her. That she had a son obviously highly educated and clearly able to support her if he wished surprised the welfare visitor.

'Edward's always been a man of words,' said the old woman grimly. 'And words don't earn you your bread unless they can be adapted to the requirements of people. Edward's too lazy and too changeable to adapt his to either the radio or a newspaper. What he'd like to do is to make hundreds of records of his own voice holding forth on his usual rubbish—and sell them for thousands of pounds for posterity. But they *are* his means of livelihood just the same. Words are his weapons—he uses them unscrupulously on behalf of any organisation who needs their men worked up to make trouble, strike or go-slow and the like. And if you don't call that despicable, I'd like to know what is! Words, words—I *hate* them, *hate* them. Sometimes when I'm listening to the radio I could scream at the endless spate of them. Words. They mean something different to each of us. To me they mean *Edward.*'

And today was Wednesday, Miss Rhodes' day for visiting this area. She would come this afternoon, as she always did.

She would come at exactly the same time and would knock on the window so that Mrs. Collins could hand her out the key, if she were too unwell to get up, and she could unlock both the front door, unless it had been left open, and the door to her patient's room. This afternoon Linda might come too. At the thought of Linda the old woman's eyes went to the window. It was no longer so grey; there was a bright ray of sunlight coming through the double net curtain which they had been obliged to hang over the window because of Neil.

She was startled by Neil knocking on the door behind the bed and asking, 'Can I come through?'

'Must you?' she asked distrustfully. She had thought him to be asleep.

'Yes, I must.'

'Oh well, come on then. Take care you don't bump into anyone—especially that old Evans. He's no fool although he's not as sharp as Mrs. Danvers. Peep round the door first and see if the coast is clear.'

He listened at her door, then slipping the latch up he closed it behind him and stood against the wall of the passage listening again. The lavatory was in the yard at the end of the passage. Just as he turned from the door the great bulk of Mrs. Danvers loomed across the hall blocking the end. She stood there with her great red mottled arms akimbo, her carroty hair pinned in curlers in rows across her head and her legs bare and obscene with huge varicose veins. Neil could not take his fascinated gaze from them. 'Not gone to work then today, Nonie?' she said excitedly. Her tongue seemed too large for her mouth and her words were slurred and half swallowed. Caught, unable to retreat or advance for fear of arousing suspicion the boy mumbled something and tried to pass her. But a great mottled red hand grasped him by the elbow and pale pink-rimmed eyes peered up at him, 'Your Gran's not bad again is she? She answered me all right this morning. Of course, one day I know she won't answer any more. . . .'

'She's all right,' mumbled Neil, disgust at her obvious gloating over the prospect of death for his grandmother making him so angry that he tried again to brush past her.

'Then what are you doing home? Not got the push have you?'

'No. Got a cold,' mumbled Neil wishing he had a handkerchief to hold to his nose.

'Give it to your Granny I expect,' she cackled hopefully. 'Why how thin you're getting, Nonie . . . nothing here at all . . .' and she grabbed the jersey in the place where Nonie's soft pointed breasts would be. 'Well well. You could do with a bit of me!' and she put both her red hands under the vast pendulous breasts bulging through the yellow openwork blouse. Bending his head and charging almost like a goat Neil managed to get past and slammed the door of the lavatory. Had he taken her in? She had dug her hands into his chest. She must have felt the absence of breasts. Had she done it purposely? Had she been listening at the door and knew perfectly well that he wore Nonie's clothes?

When he returned to his grandmother's room she was trying to discourage old Mr. Evans from entering. . . . 'No. No . . .' she was repeating, 'No. I don't want anything at all today, Mr. Evans.'

'Got a cold, has she? I heard her telling Mrs. Danvers. She ought not to go out there in the draught,' he was saying as Neil tried to dislodge his arm from the doorway and get through without inviting him to enter. 'Where's all your pretty hair gone? Not cut it off have you? A woman without hair is a woman without beauty I always say. . . .' His quavering voice rambled on long after Neil had shut the door. They heard his shuffling steps go down the passage and up the stairs.

'He hasn't gone to his own room, he's gone into hers . . . they're putting their heads together. . . .' said his grandmother worriedly, 'You would have to bump into *her*.'

'She won't do anything, will she? She's too fat and lazy . . . .' He could still feel her fingers pressing into his chest and he was terribly uneasy. His grandmother didn't reassure him. 'Don't make any mistake about her. Fat people are not always good-natured. She's spiteful and never misses an opportunity to make a bit. She's a ghoul in spite of her size. And that old Evans remarking on your lack of hair. I don't like it.

Pull that lock out a bit more in front . . . here . . . let me do it.' She pulled out the wisps of fair hair.

'She wouldn't *do* anything about me, would she?'

'Only if she thought I'd pay her to hold her tongue . . .' said the old woman with a sigh.

'I wish I could get you away from here . . . it's so dreary and dirty. You want to go back to the country, don't you, Gran? I wish I could get you to a place with a little garden.'

'You're going to be on the run for years. No use you thinking about gardens—or me either for that matter,' she said wearily. 'And they'll probably be listening at the door—you'd better get back in there for a bit.' She was tired—the influence of the drugs still about her.

CHAPTER IV

THROUGH the two pots of geraniums, when the light was good, Mrs. Collins could see the piece of waste ground left from the bombing in the war. Tall willow weed and grass grew in profusion amongst the fallen masonry and stones. Most of the rubble had been cleared away—but now, more than ten years after the end of the war, there were still the ruins of some houses, an archway, odd walls, and the deep foundations of what had once been a block of flats. The barbed wire erected round the site did not prevent the children from playing there. They had taken it over as a playground, finding it far more exciting than the streets in which they lived, and watching them at play there had become more than a pastime for the old woman—it had become almost an obsession.

She knew all the children by sight, and from watching them at their games she had learned to know all their characters. She knew that Sandy cheated, that the one they called Ludi was a bully, that they called the little negro boy Sambo and pulled his tight black curls but loved him. She knew that little fat Cissie wet her pants, that Emily with the flaxen hair was a nasty little girl who was always telling smutty secrets in corners, and that the sisters with long pigtails were quiet and shy, and that bright-faced Linda was the darling—the leader of them all.

Linda was the only one of all the children who played on the bombed site who was known personally to Mrs. Collins. One afternoon, a few months previously, the ball with which Linda and her friends were playing had been thrown high across the street, right over the little fence and down the sloping piece of ground to the semi-basement on to which Mrs. Collins' window opened; and after it, laughing, tumbling, bright as the sun itself had come Linda. She had picked up the ball, and because she was a child both alert and inquisitive she had noticed the geraniums and Smokey the cat who curled up on the sill between the two pots in the afternoon sun. She had stood on tip-toe to stroke Smokey and to see if the geraniums had any scent—and in doing so she had caught sight of the old woman lying in the bed. It had been one of Mrs. Collins' bad days when she was not able to sit in the basket chair. Through the dingy pane the child had smiled and waved her hand, and as she ran up the few steps again she had turned back and blown a kiss to the old woman watching her.

After that Linda had come again and again. The window just below the street level, with the geraniums and often Smokey curled up outside his mistress' window, seemed to have some strange attraction for her as she would timidly peer in the window. One day she had tapped on the glass pane and had waited until Mrs. Collins had managed to get it open. The late afternoon sun had been streaming in—it only came to the dark little room just before it began sinking low in the heavens, and the child had found an empty box on which she climbed so that she could talk comfortably with her head and elbows on the window sill. She was a gay child, full of inconsequent chatter, bits of news about her playmates and neighbours. To the old woman, imprisoned now in the small dark room, alone all day, the child was like some bright gaily-plumaged bird from another warmer brighter world. In the brilliant colours in which her mother dressed her, and with her dark eyes and flashing smile, she was curiously exotic for these drab streets.

Mrs. Collins' own daughter, now in Australia, had been a large dull respectable girl, and her dead daughter, Agnes, had been ugly, with spectacles and teeth that protruded. Nona, her granddaughter, had been sweet, but quiet and rather cautious. This child, daring, full of adventure and fun, was the kind of little girl which every man and woman would have been glad to have been blessed with. Beautiful as a cherub with tangled deep gold curls and great wide-set dark eyes, she had a skin of dark tea-rose. There was something so vulnerable, so transient, in the bloom of the skin, the curve of the full little mouth and the dimples which creased her face delightfully, that she could not pass unnoticed anywhere. But it wasn't the face, beautiful as it was, which held the old woman in thrall—it was the child herself.

She had come into Mrs. Collins' life as a brilliant butterfly unexpectedly comes through a window, and there had been an immediate understanding between the old woman and the child. Now scarcely a day passed when Linda did not come standing on tiptoes on the box to chatter to the sick woman. She brought her drawings from school, her maps, her needle-work, the first daisies, the first chestnut buds from the old tree amongst the ruins; these and all her small childish treasures were brought for inspection and approval. If Mrs. Collins felt well they would play games—halma, or ludo, fighting out exciting contests to the finish. If it were wet, Linda would climb in the window and curl up on the end of the bed and they would tell each other stories. The child had a vivid imagination and her stories were a source of great amusement to Mrs. Collins.

Linda was left alone all day, for her mother went out to work. A pretty woman with the same wide-set dark eyes and dark gold hair as Linda's, she had not been married to the child's father.

'She's a good child—never given me a moment's trouble,' she would say to Mrs. Collins, when the old woman praised Linda's beauty and intelligence. Linda was almost ten; she had been born just after the end of the war. Her father had never seen her, having returned to America without knowing of her existence.

'He had a wife and family back there in the States—he never deceived me about that. He was good to me, but I always knew it couldn't last. If he had known about Linda he'd have done something—he loved kids,' she had said disinterestedly when Mrs. Collins had asked about Linda's father.

'Do you ever hear from him?'

'Christmas and on my birthday he sends a card.'

'And you've never told him about Linda?'

'No. He had children already. I knew that.'

'What have you told the child?'

'That her father was killed in the war.'

'Well, I think it's wrong. Her father should know about her. Any man would be proud to acknowledge a child like Linda.'

She did not tell the mother that she did not like the way Linda was left to her own devices every day after school. What was the use? Hadn't she herself been obliged to leave Nona and Neil in the same way when she had been out at work? But of course she had had Len. He had always been a rock of a boy. If he promised a thing he did it. Nothing could have lured Len from the straight path of duty. He had been the reverse of his father. He had been a grand boy. Several tears spilled from the old woman's eyes at the thought of his untimely death—they rolled unheeded down her woollen jacket buttoned high and tight to the neck. On Len she had lavished all the affection which her own son Edward had thrust from him from an early age.

Since Len's death Linda had come to mean even more in Mrs. Collins' life. She lived now for the afternoons when the little girl would come; and the short hour which they spent together was for the old woman the highlight of her monotonous dreary days. The child brought life, vivid pulsating life into the room. She always came with the sun—and with shouts and shrieks of laughter. She was already showing at ten the signs of a ripe and voluptuous beauty, with something so foreign and exotic in her that the old woman did not care to think of her playing in the streets so freely and crawling about in those ruins across the street—there were eyes in the drab neighbourhood which would soon become aware of her.

'Was her father a good-looking man?' she had asked the mother.

'Wonderful looking. Blonde—and yet dark . . . Linda's like him.'

The house was very quiet now. Neil must have fallen asleep—there hadn't been a sound since he had turned once or twice on the narrow cot. The clock from the nearest church struck ten. A sparrow came and perched on one of the geraniums. He was so near Smokey that she held her breath. Smokey had opened one eye. Years ago she had waited breathless for a sparrow to perch on her wrist in Regent's Park—that had been when Jim had been courting her and had brought her on her first visit to London. Jim had been killed in the First World War. . . . She remarked the shining line of the sparrow, its quick grace, the sudden movement of Smokey—and it was gone.

Shuffling steps sounded along the passage in the hall, a pause, a heavy breathing, then old Mr. Evans' voice, 'Mrs. Collins . . . Mrs. Collins . . . going out now . . . . Can I get anything for you? Any little bit of shopping?'

'No, thank you, Mr. Evans. Nonie'll go presently—she'll be here today because of her cold and she'll bring in all I want.'

'It's no trouble. No trouble at all. If you'll just tell me what you want.'

'Nothing, thank you,' she said firmly. The old man would go on repeating his offer for some time. She was sorry for him— and often shut her eyes to the purposely-forgotten change— or to commodities for which he took the money and never brought her—but there were limits. One's purse set a limit on compassion. She was herself too poor to be blind too often. All he wants is a few pence—when his miserable bit of pension is gone and he's got to wait for next week's he gets like this—always trying to squeeze a few pennies out of Mrs. Danvers or me. If I had no family I'd be driven to something similar.

A boy went by whistling a tune from *Kismet*. A song they were for ever plugging now. Now, that's started me off again, thought the old woman. I'll have that tune running through my head all day.

The radio stood on a cupboard by the bed. She had only to turn the switch. Nona wanted to get her the television—but she didn't want it. They had quite enough to pay for, saving up for Australia. They wanted to pay their own fares so that they would be free to do as they liked about settling. She did not want the radio this morning—she wanted to think, about Neil. What had she done promising to assist in getting him away like that? *She must have been mad.* Nona had been so insistent, so desperate in her plea for her twin. She had looked quite distraught when she had threatened her grandmother. The old woman was powerless against this strong tie between the twins. It had always been like that—from early childhood. The two were wretched when separated. They never had been separated for more than a day or two because one could not bear to be parted from the other. During the war, when they had been evacuated to the country, they had inadvertently been sent to different families and both had been ill with misery. It had, as usual, been Len, placed in still another house, who had managed to get them accepted in a family willing to take them both.

When Neil had been called up Nonie had been frantic, but all her protests and tears had been unavailing; Neil had been taken. For the first few weeks his twin had moped and fretted herself into a frenzy over him—and then the boy had suddenly turned up at home—had simply walked out because he couldn't stick it, he had said. She could see now the scene when, having resisted all the girl's desperate appeals to get her twin away, to hide him from the police—she had handed him over to them. She could see Nonie clinging, sobbing to the boy and the two embarrassed policemen having to remove her forcibly. Horrible! And the second time had been almost as bad. And of course the girl blamed *her* for not having helped her grandson. She had been bitter and resentful, saying that the old couldn't understand the changing world and the new outlook of the young. They were all sick of war, of soldiering and the talk of bombs.

The old woman sighed; she saw it all too well—but what could she do? The law remained unchanged—military service was obligatory, whatever those liable to be made to fight thought about it. It had been Len who had encouraged his friend Charlie Kent's friendship with Nonie. Len had been wise beyond his years, had always carried the burden which his father had refused to accept. Len said that neither twin would be able to stand on their own feet until one of them had married. And Nonie and Charlie had been instantly and mutually attracted—just as she and Jim had been. Only Neil, when he had been told by his brother of the forthcoming marriage had come rushing home again, as wild and desperate as Nonie had been this morning and had made another scene, shouting that Charlie Kent was too rough and insensitive for his twin, that Nonie could never be happy with him. Well, there it was. They were happy enough, planning to go out to her sister in Australia and loving each other when Charlie was not away on long runs. It was Neil who caused the rifts between them. She was positive that Charlie would refuse to help his young brother-in-law, that, like last time, he would insist that he be handed over to the Army authorities. And with Len dead it was no use denying that she herself felt differently about forcing the boy back. He was her only remaining support; for Nonie belonged to Charlie, and, frail as he was in character, Neil was devoted to his grandmother.

From the street above came the sounds of the dustmen. The clatter of dustbins, the shouts of the men as the great dustcart halted outside each house for them. Down the steps came two lumbering figures. Up they went with the laden bins on their backs. When they returned with them empty, one of them tapped on the window—'Hello, Ma! How be doing?' She pulled herself up and, pushing open the window, smiled as the great dirty face grinned in at her. The second man turned back and waved too. 'Cheerio, Ma! Chin up!' he called.

They never forgot her. Always knocked on the window or called out a greeting to her. One of their grins and quips was worth more than all the advice from the welfare worker or the doctor. When she watched them lumbering up the steps with the loaded dustbins on their backs, she would think with rage of her son Edward. He had never carried a thing in his life, except himself—and even that unwillingly.

This is my life now—it has come to this, she thought whimsically. To lie and wait for the milkman's clatter, the postman's knock and the dustmen's greeting. For what else do I do? Watch the geraniums flower—the sparrows preen themselves, and wait for the clock to strike. This is the pause—the lull for the gathering of the forces before the last round.

She shut her eyes for a while and, dreaming a little, dozed. The pain was quiet—the Monster sleeping. When she opened her eyes again the space between the geraniums was blocked by a large grey blur. Was it the dustmen come back again? But it wasn't the dustman's face. It was the large grey cat. He had reared himself up, and was on his hind legs pressing his face against the window pane, rubbing his ears against the glass lazily and luxuriously. He blocked out the light . . . 'Smokey . . . Smokey . . .' she called softly. The cat listened, ears up straight, then began rubbing his head against the glass again.

'You missed the sparrow. . . .' she said with satisfaction, and smiled. Presently, in spite of her apprehensions she drew up the covers and slept.

In the cupboard-room next door, in his sister's jeans and sweater, the boy slept too. He had flung himself on the old iron bed and, tossing uneasily in his sleep, had pushed off the head scarf. Even so, with the delicacy of his features and face accentuated by the powder and lipstick which his sister had applied, he could have passed as a girl. Only his ears gave him away—large and red—they were unmistakably those of a boy.

CHAPTER V

NONA, ARRIVING late at the store, was frowned upon by Mr. Durton, the manager. He was a small pink-faced lewd old man who liked to put his hands on all his young assistants, and if possible on the younger women customers. He was in charge of the bacon and ham counter, and wore a filthy blue-and-white striped apron on which he wiped his hands, the tins which he was opening, and frequently, if necessary, his nose.

The assistants, of whom there were six, wore white overalls, but being allowed only one clean one a week they could better have been described as grey. The grocery store belonged to a chain, and Durton had been the manager of this branch for thirty years. Thirty years too long in the opinion of the girl assistants, who loathed him and his unsavoury habits.

Nona, in charge this week of the sandwich counter, from which they supplied the local offices and public house with ham-rolls and snacks, was a favourite of Mr. Durton's, although she resisted his straying hands and loathed his dirty apron.

As soon as she had arrived this morning there had been trouble over the opening of a new tin of ham. Young Wally was supposed to help with this, but this morning he had been sent to the bank. Nona, putting her counter ready for the day, had found that a new tin must be opened.

She went down to the cellar and brought up a heavy eight-pound tin and went to ask the manager about getting it opened. Should have been opened and ready by now,' he had snapped. 'It's almost half-past nine. You were late this morning, Miss Collins. A customer's been waiting for some time. Young Wally's gone to the bank, and I've no time to open tins now—I've got all the accounts to do with the cashier.'

Nona got Joan to help her with the tin. They could not get the ham out; it stuck fast and no amount of shaking and coaxing would persuade it to slide out gracefully on to the marble counter. 'Here—let me give a hand,' said the waiting customer. He went behind the counter and took the tin firmly. 'Got a cloth?' he asked. Nona handed him a grubby tea-towel and with much laughter and encouragement he got the ham out—but not whole, alas—it was broken.

Mr. Durton chose that moment to come out of the cashier's office. He frowned when he saw the broken ham and heard the girls laughing with the customer.

'Now then, now then. Enough of that noise. You girls get back to your work—the ham's out now—and very carelessly too.'

'I'm sorry,' said Nona meekly. 'I'm not used to it.'

'I am,' said the customer. 'Got tins like that in the Army—
bully beef . . . terrible job to get 'em out. We had a cook who
was a dab at it. Had 'em sliding out like peas from a pod.'

Nona, buttering rolls and slicing the ham, looked up at
him.

'In the war?' she asked.

'Yes. Fine life it was. Never had a decent job since. Wish
I was back again. But they wouldn't have me now—too old.'

So some people actually liked the life she thought, as she
pressed the ham between the halved rolls and wrapped them
in greaseproof paper.

'I've got a young brother doing his National Service—he
hates it.'

'Pity,' said the man. 'Best time of your life.'

That's what they say about school, thought Nonie, putting
the six rolls in a bag. She had loved school—but Neil had
hated it.

'My elder brother was killed in Cyprus,' she said, handing
him the bag.

'Bad show that,' said the man. 'Ought not to send young
Servicemen out there. Should keep that for the Regulars . . .
how old was he?'

'Nearly twenty-one—he'd almost finished.'

'I'm sorry,' said the man simply, taking the bag and handing
her the money.

She began slicing ham in the bacon machine, and was
obliged to take it out when Joan wanted to cut some bacon.
The van arrived with the trays of buns, pastries and tarts, and
the morning's bread. There was nowhere to put them. 'Come
along and get them unloaded,' shouted Mr. Durton from the
cashier's desk. He was irritable because Nancy, the cashier, had
lost three pounds which they couldn't trace.

'What a silly sort of shop this is,' said Joan crossly, leaving
the bacon to help unload the trays of food into the window.
'The new self-service ones are much better. They've got a
place for everything—and they're clean too—with all the new
refrigerated cupboards. Not old cellars full of beetles and rats

like these are. If people saw where we keep the food they'd never come into the shop.'

'Wait until the Sanitary Inspector comes again,' said Nona. 'He said last time that if storage space wasn't improved he'd have to take action.'

'He'd better take action over old Dirty's apron,' said Joan, 'it's thick with grease—and so are these overalls. Funny how he always gets the tip when the inspector's coming. We always get clean overalls that day—and he wears a clean apron, the old beast.'

'Hurry up and sign for those trays. Have you checked them?' called the man of whom they were talking.

'Got eyes all over his head like a beetle he has,' said Joan. 'Come on, Nonie, you call out and I'll check.'

The morning wore on but to Nona it was a torment. Nothing went right. She cut her finger badly, slicing sausage and was grumbled at by Durton for not using the machine.

'It was in use I couldn't keep the customer waiting while several pounds of bacon were cut,' she said helplessly.

'You're all het up today. What's the matter with you?' he asked. Start late, end badly—that's what I say. Time lost can never be regained.'

There seemed to be no lull in the morning's work—and all the time the thought of Neil ate at her. *Would he be all right? Would anyone come?* Would Gran let them in if they did? Half-way through the morning she remembered with a shock that today was the day when the social worker usually visited Gran. She felt frantic with anxiety and at lunch-time, when she had forty minutes free, she went to the nearest telephone booth.

It was difficult to find out about Charlie. He was often away for the night—and on long runs no one knew when he would be back. The depot where the lorry which he drove for a firm of sand and gravel merchants was kept was a large yard with a small shack used as an office. In this the foreman sat checking the runs and the loads. It was this man who answered Nona when she hesitantly asked for Charlie. 'Wait a minute—he's due in now—hold on, I'll see if he's arrived.'

She held on in the hot airless telephone box ignoring the repeated rapping on the glass of an impatient elderly woman waiting to make a call. At last there was a breathless hurried voice again. 'Wait a bit, missus—Charlie's in—he's coming as fast as he can.'

The woman began rapping with her umbrella. Nona opened the door while still holding the receiver to her ear. 'If you do that you'll break the glass,' she said. 'Can't you see I'm still waiting for my call?'

'You've been more than three minutes,' snapped the woman.

Nona shut the door as Charlie's slow throaty voice came over the wire. 'What's the matter? Anything up with Gran?' he asked.

'Not Gran, Charlie,' her voice was lowered. 'Are you alone there? Can anyone hear?'

'Only the foreman and he's doing his football pool—what's up?'

'Charlie—can you get off early tonight? *Please try*— it's *important.*'

'What's up, Nonie? Let's have it.'

'Neil.'

She heard an angry incredulous gasp. 'Not back again?'

'Yes. Charlie, try and get back early so we can talk it out in our room before I go into Gran's.'

'I'll try—but why all the fuss? He'll be fetched back same as last time.'

'*No,*' said Nona sharply, 'he's got to get away this time. *You come home early.*'

'All right. I'll try . . . but it's no use. You should know that, Nonie. *They'll get him.*'

'Listen, Charlie! I'm going to get off early too. I'm going to say I'm sick. I'll be waiting for you in our place.'

'O.K. But I won't promise anything, Nonie. You know how I feel about Neil.'

'Charlie you *must. Please.* Get back early.'

But he had hung up with an angry exclamation, and Nona gave up the telephone booth to the irate woman waiting for it. Charlie was angry just as she knew he would be. He'd never even asked her how she was, although he'd been away two nights up north. He had been furious last time Neil had quit. Couldn't understand why the boy couldn't take it. It was useless trying to make anyone understand things which only her twin and she herself shared.

But this time Charlie had *got* to help. Gran had said so. His lorry was the safest and best way of getting Neil out of the country quickly. Gran had said she must persuade her husband. They didn't realise how difficult it was going to be to get Charlie's promise of help. They knew nothing of the troubles growing up between Charlie and her. Nothing of the doubts, suspicions and miseries arising constantly now between them. Charlie didn't like Neil—never had. Perhaps it was because he was her double and it irritated him to see a boy in the image of the girl he had married. Perhaps it was the fact that she and Neil shared so much that no one else could. Each always knew when the other was unhappy, each could read the other's thoughts when near one another. The sympathy between them was something which she couldn't explain any more than Neil could.

Charlie was not only jealous of Neil's emotional pull on his wife; he was impatient and angry with Neil's fear of everyone and everything. He was afraid of nothing himself and simply couldn't understand anyone who was. To him Neil was not his wife's adored twin brother who was not cut out for Army life—he was just a miserable yellow-bellied coward who quit.

CHAPTER VI

'THERE'S A LETTER for you, Mrs. Collins. I found it on the mat,' said Alison Rhodes, as she cautiously opened the door of the patient's room. She entered hesitantly, although Mrs. Collins had passed her the keys out of the window, for this was one of the homes in which she was never sure that she was welcome. Lately she had felt that old Mrs. Collins was perhaps not so resentful of her visits as she had been at first. She had liked to believe that there was a slight lightening of the face, an almost imperceptible relaxing of the tautness of eyes and mouth when she was greeted—but she was never sure.

'A letter? That'll be another one about Len. I don't know that I can stand any more, Miss Rhodes. It's strange how few stock phrases there seem to be when anyone's dead.' Nothing in the old woman's calm demeanour showed the violent agitation which this visit was causing her. Behind that frail door was Neil—and Mrs. Collins neither knew nor trusted the visitor enough to confide in her. She stood up from the old wicker chair in which she sometimes spent the afternoons and Miss Rhodes said hastily, 'Sit down, Mrs. Collins. Please don't get up. How are you today?'

'Same as usual—dying,' said the old woman grimly, and this time there was no doubt about the smile. It flashed like silver from the sunken eyes and the old, still-beautiful mouth.

Miss Rhodes placed a big square envelope on the table and accepted the chair her patient offered. She had noticed the crest on the back of the envelope.

'I think this letter is from the Palace,' she said gently. 'Aren't you going to open it?'

Mrs. Collins' heart gave a great jump—it was as if it gave a last cry for Len—but she said quietly, 'Then it'll be about the medal for Len. The Colonel wrote me that I'd be hearing soon. Len always gave me as his next-of-kin, you see. What was the use of giving Edward, his father? Never know where he's likely to be.'

She did not open the envelope at once but kept it in the palm of her hand. 'Seems a pity to tear it open, might interfere with the battle,' she said smiling whimsically. Would you be very kind, Miss Rhodes, and get me a knife then I can slit it open?'

'Interfere with the battle?'

'For the Crown,' said the old woman, smiling again. 'Didn't you learn it as a child? . . . "The lion and the unicorn fighting for the Crown: the lion beat the unicorn all around the town. . . ."'

'Oh, yes . . . I see now,' and Miss Rhodes smiled too.

She has a dimple, thought the old woman. What a pity she doesn't smile more often.

She looks quite human today, how could I ever have been afraid of her? thought Alison Rhodes. Oh how I wish I could tell them—make them feel that I *care*. That I don't do this just for the sake of work: I do it because I want to help. I long to tell them . . . but my words come out in the stiff meaningless jargon of all these Social Services. Why, oh why, haven't I got the easy flow of words which this old woman's son has? *Why?* When I long so passionately to help?

'Shall I find the knife in the kitchenette?' she asked, getting up from the small prim chair which Mrs. Collins always placed for her. The old woman's manners put those of many of her fellow workers to shame. No matter how ill she was, there was always the chair and a tray of tea at hand.

'Don't bother. I can use the scissors—look!' She picked up the large pair of scissors with which she cut the wool for the rugs she made, and with one blade she slit the envelope. From it she slowly drew a letter on stiff white paper, which also displayed the red lion and unicorn at the top.

'I have the honour to inform you that the Queen will hold an Investiture at Buckingham Palace . . . at which your attendance is requested. . . .

'I am desired to say that you should arrive at the Palace between the hours of 10 o'clock and 10.30 o'clock and this letter should be shown on entering as no other card of admission is issued.

'Two guests may accompany you to the Ceremony. . . .'

Mrs. Collins put the letter down on the table and turned her face away. With a tremendous effort she regained her usual composure and handed it to Miss Rhodes. 'It's about Len's medal—the Military Medal,' she said tremulously.

Miss Rhodes took the letter. . . . 'The twenty-ninth . . . that's the day of the Investiture. What a wonderful experience it will be for you, Mrs. Collins!'

The old woman did not answer for a long time. Her eyes were on some faraway place, then she said, 'Yes, it will be wonderful. I should dearly love to see the Queen, God bless her.

But it's a long way off—anything can happen before that.' And she thought wildly, Yes, *anything* with my grandson hiding behind that door. Why, oh why, does he have to turn up *today* of all days? Why is it always like this? Aloud she said, 'Shall I have to answer this immediately, Miss Rhodes?'

'As soon as you can. They have to know whether or not you'll be there to receive the medal. The instructions are enclosed with the letter. Shall I see to all that for you? Whose names would you like for the tickets for the two guests?'

'I don't know that I'll be able to go. Some days I can't move—let alone walk.' In her mind she was thinking frantically that perhaps by then none of them would be able to go.

'I could drive you there in my car. I'm sure Nona will be able to get off work to accompany you. I suppose your grandson Neil won't be able to get leave?'

'It's very good of you, Miss Rhodes. I'd dearly like to go. But it's a long way off. No, Neil won't be able to come.'

'Only six or seven weeks.'

'That's a lot when one's days are numbered.'

'All our days are numbered,' said Miss Rhodes sighing.

'I'm always thinking about my childhood now,' said Mrs. Collins musingly. 'I suppose I long for the country and the trees and flowers. I'd love to see the country again and smell the grass.'

'I'll drive you there one afternoon. You'd like to see my mother's garden, wouldn't you?'

'I would indeed. I lie here and look at the children on that bomb-site opposite. I know them all. Do you know, Miss Rhodes, I get quite excited at their games. I join in them—in their hide-and-seek and their follow-my-leader. I suppose I'm returning to my second childhood. . . .'

'Were you very happy as a child?'

'Yes, I was. I was brought up in a Home—or rather several Homes—with my sister Liz—and yes, we were happy enough. Don't believe all you hear about the frustrated children without parents nowadays. We were better off without ours—we never missed what we'd never had.'

'It's such a lovely afternoon. What a pity you can't see the sky from here!'

'I can see the children and my geraniums in the window— and Smokey, the cat. Can't have everything, can we?'

'How's the rug getting on?' Miss Rhodes picked up the grey rug on which her patient was working. 'How quickly you work, and how beautifully. It's almost finished, I see. I have a customer for it—did I tell you?'

'You did. Thank you.'

'Have you seen your son again, Mrs. Collins?'

'Last week. He's begun coming quite often. Since Len's death he's been here three times. Edward never comes unless he wants something.'

'Perhaps he feels that you need him now that your eldest grandson's been killed.'

'It's not that. You've met him, Miss Rhodes. You know how he talks. Words, words, words—like the radio. Only Edward has no time signal to stop him. Last time he was here I had a feeling that he was edging on to religion. He's never been on to that yet. That would be the last straw.'

Alison Rhodes said nothing to this, but by the way she set her lips Mrs. Collins saw that she felt her to be hard on her only son, just as Nonie did. Nonie always defended her father.

'We're all different,' she said rather primly. 'Your son sees things from a different angle to yours.'

'Edward sees things from whatever angle suits him best— and that angle is left or right, whichever is most advantageous at that particular time.'

'But he must be very proud of his son. Why, the newspapers were full of your grandson's heroism.'

'Not at all. Edward rather despised the boy for doing his National Service so willingly. He considers that his death was legalised murder by the State. I'm quoting *him*, Miss Rhodes—those are not my opinions. That's why I won't have Edward going to the Palace to get Len's medal. Edward's by way of being a Communist—or was. No Communist, whether he's my son or not, is going to handle Len's medal.'

Miss Rhodes felt uncomfortable. She felt for the old woman but she thought her hard on her son. She opened her notebook and began the routine questions. To all of them, the patient replied with a little smile of amused tolerance, if not disdain, and the girl thought despairingly. Now we're poles apart again; she likes me as a person and hates me as an official visitor.

'I'll bring you some more wool. You'll be needing canvas for a new rug, too. What colour will you make next time?' she asked, looking at the old fingers which, although knotted and deformed with rheumatism, could still work so quickly and so well.

'Any colour which sells. I leave it to you, Miss Rhodes.'

'And how's your granddaughter, Nona?'

'Pale—this warm weather tires her in that stuffy shop.'

'Must she go on working now that she's married?'

Miss Rhodes knew Nona, and often bought her groceries from the shop where she was employed.

'Charlie earns treble what my Jim earned when we had three children to feed and clothe. But they're saving to emigrate to Australia—that's why Nona is working.'

Miss Rhodes looked round the small dark room. It was neat and cleaner than many which she visited, in spite of the fact that Mrs. Collins was often confined to bed for days at a time. A round table—a small sideboard, and on the mantelpiece a pink china swan. Her attention was caught by some bright blue tissue paper on the sideboard. On it lay a mango. Miss Rhodes could not help looking at it. Strange exotic fruit to find in this dingy little room.

'Looking at the mango? That's Edward. He says it will take me out of this room to the land where the sun always shines—to India. Every time he comes he brings some outlandish fruit and gives me a long discourse on the country from which it comes. I asked him if he could bring me a fruit grown in the land to which Len has gone—and where I shall soon be going—that's the only geography in which I'm interested now. Do you believe in an after-life, Miss Rhodes? There's been a lot of articles by famous people in the newspapers about it.'

Alison Rhodes shook her head—she had no wish to be drawn into a discussion on the possibility of a hereafter.

But the old woman persisted. 'That Joshua Taylor is so certain of the after-life that he's quite shaken me. I've got to think about it again. My time here's getting short.'

'That's your negro friend isn't it?'

'Yes. Edward brought him here one evening last year. He's called several times since. He's got something—a kind of hidden strength as if he knows what's wrong with civilisation and is laughing at us all for our blindness.'

'You mean he's got some new kind of philosophy?'

'The kind on which you and I were brought up, Miss Rhodes—Christianity. It'd be strange wouldn't it if those so-called heathen for whom you and I were made to put our pennies in the missionary boxes should be the ones to bring healing to our present state of chaos?'

Miss Rhodes drew in her breath sharply. Mrs. Collins had the power to disconcert her with such statements. She had seen the negro, Joshua Taylor, a huge man with a magnificent head and the treacly-smooth voice of his race. He was said to be doing quite remarkable work in the district. The social worker in her resented him. He had no status; there was no label to be pinned on him. He came under no official health, social or religious organisation; and yet in several homes in this district she had heard him spoken of with both interest and respect.

'You could see the Rev. Palmer if you wished, Mrs. Collins,' she said stiffly, 'You've only to say the word.'

'He's a paper creature. No blood in him. He makes me impatient. I like that great black man. I sit here and look at him so neat and respectable in my basket chair and I picture him a few generations ago in the jungle leaping about savage and half-naked . . . and now he can recite the whole Bible to an old sick woman who learned it by heart as a child. I think it's extraordinary. It makes me chuckle.'

Miss Rhodes found the subject distasteful. If the old woman knew she was dying—and she was no fool and must realise it—

she ought not to be so frivolous about it. She was determined to change the subject and reverted firmly to the mangoes.

'Have you tasted the mangoes, Mrs. Collins? What an original and charming idea of your son's.'

'Nonie and I ate one—he brought two. Tasted to us like turpentine. I'd rather have an apple any day.'

'What other fruit has he brought?'

'A Chinese gooseberry—looked like a huge woodlouse unrolled. He brought a persimmon too. I liked the persimmon, but I was bored by Edward's long geography lesson. Does he think that no one ever listens to the radio or reads the newspapers?'

Miss Rhodes said eagerly, 'But Mrs. Collins, your son is quite exceptional.'

'*Was*' corrected his mother grimly. 'When he was twenty it was exceptional to think as he does. Now he's forty-eight, it's just pathetic. I've heard the same tale in a different setting from Edward ever since he was twenty.' She picked up the envelope with the red crest on it again. 'He'll start off again as soon as he sees this, and I know exactly what he's going to say. Sometimes he doesn't come for months—but when he does he starts off exactly where he left off the last time. I could address any of his meetings for him. He's only got one record and it's a long-playing one.'

Miss Rhodes got up to go. She was dressed quietly but well. The old woman always noticed her accessories—bag, hat, gloves and shoes—all unobtrusive but expensive. She was slim and could have shown her figure to better advantage—but Mrs. Collins preferred her quiet slenderness to the blatantly vital statistics of the young women of the street, whose tight jerseys and tighter trousers hid nothing.

'I've taken down the particulars of the Investiture,' she said. 'I'll see to it all for you. Is there anything else I can do for you, Mrs. Collins?'

The old woman shook her head. 'Thank you, you're very kind, Miss Rhodes.' There was no gratitude but rather an unwilling acceptance in her face and voice, and an unmistakable wish for the visitor to go.

'Goodbye then, until next week,' Miss Rhodes was saying. 'No, please don't get up. I'll let myself out. . . .' When, suddenly, with a terrific thud, the door behind the bed shook, then burst violently open, and there fell into the doorway a figure which appeared to be enveloped in blankets and to have its legs caught in the wire frame of a broken bed.

CHAPTER VII

ON THE NARROW cot on which Nona often slept when Charlie was away, or when her grandmother was suffering more than usual, Neil had been in an uneasy dream. The centre of a class of his fellow Servicemen, he was demonstrating rifle-drill, loading, unloading and reloading his rifle. 'Safety catch forward, open breech, place charger in guide, force rounds into magazine, close breech, apply safety catch, watch front.' He heard himself repeating the rule as he complied with it.

'Collins, you there—what is the object of weapon training?' The sharp voice made him jump to attention, his rifle, as always, forgotten. . . . 'The object of all weapon training is to teach all ranks the most efficient way of handling their weapon in order to kill the enemy, sir. . . .' *In order to kill the enemy . . . in order to kill the enemy. . . .*' chanted the class, louder and louder, closing in in a circle upon him. . . .

But Len hadn't killed the enemy. The enemy had killed him, and it had been Len who had worked so hard at instilling the hated rifle drill into his brother. He had explained again and again loading, unloading, maintenance and firing. You know it perfectly well—I can't understand what you're worrying about. But Len couldn't know the fumbling, groping, stupid idiot which the loud authoritative voices made of his brother.

'What is the object of maintenance, Collins?' boomed one of those very voices . . . and he heard himself repeating the answer. . . . 'The object is to teach the soldier from the beginning that he must take proper care of his weapons so that they are always at maximum efficiency for killing the enemy. . . .' *'For killing the enemy . . . for killing the enemy. . . .'* chanted the

ever-encroaching khaki circle of the class. But there was no
enemy; this was not even an exercise . . . it was all so stupid.
Or was *he* the enemy? The approaching faces of the khaki
men grew larger and larger and more and more menacing.
No. *They* were the enemy —*they* with their stupid grinning
faces. He must kill . . . he *must*. That was surely what they
wanted him to do.

One lay down to kill. It was all in the orders. 'Long pace
forward with left foot to right front; rifle into left hand grasped
at point of balance; left arm extended, legs well apart; load as
already taught.'

He took the long pace forward with his left foot to right
front . . . he would *kill* them . . . *kill* them . . . that would wipe
the grins off their faces. . . .

'*Always examine your rifle before use to see if it is loaded. . . .*'
It was Len's voice . . . the same voice which had told him patiently that whether or not there was an enemy didn't make
any difference; you had to learn what to do in case there were
an enemy. 'Len!' he shouted, 'Len! Help me! There's too many
of them. *Help* me!' and he awoke with a violent jerk dripping
with sweat, his hair damp and clinging to his head.

He heard voices again and slowly sat up. But now he realised that the sounds came through the thin door between the
room and his grandmother's. The voice talking now was not
Len's. He had been dreaming as he always did . . . dreaming
that he was doing the rifle drill which he hated and feared. He
put his wet face in his hands. His grandmother was talking to
someone who was in the room with her. And suddenly new
terror came crowding in on him. Was it that horrible Mrs.
Danvers? He pulled the head scarf up over his short hair and
crouched up on the bed listening. So confined was the space
in the dark closet-room that by moving to the far end of the
cot and bending his head down he was on a level with the
door knob. There was no keyhole; it had been covered over on
the far side with the wallpaper of his grandmother's room. He
leaned down. He could hear two distinct voices but he could
not hear all that was being said.

It was a woman talking to his grandmother. A rather high voice—one which belonged in Neil's category to the classy ones. Clipped and clear—and somehow with the same ring of authority as those which hectored him. His grandmother had warned him that Wednesday was the usual day on which the visitor from the Health Service came. Must be her. 'If she comes don't you stir,' his grandmother had said, 'she's rather an officious young woman.'

His grandmother must have got up to let her in. What were they talking about? He leaned even further over to get his ear right against the place where the keyhole used to be. The weight was too much for the balance of the rotten old bedstead and suddenly with a terrific crash the whole frame collapsed on to the floor and he was thrown violently against the frail door. Built originally as a cupboard, it could not withstand the impact and burst open so that he was precipitated through it, while at the same time Len's picture of the Queen crashed down on to his grandmother's bed.

Miss Rhodes, exclaiming in alarm, sprang to help him, pulling him from the tangle of blankets, pillow and steel spring frame. The scarf fell from his head again and, helped to his feet, he stood there shaken and agitated. Miss Rhodes looked from the scarf which he snatched up and began twisting again round his head, to the jeans, the jersey and the plimsolls. Across a chair in the wretched little room now revealed was a khaki uniform. He saw her looking from it to him. 'You're Neil!' she said accusingly.

This was the twin brother, Nona's double. She had heard about him so often. There had been all that trouble over him deserting some months ago. Old Mrs. Collins had been horribly upset when the police had come for him to hand him over to the Military Authorities. And that had not been the first time apparently. He had done it previously, a few weeks after he'd been conscripted.

She looked curiously at the lipstick on his mouth and at the fair waving hair—so like his sister Nona's, and disgust for a fear so great that it could use a girl's cosmetics and clothes as a disguise was visible on her face. 'I'm afraid that bed is broken, or has the frame only slipped out of the socket? Let's have a look, shall we?' she said brightly to hide her discomfiture. 'Take that end of the frame; I can just squeeze in here. Now, if we lower it gently together, I think we can get it back. . . . Now . . . heave . . . lower gently . . . there that's got it. It's in!'

Triumphant at achieving a constructive task she mechanically picked up blankets and pillow and folded them neatly back on the bed. Mrs. Collins' voice, harsh and commanding, made her turn from scrutiny of the boy, now flushed and even more agitated.

'What's going on in there, Miss Rhodes? What's happened?'

'Only the bed, Mrs. Collins. The frame slipped out of the sockets. We've got it back now. Neil's got a bump, I'm afraid.'

So she knows it's *him*, thought the old woman. That's the first one to know and there'll be others. Can't hide much in this dump.

'Come in here, Neil,' she called authoritatively, 'and make Miss Rhodes a cup of tea.'

'I ought to be going, Mrs. Collins,' said the visitor nervously. 'I've still got three more visits on my list.'

'Leave them be,' said the old woman grimly. 'They won't break their hearts if you don't turn up.'

The young woman in the neat dark suit and the small beret smiled a little. 'I'm sorry you feel that way about us, Mrs. Collins. We try to help.'

Mustn't alienate her, thought Mrs. Collins quickly. She's seen Neil—she knows he's hiding. What was the little idiot doing to break the bed like that? Trust him to do something silly. Aloud she said quietly, 'Sit down, Miss Rhodes, and listen to me.' And at the same time she gestured to the boy to disappear into the kitchenette.

She's got nice eyes, thought Mrs. Collins, studying the closed earnest face of the young woman who had sat down again on a small stiff chair. And pretty hair. Why do they all have to put on this falsely bright manner—as if we were all mental defectives or children to be humoured?

'Miss Rhodes,' she said aloud, 'let's face facts. I'm not one to beat about the bush and I hate lies. I admire you for doing this work, but today you've seen something you were not meant to see—through an accident. You're here—in my room, not because I invited you into my home, but because I've had at times to ask help from the State. For that help, small as it is, I've had to pay in the intrusion of my privacy whenever the State feels like violating it.'

Miss Rhodes said quickly, 'No, no, Mrs. Collins!'

'*Yes.* If I were a wealthy old woman I could live in filth—as many do—or in sickness or neglect and no one would trouble about me. But because the pension towards which I've contributed all my working life is not enough to keep me, and the State has had to supplement it, any young thing like you—no offence intended—has the right to come in here and visit me and write a report in your neat little book.'

The young woman's face turned pink with embarrassment, but she did not reply.

'I'm not complaining,' went on the old woman. 'Indeed I appreciate all that you do. You look at the floor—at the bed-clothes. Oh yes, I'm not blind. If they were dirty you'd go back with a bad report to your head office and soon I'd be carried off to a Home for the Aged or the Sick, where I'd be forcibly washed and kept in a carbolic-scented ward. Well, the floor in this room is still clean and so are the bedclothes and I'm dying just as slowly as it suits the disease which is killing me. *I've no complaints.* You do your duty and I'm grateful to you. But what you've just seen—that's *not your business.*'

'You mean your grandson is absent without leave again?'

'He's quit again,' said his grandmother with a sigh, 'although he gave me his word last time to stick it out until the end.'

'But,' faltered Miss Rhodes, 'aren't you going to send him back before they fetch him back?'

'What's the good? It'll happen again and again unless he's locked up permanently in the glass-house. *He's a quitter.* He's no use to them. No use at all. There's no harm in the boy; in fact he's a good law-abiding boy until they try to make a soldier out of him. Neil's not cut out for soldiering. Why *can't* they see it?'

'But what are you going to *do* about it?'

'It's better that you don't know. I don't want to get you mixed up in this. No. Be a good girl and don't ask me—and forget that you've seen him. You must. *Will you?*'

'Mrs. Collins,' said the girl earnestly, 'do think carefully what you're doing. It's aiding and abetting a deserter.'

'So what?' retorted the old woman. 'I gave them Len, didn't I? And I've sent this chicken-livered boy back twice. If I send him back again he'll only run away again as soon as he's released from jail. He gets longer and longer sentences—harsh savage sentences—and so it'll go on. It makes me frantic that no one sees the stupidity of it. *The boy's got no guts!* His brother had them all. Neil's been fashioned without any—he couldn't kill a fly—I've found him taking endless trouble to save a spider or a bee. If he's got guts he hasn't found them yet. And he's Len's brother. Isn't it strange?'

'Your granddaughter—does she know he's back?'

'Yes. Who d'you think fixed him up in those clothes but her? She's his twin—they're as alike as a pair of vases—one of them chipped. She loves Neil with a passionate intensity that frightens me. She feels what he does—suffers what he does—and can't bear that he must endure what she is spared. She attacked me violently this morning—almost threatened me that if I don't help him this time she'll go away with him—and leave me.'

'But she's married. She must leave her twin to his own life—they are no longer children.'

'What's the use of you or I thinking that? I tell you that no one but twins can understand this extraordinary sympathy—this terrible bond—as if they share one mind, one soul. I tell Charlie the same thing. He's jealous of Neil—horribly and unjustly jealous—but what can I do? It's always been the same.'

'I think you'd be helping them both if you sent your grandson back, Mrs. Collins. It's your duty.'

'I' m too old to be told what is my duty any longer. I must decide that for myself now. What matters now is *you*, Miss Rhodes. Are you going to forget what you've seen by chance this afternoon?'

The girl stared at the old woman. The enigmatic look was back there again—the faintly derisive look which said, 'I don't really care what you say or think. I've lived so long that I can put things into so much better perspective than you can, my girl.' It disconcerted her again, so that she faltered a little as she answered. 'I shall have to think it over, Mrs. Collins. . . .'

Not a flicker on the impassive old face showed the anguish underneath it. She could hear the chinking of crockery in the kitchenette. I know he's listening . . . he must be, the grand-mother thought, and she called softly, 'Neil, Neil—where's that cup of tea?' That he had been listening was proved by the way his eyes went straight to the girl's face. He had a dish towel over one arm and she was struck by the fact that for a moment she had thought it was Nona coming in. 'Miss Rhodes . . . is she going to give me away?' he blurted out, his face paling at the very thought of it.

'I don't know,' said his grandmother tersely.

'*Are* you?' asked Neil, and the girl could not withstand the urgent anguished demand in his face.

'I don't know . . .' she faltered.

'Get Miss Rhodes a cup of tea,' said his grandmother quietly.

'I really think I'd better be going—I've three more visits to make,' she said again.

'Leave them be. They won't miss you. . . .'

She was angry with the girl and wanted to hurt her, and as she saw the colour flood the small face, she said quickly, 'No, that's not true. They *will* miss you—as I'd do now if you didn't come. I mustn't keep you.'

'I wrote to my mother and asked her if I could bring you down to see the garden,' she said. 'You'd like that, wouldn't you?'

'Thank you.' There was no enthusiasm in the reply and Alison Rhodes was piqued. The old woman had been so inter-ested in her mother's garden. She had told her about the rock gardens, the water-garden with the little bridge and the step-ping-stones, the rose gardens and the long herbaceous borders. It's this wretched boy, she thought angrily. Just as I was getting somewhere with her at last, he must come crawling home like this. He's utterly selfish and worthless. . . . He ought to go back and learn his lesson. . . .

'Is there anything you especially need?' she asked perfunctorily, picking up her notebook and gloves.

'Only a brand-new body instead of this rotting old carcase,' was the grim answer.

Alison Rhodes could not bring herself to speak to the youth busying himself with the tea. She felt no pity for him. All her compassion was for the old woman on whom this burden must fall. 'Don't get up,' she said quickly, 'I'll let myself out—your grandson had better not go near the door. . . .'

But Mrs. Collins had risen and stood stiffly by the chair. Something hostile had sprung up between the two women suddenly, so that their glances, as they met, measured and appraised one another. What *is* she going to do? each asked of the other, as they shook hands politely.

'Here's the tea,' said Neil, coming in with a plate of biscuits balanced on his arm and the teapot in his hand . . . and was relieved to see the visitor slipping out of the door. They heard her start up the engine of her small car; it started easily and she drove off quietly. From the window below street level, everything appeared elevated and distorted. They watched the car move away with the same ease and efficiency which marked all Miss Rhodes' movements. When the last sound of it had died away, Neil said agitatedly, 'What'll she *do*? I didn't like her. Will she go and split on me? *Will* she? She may drive straight to the police station now. . . .'

'I don't know,' said his grandmother. 'It's a thousand pities that she saw you. How could you be so stupid as to fall in like that? What were you doing? Listening, I suppose.'

He nodded. 'I woke up from an awful dream and heard voices. I had to know who it was in here with you.'

'Curiosity killed the cat. It may well have put paid to your escape.'

'You don't think she will really go to the police?'

'I don't know what she'll do. She brought *this* in with her.' She held out the Investiture letter, and she knew from his face that he felt keenly the fact that it had arrived on the same day as he had. He was sensitive—perceptive—as a woman is, she thought. He is imaginative, too—that's why he suffers so.

He looked up slowly now. 'You must feel pretty bad about this—and me coming home like this. Len was always brave. . . .' he said chokily.

'Brave people know fear too, but they overcome it. Can't you, boy, can't you?'

Amongst the fallen masonry, the tall grass and the fire-weed, the children were playing on the bombed-site. They were playing hide-and-seek. The sun made long slanting shadows which in the dark corners of the former houses were mysterious and compelling. They were a little afraid of the deepest ruins, the foundations of the building, which had once been a block of flats. The barbed wire put up to keep them away from the place was no obstacle to their adventurous spirits.

Linda and Cissie, hand in hand, were in one of the darkest corners hiding their eyes and counting a hundred before they called 'Coo-ee' and went to look for those who were hiding. 'Ninety-one, ninety-two, ninety-three, ninety-four, ninety-five . . . Ooh! look, Linda, there's a man!'

Cissie clutched the bigger girl nervously. Linda, conscientiously keeping her eyes shut until she reached the century, gabbled through the last numbers and opened them. Yes, there, where Cissie was pointing, was a man—and what was more, he was a soldier. He lay there in the shadows almost hidden in the thick long grass. He was dark—and his eyes were looking right at them. There was something menacing and threatening in that glance, although he was smiling, and Linda drew back and pulled Cissie more closely to her. They stood there staring at the man and he at them. He was young—but big, and his skin was brown and sunburned. His hair was dark and thick and there were bits of grass in it from where he had been lying. He didn't move, but still looking at them, he said, 'What are you staring at? Haven't you ever seen a man before?'

The little girls giggled and remained dumb. From all around them came the voices of the impatient hidden friends, faint coo-ees to assist the seekers in their search.

'Go on—get hunting again,' said the man roughly, 'You haven't seen me—I'm hidden too. Understand? You never saw me. *Get me?*'

Linda nodded. Her throat was closed suddenly. She couldn't look away from the man—there was something so strange and compelling in his dark eyes.

'You're a pretty little girl—I wouldn't like anything to happen to you—so you keep your little mouth shut . . . see? *You haven't seen me.* Got it?' Linda nodded again. 'And nor has she. . . .' pointing to Cissie. 'You keep her mouth shut, too—get it?'

Linda nodded. She stood poised now for flight. She'd been told about men—never to let them touch her. This one caught hold of her bare leg now and gave it a vicious pinch. . . . 'That's just to keep you remembering . . . now *beat* it.' The pinch hurt, but the child was too alarmed to cry. She seized Cissie's hand tightly, and pulling her roughly away, tried to raise her voice to cry 'Coo-ee—Coming . . .' in answer to the more impatient cries of those she should be seeking . . . but no words would come. She gave a sound which was a strangled gulp and turning, fled, dragging the fat Cissie with her.

CHAPTER VIII

NONA, HARASSED and distraught over Neil, could not bring herself to go straight back to the grocery store after telephoning Charlie. She found herself wandering towards the river. The street emerged on to an especially sordid scene. It was low tide and the house-boats showed their draggled muddy bottoms, and on the slimy mud where the tide had receded was an unpleasant collection of discarded objects—old tins, a hat, a bicycle wheel and something that looked uncommonly like the carcase of a cat. Sickened, she turned away in disgust to a group of swans and began throwing pieces of her sandwiches to them. There was one swan smaller and more timid than any of his fellows. He got nothing. Every time she tried to coax him near enough to take a piece of bread the stronger birds chased him away. He's like Neil, she thought wretchedly, he doesn't stand a chance with these toughs. They were dirty too, their white beauty sullied and muddied. Everything was soiled and stale.

Neil . . . what was going to be done about Neil? If only Len had not been killed. She had still not got over the shock of his death and the fact that the whole basis of the family's stability had gone with him. She could still hear the anger and scorn in Charlie's voice . . . he had said flatly that he would not help. Perhaps Gran could persuade him. Gran admired Charlie, she liked his strength, his gruff rough ways. But she knew that things were not right between them. How was he to be got away if Charlie would not help? He doesn't know pity . . . he's never needed to, she thought. It's all been straight-forward for him. What he wants he takes by sheer brute force. In spite of the physical tie between them she felt that they were inevitably growing apart. Apart. Her grandmother had used that word. She was aghast at the old woman's perception. I lie in his arms, my skin next to his skin, my heart beating to his beats, striving for deliverance—escape from it all—and yet we're strangers really. I don't know what he thinks, what he seeks in me except perhaps this same terrible delight and release. And when that has gone? They say it goes. What then? Does he wonder about me as I do about him? Does he wake afterwards and look at me as I do at him and say to myself, What am I doing lying with this man? Why just *this* one? Does he lie with other women when he's away on those long runs, three or four nights a week?

Why had Neil chosen just this time to come home? Things had been getting a little easier. After that last time Neil came back Charlie didn't speak to me for weeks. He took me in silence, in monosyllables . . . outraging me . . . degrading me. And yet I can't deny myself or him. If this awful thing be-tween us is love then I love him . . . *I love him.* And I want his child . . . but he won't agree. Every time Nona begged to have a child, Charlie's answer was always the same—'Wait until we get to Australia!' She wanted a child terribly—how Charlie felt she wasn't sure. He was good with children, but had no patience and little tenderness. He laughed at her fantasies, her imagination, just as he laughed at Neil. But he was capable of tenderness; she had learned that herself, as had her grandmother when in great pain. He seldom came back from a long distance trip without bringing the old woman something.

But Neil didn't like Charlie Kent. Charlie, he said, was too rough and too crude for Nonie—he wasn't good enough for her.

Mary, the family's young friend who had been at school with the twins, had tried to console him. She had been fond of Neil, and Nonie had thought for a time that perhaps it would be the making of her twin. If he were engaged to Mary, surely it would make all the difference to his wretchedness during his National Service. But it hadn't worked out that way. Something had gone wrong between Neil and Mary just as it was now going wrong between her and Charlie. Mary had gone to live with a fat, balding, middle-aged car dealer who had taken a fancy to her. She had got tired of Neil's sordid troubles in the Army.

Nona's love for her twin wasn't in the least like anything she felt for anyone else. It was an anguished tenderness. She not only loved Neil, she suffered his pain, his misery, his humiliation, was tormented by his agonised indecisions and bewilderments. She had two lives, was two persons, she lived in him as he did in her—or was it that she and Neil had really only one life between them? She was *him* and whether she liked it or not that weak frightened side of him was *her* too. Why had she been able to overcome it and he not? Why had the distribution of such qualities been so uneven when all the external basic similarities were shared by them both?

Charlie, good-natured and generous when it suited him, had a violent, jealous nature. He was jealous not only of men but of everyone—of Mary, of Joan, of Len, of her grandmother, for taking so much of her time, but most of all it was jealousy of Neil, her twin, which was tearing them apart. 'Your feeble shadow, your weak-kneed identical . . .' he would call

Neil contemptuously, although he knew that he hurt her terribly by doing so.

Before they had been married he hadn't said these things, even if he had thought them. That was one of the horrible things about marriage. Nona had discussed it with her grandmother. 'If you girls would only realise that marriage means scrubbing your own steps for nothing instead of other people's for money, you'd think twice before you did it,' was the old woman's acid comment. 'It's the fact that he need not pay you for what you do for him that makes a man think he's entitled to say and do what he likes.'

It was Len who had persuaded her to marry. He had always said that Neil would never do anything until his twin was married and he was forced to manage without her. Len had been Charlie Kent's friend.

Charlie had immediately made it clear that he had no intention of taking Len's place in the home. He hated responsibilities, especially if they were not of his own making. He wanted to get to Australia, and nothing else interested him. He was blunt and tough, never promising anything which he couldn't carry out, never boasting anything which he couldn't achieve. He would get to Australia all right—even if he went alone. Nonie had no illusions about that. Sometimes she wondered if the fact that she had a well-to-do aunt in Australia, who was willing to give them a start out there, had had something to do with his impatience to marry her. Did he really love her? She tormented herself with the question sometimes. Or was he tired of her already.

The clock struck two. She would be late again at the store but she felt that she didn't care as she retraced her steps back there. It was hot and airless in the midday warmth, and the smell of the food sickened her. On edge and nervous, her mind in that small sombre room with the papered door behind her grandmother's bed, she could neither keep her attention on her work nor find her usual gay retorts to the manager's bullying. At his third sarcastic remark on her lack of attention to the customers, she shouted, 'I'm leaving, I'm packing in—a week from tomorrow.'

She shouted it across the shop and over the heads of the open-mouthed customers waiting to be served. They loved it. What! One of the young chits saucing that dirty old manager.

'Notice accepted, Miss Collins—or rather, Mrs. Kent,' said that gentleman—using Nona's married name sarcastically. 'But for this week you'll kindly carry out your duties.'

'Nonie, you don't mean it?' Joan was aghast. The work was hard, the floor of stone, the draught from the ever-open door something frightful, but they had fun and the pay was not too bad, and although old Dirty could be sharp-tongued and mean, he was quick to forget. A girl might have a much worse job, and Nonie had said that she liked it.

'I'm going to work in a library in a big store,' said Nonie casually. 'Been trying to make up my mind to give notice for weeks. I'm sick of ham and bacon and butter and of making sandwiches and rolls for the empty-bellied. I love books—I've always wanted to work in a library.'

'I think that's wonderful—however did you hear of it?'

'Miss Rhodes—she's a social worker who comes to see my grandmother—she put in a word for me. I passed my G.C.E., you know. It's a pity for me to be serving bacon and butter when I passed that. But this is near home—and now I'm married that means a lot.'

'Miss Collins, will you kindly stop chattering and get on with your work. If you've no customers there are all those shelves to be cleaned and dressed. Go down in the cellar and start bringing up some tins; we're very low on soups and vegetables.'

Nonie went down to the dark dirty cellar and began taking tins from the cases. Sitting down on a packing-case she lit a cigarette and studied her long slim legs. It had taken all her control not to have shouted something at old Dirty. He knew perfectly well that it was not her job to fetch up tins for the shelves. Wally did that—and old Pete. Neither of them was ever there. Pete and old Dirty were forever placing a shilling here and a half-crown there, and it was old Pete who went out to give them to the shoemaker who ran a small bookmaker's business. Young Wally with his round red face and goggling eyes was always at the bank or delivering goods on his bicycle. She could not get Neil out of her mind. She felt frantic with anxiety whenever she thought of him.

It was strictly forbidden to smoke during business hours. Nonie heard footsteps coming down—old Dirty's she supposed. She stubbed out the cigarette and pushed it under a case as the manager descended into the murky cellar. She sat quite still on the packing-case. His small boat-shaped eyes squinted at her in the dimness, then he switched on the light. He sniffed suspiciously at the smoke. 'Well, you're busy I must say,' he said sarcastically. 'What's the matter with you today? Always my little sunshine. Nonie, I always say—that's the girl for me. What's come over you, girlie? Giving me notice and all....'

'I don't feel well,' said Nonie coldly. Inwardly she was trembling. (I won't take it back ... I won't! I want to go to that library. I won't take it back....)

'If you're not well you'd better go home,' he said kindly, patting her arm so that his hand strayed beyond it and across to her breast. 'Run along home—and take one of those tins of salmon for your Gran.'

Nonie gulped. She simply couldn't bring herself to push away his hand. Although sick at the thought of those unclean fingers exploring under her overall, she simply could not get up, push him away and walk up the stairs. He picked up a tin of salmon. 'You take that to the old lady. She'll relish a bit of salmon ... won't she?'

'Yes ... thank you, Mr. Durton....'

Coward, coward.... Talk of poor Neil, she thought fiercely, he's not the only yellow one.... She drew a breath. 'I don't feel bad enough to go home,' she said calmly. 'We're short with Millie away and there's a lot to do filling the shelves. I'll take an aspirin with my cup of tea.'

'Then we'll say no more about the notice.... You like it here, don't you, Nonie?' His hand strayed further.

'It suits me all right,' said Nonie desperately. Then, thinking of Neil and of how he was despised for doing exactly what she was now doing, she stood up abruptly, almost knocking the man over, and said firmly, 'Mr. Durton, thank you, but I won't take this tin, and I do want to leave. I've got a chance to work in a library—I've always wanted that. A girl ought to better herself. . . .'

'A married woman, not a girl,' said the manager nastily. 'When I married I wouldn't have allowed my wife to go out to work. These young fellows now—half of them live on their in-laws—and lots of them on their wives.'

'Charlie doesn't live on anyone but himself,' she retorted angrily. 'I'm working to save up to go to Australia. You know that.'

Joan came down the stairs. 'Want some tinned beans. What, are *you* down here?' She looked suspiciously at the old man and at Nona. There was something going on. Probably old Dirty had been at his tricks again. Nona picked up some tins, 'Here's some beans.'

Joan looked at her. They both giggled suddenly at the idea that each was thinking the same thing.

'That'll do, Miss Collins—the notice can remain.'

He picked up the tin of salmon and replaced it in the case.

Why did I do it? *Why? Why?* Gran'll be upset—she'll miss the tins and the tit-bits—and she's no opinion of libraries because of Father always quoting from books. . . . And the pay'll be less just as we want money with Len gone. Why am I like this today? Why? Is it only Neil—or is it me?—or is it Charlie?

It was just before they closed that Miss Rhodes came in. She looked quickly round the shop and made for Nona. Good afternoon, Nona. I've just come from your grandmother.' There was a pause. What's she going to say? Does she *know*? *Why's* she come? Aloud she said, 'Good afternoon, Miss Rhodes.'

'I want some cocktail biscuits—some cheese-flavoured ones,' said her customer briskly, seeing the manager eyeing them inquisitively. Nona went to find a tin, only to discover, as with the ham, that a new one had to be opened. She placed the large square tin on the counter, took a knife to cut through the airtight binding.

'You've cut yourself,' observed Miss Rhodes.

'Did it this morning opening a tin of ham.' Nona did not look at the social worker; she kept her eyes on what she was doing.

'Your grandmother,' began Miss Rhodes, 'is upset today. Something is worrying her. She ought not to be worried. She's really *very* ill. You know that?'

How I hate her, thought the girl, cutting deftly round the tin, as if I didn't know that Gran's not got much longer. What does she think of us? That we're callous and devoid of any feeling?

'You can't stop people worrying,' said Nona, looking up suddenly so that Miss Rhodes got the full impact of the eyes. Strange, slanting, intelligent eyes, hazel and black-ringed. They made Miss Rhodes faintly uncomfortable; they were so like that boy's.

'I saw your brother,' she said abruptly. The knife slipped and Nona just saved her thumb from being cut.

'And?' she said evenly. How *could* he? How could he? I might have known it would happen like this. Neil's not the one to get away with anything. . . .

'He fell into the room. I wasn't *meant* to see him. The bed gave way and he fell against the door.' She did not add that he had been obviously eavesdropping, leaning all his weight on one corner of the bed.

The tin was open. Nonie removed the paper shavings, the protective pads. 'Half a pound?' she asked.

'A pound.' She began to weigh them out.

'I've packed up here,' said Nona. 'Gave my notice this morning.' She expected Miss Rhodes to say that there was that library job and that she would put in a good word for her. But Miss Rhodes said nothing, except, 'I expect you get tired of working with foodstuffs—especially in summer.'

Nona put the biscuits in a bag, her hands were trembling. I must ask her. I *must*, she thought agitatedly. I can't go back to Gran and say I've packed up, when there's no other job in the offing. But there were jobs enough for the asking. No one wanted them. They all wanted bigger wages than the shops could give. She could walk right into another one of this sort this very afternoon. But she wanted that library one. If she got experience, she could work in a library in Australia.

'Miss Rhodes,' she began nervously, 'you mentioned once to me about a library job. Could you help me to get it? I do so want a change. Half a pound of coffee—continental roast.' Nona fetched the beans, put them in the mill and began laboriously to grind them.

'Good gracious. Haven't you got an electric machine for that?'

'One's on order, madam. Been on order some time,' came the suave voice of old Dirty.

So he's listening, thought Nonie desperately. Does she know about Neil? *Does she?*

'Been on order ever since I've worked here,' she said.

Above the noise of the grinding she looked anxiously at Miss Rhodes for an answer. When it came Nona could have hurled the beans to the floor in her disappointment.

'I'm afraid that job's filled,' she said calmly. 'It was some time ago you know. You didn't seem keen. About your brother, let me give you some advice; that's why I really came in.' Above the noise of the coffee mill she said, speaking quietly and carefully, *'He must go back.* There's no question about it. You're committing a felony in harbouring a deserter.'

Nonie stared contemptuously at her, scooped the ground coffee out of the drawer, poured it neatly and expertly into a red bag, 'That's three and ten—it's the best roast,' she said non-committally, 'and four shillings the biscuits.'

Miss Rhodes looked at the set face. She's not giving anything away, she's a pretty kid—horribly pretty—the sort that men like—Rodney, for instance, would love her. At the thought of Rodney, and tonight's date with him, she felt agitated. She no longer looked forward to those evenings with Rodney. He wasn't really her sort—but she could no longer choose her sort because they chose others, girls more like this little twin sister of the deserter. Rodney was too highly coloured, too synthetically glossy, too sure of himself. She didn't like him really, but he took her out, and she had to have an escort. She couldn't go out alone.

Rodney was in advertising, and he looked somehow like one of his own lay-outs for an advertisement of himself. Even his car was flashy, his hair an advertisement of the virile he-men in women's magazines.

Because her mind was on Rodney, she did not notice Nonie's pale face or the worried lines on her usually smooth forehead.

'I took your grandmother some more wool,' she observed as the girl handed her a slip for the cashier.

'Thank you. She gets through it very fast.'

'Yes. That rug will soon be finished.'

'When your brother has gone back, we'll see what can be done about that library job. They're particular there of course. They expect—and get—good references.'

So she's not going to play unless I do. *When your brother has gone back.* What does she mean? What's she playing at? Oh, why did Neil have to let her know he's there? *Why?*

She replaced the biscuit tin lid listlessly without bidding Miss Rhodes goodbye.

I suppose she's upset that I know about the brother. These young girls are all the same—no manners, no interest in their work. . . . Miss Rhodes gathered up her parcels from the counter and left.

Nonie, replacing the biscuit tin on the shelf, saw that the manager was staring interestedly at her. What's she going to *do* about Neil? I didn't like her manner; it was almost threatening. She felt that she couldn't stand one more minute of the smell of pig—bacon, ham, sausages, lard. Poor pigs, they have a lot to answer for, she thought, but the people who bought them had even more. I've got to get out of here. . . . She leaned against the marble counter for a moment. Then she said fiercely, Pull yourself together, you miserable jelly-baby. You're no better than your twin. She took several deep breaths and said quickly and loudly, 'I'm going now, Mr. Durton. I'm sorry but I'm wanted at home. Miss Rhodes has just come to tell me so.' And before the manager could recover from this impertinence, she had rushed through to the corridor where they hung their coats, snatched hers, and darted through the side door to the street.

CHAPTER IX

MRS. COLLINS, exhausted by Miss Rhodes' visit and its consequences, took to her bed again. She had been up for several hours in her basket chair and her back hurt. Neil was finishing his bread plastered with raspberry jam and gulping down the last drop of tea. His grandmother watched him take the tray back to the kitchenette. He loved messing about in the kitchen. Nona liked to tinker about with Charlie's motor-cycle. She would spend all Sunday mornings out at the back working with Charlie on the machine while Neil would be blissfully happy cooking the midday meal for them all. She heard him washing up the cups and plates. Nona would have left them until she was obliged to do them.

Remembering that her neighbours would be wondering why she had not had her radio on all day she switched it on, amused at her efforts at deception. She tuned in to 'Music while you work'. She liked music and enjoyed this programme. Her husband Jim had had a fine voice with the same magnetic quality as their son Edward's had. But Jim had used his to sing in a famous choir, not to go round the country stirring up trouble in the industrial areas as Edward did.

She was late in switching on because of Miss Rhodes' visit, and almost at once the music ended to be followed by 'Mrs. Dale's Diary'. She listened for a few minutes to the imaginary difficulties made in order to be overcome in the life of the fictitious doctor's wife. Words, more words . . . sometimes she couldn't stand them, but today she wondered what Mrs. Dale would do in her place. Now, here's one for you to solve my girl! What would *you* do? Send him back between two guards to the glass-house, to the possible year in a civil jail? Send him back to the reveille at 5 a.m., to the relentless harrying and chivvying, to the never-letting-up of the sergeant's enforced discipline, to everything done at the double, of never being allowed to stop for one moment from the stone-breaking, the sack-sewing, the scrubbing of cells, the cleaning of equipment? *Would you, Mrs. Dale?* Yes, perhaps you would—as I know I ought. *As I've done twice already*. But what's the use? It didn't do Neil a bit of good, not a bit. And what would he have done had he been sent to Cyprus, I wonder? Neil's the sort who can only go in for imaginary heroics just as you have to deal with these imaginary problems. But Jim always said that it was just that sort who actually did achieve real heroism in *his* war—the First World one.

I'm in a real mess, she worried. How can I go and fetch Len's medal with it on my conscience that I've helped his brother to desert? *What would you do about that one, Mrs. Dale?* She switched the programme off impatiently. Compared with the urgency of her own problem it all seemed too trite. Everyone was too kind and helpful. People weren't like that in real life, not a bit. They were more like Mrs. Danvers who was probably listening outside the door now; and like old Mr. Evans who was always robbing her of her change . . . and here she was talking away to herself as much as Edward talked to anyone who would listen.

'Neil,' she called softly. He came in, apprehensive and anxious. His face was drawn and old. The thinness of his cheekline, the sharpness of the jaw, the horizontal lines across the normally smooth forehead and the tight Adam's apple when he swallowed nervously had a vulnerability as potent as that small white bit at the nape of his neck. She felt another agonising wave of pity flood her, but thrust it away relentlessly. Pity had never been anyone's friend.

'You've slept, eaten, and you look better,' she said evenly. 'Now sit down, Neil. We'd better get talking about your plans. There's one person knows your identity—and almost certainly two. Mrs. Danvers will have said something to Miss Rhodes about her suspicions.'

'Damn Mrs. Danvers,' he said angrily. 'What's it got to do with her?'

'There's no privacy when you're old and sick any more than there's any up at your camp. We all know one another's business here. What else is there for us to do? Your desertions and arrests were the highlight of their lives here. They're, always on the look-out now. It's no use blaming them, it's your coming back which has upset the apple cart.'

'I'm sorry,' he mumbled.

'Supposing every lad who couldn't get on up there ran away? It'd be like one of those strikes your father's so fond of working up.'

'It wouldn't be a strike, it would be a mutiny . . .' he said sullenly.

'When I was your age I was working in the Home where my parents left me. I scrubbed, washed, mended and ironed for all the younger children. I was at everyone's beck and call. I got up at five and fell on my bed after eleven at night, often too tired to undress. I didn't run away—there was nowhere to run to. . . .'

'Things were different then,' muttered the boy. 'It wouldn't be allowed now. That's what gets us. Only the Army dare treat humans like that. The Trade Unions don't help the conscripts. . . .'

'Don't start talking like your father. When he gets on to Trade Unions I switch off. I stop my ears.'

'A lot of what Dad says is sense. . . .'

'And most of it is drivel, cheap stuff you can read in any Red rag, if you're stupid enough. If I thought you were going to start talking like your father I'd send you back right now.'

'I wouldn't go,' he said defiantly.

'You'd have to,' said his grandmother flatly, 'as you did before. Let's quit this shilly-shallying. *Why did you desert again?*'

He did not answer but sat there swinging one leg against the bedpost. 'Don't do that. They'll know there's someone here. I don't go knocking my feet like that. . . .'

'If I tell you . . .' he began, 'will you promise . . .' when a shadow fell over the window and a child's voice was heard singing 'Angels Ever Bright and Fair'. The words fell high and clear on the heavy air and increased in volume. The singer was evidently coming nearer. Then light skipping steps approached as the song continued. . . . The last words, 'Take, Oh Take Me to Your Care' were run without a pause into . . . 'Gran Collins!

Gran Collins! . . .' and a child's face was framed between the geraniums.

With the movement of the hunted, Neil had dropped down on the floor. . . . 'Gran Collins, Gran Collins, can I come in?'

'It's the child Linda. Keep down there and crawl into the room next door. She's sharp. You can't fool her.'

Neil began crawling along the floor on his stomach, like a worm, making for the door behind the bed. His grandmother began rolling herself over to unfasten the window latch again. In spite of her anxiety her face lit up at the sight of the little girl standing outside. She unfastened the window again, and the child repeated her question, 'Gran Collins, Gran Collins, can I come in?' And the old woman answered as she was expected to do. The formula for every visit were the words of the story of the three little pigs and the wolf. 'No! No! by the hair of my Chinny Chin! . . .' And after three times the child would cry, 'Then I'll huff and I'll puff and I'll blow your house in!' And with a shriek would jump on to the bed.

She stood now on the window-sill, framed provocative and laughing against the light, making huffing blowing noises, then she dropped lightly, and with a final shriek, on to the end of the bed. 'There . . . I won't eat you up today . . . I'm going to tuck you in properly. Look, I've brought you some flowers.' She handed the old woman a wilting bunch of white carnations.

'Lovely, darling. Where did you get them? From your old friend with the barrow?'

Linda nodded, her lips set tightly. She often brought flowers to Mrs. Collins. They were always short and usually white. White ones probably faded more quickly than any others. That old man with the barrow must have taken the same liking to the child as she had herself, thought the old woman; he was always making her presents of these bunches of tired flowers.

'Shall I get a vase?' Linda jumped off the bed and took from the chimney-piece a pink and gold china swan. 'I'll get some water for them. . . . Did you have visitors?' she called, with the tap running wildly. 'I couldn't make you hear today, I had to ask you twice. Through the curtain it looked as if there was someone else with you. It looked like Nonie. Why do you have a curtain today? Don't you like to see out any more? Was it Nonie?'

'Yes, but today I had a headache—the light was too strong. Miss Rhodes was here this afternoon. Nonie's at work.'

'She didn't come out,' said the child, astonished.

'Yes, she did,' smiled Mrs. Collins.

'But she'd have gone past us playing over there.'

'She probably went up to see Mrs. Danvers.'

How inquisitive children were. The old woman was nervous of those bright curious eyes. What terrible and ruthless spies they would make—and did, it was said, in the Iron Curtain countries. Inexorable . . . that's what they were.

Linda put the white carnations in the pink and gold swan. Hideous thing it was, thought the old woman, but Neil had won it at a shooting gallery in the Festival Gardens when they had first opened. Strange that he could win anything shooting in such places and become a fumbling terrified clot when he had to fire blank cartridges in the exercises up there at the camp.

Linda placed the swan on the table by the bedside delightedly, 'Sick people should always have flowers. . . .'

'Why?' asked the old woman smiling at her.

'To help them get used to having to go to heaven. Heaven's full of flowers—*so's the cemetery*!' The last words were shot out almost defiantly and, startled, Mrs. Collins looked at the small face bent down to the carnations.

'Where have you been playing? I didn't see you over there,' pointing to the waste ground, 'this afternoon.'

'We were playing hide-and-seek only there was a man there. I didn't like him. I was scared. He was a soldier and he told me if I didn't forget I'd seen him I might get *hurt*. He said he wouldn't like anything to happen to me so I'd better forget. So I have forgot—almost. But I was frightened, so was Cissie—he had such funny eyes.'

'Where was this?' Mrs. Collins was alert now.

'Over there. . . .' She pointed to where the old woman had pointed just before. 'He was lying in that deep bit of the ruins. He was quite still—as if he were hiding.'

'And he was a soldier?'

'Yes, He wore clothes like Cissie's brother and Neil.'

The old woman drew in her breath sharply. What now? What? For some reason she felt a stab of fear. A feeling of acute danger warned her to go carefully.

'Linda,' she said calmly, 'that man was quite right. Forget you've seen him. You don't want to get hurt, do you?'

'Do you know what that man was doing?' asked the child slyly. 'He was watching *this* house.'

From behind the door there was a faint sound—a sigh or a gulp. Linda swung round. 'I heard a noise . . . from there, behind there. . . .'

'Mice,' said the old woman soothingly, 'and the wind comes through the skylight.'

'Mice! I love mice! Oh, look! The Queen's crooked. She couldn't sit crooked on her horse . . . there now . . . that's better. . . . Lovely picture, isn't it? Why doesn't she wear her crown?'

'Because she only wears it on very special occasions.'

'In the history books at school all the kings and queens wear crowns.'

'They used to but now it's changed.'

She drew her breath while the child stood on tiptoe to straighten the picture which Neil's fall had knocked down. Would the boy have the sense to hold his breath? Would Linda take it into her head to open that door behind which he cowered? She often did. Not by a sign did she betray her anxiety. That was fatal with children. They were clever and knew intuitively when you didn't want them to do something. The knowledge was sufficient to make them want to do it. She must head her off—away from the door.

'What's the time?' she asked quickly. 'What does the clock say, Linda?'

Linda went and stood on tiptoe to look at the cheap alarm clock on the chimney-piece. 'Ten to five. . . .' she said swiftly. 'If I turn the clock up the other way it'll be five to ten. Which will you have, madam?'

'I think ten to five will suit me all right,' said the old woman, entering into the game they played together. 'That silly clock loses . . . it must be five by now. Listen and see if you can hear the church clock strike the hour. . . .'

What a fool I am to suggest her listening with Neil next door like that. Why can't he learn to hold his breath and not to cough . . . ? From across the street came the first chime of the clock.

'One!' said Linda, 'Two . . . Three!' She opened her mouth to say 'Four', but a loud ring at the front door startled them both. The child looked at Mrs. Collins. . . . 'Shall I open the front door?'

'No. It won't be for us. It'll be for Mrs. Danvers. . . .'

They heard the shuffling steps of the heavy old Mrs. Danvers. . . . 'She'll open it. Well, my darling, did it strike five?'

'Mrs. Collins . . . Mrs. Collins . . . Someone for you. . . .' croaked Mrs. Danvers.

'Who is it? . . .' apprehension sounded in her voice in spite of her care. 'Who is it?'

The answer, when it came, brought with it a stab as sharp as any the Monster himself could give. But her own apprehension was as nothing to the reaction of the child beside her. There was gloating, almost love, in Mrs. Danvers' answer. Not love for her neighbour, but delight that it might mean trouble for her. Linda, trembling and white-faced, clutched at the old woman frantically. . . . 'Don't let them in. Please, Gran Collins, don't let them get me. I'll never do it again, *never*. Only don't let them take me away. *Please, please.*'

What had Linda done to turn into a bundle of shaking terror at the sound of the word 'Police.'

She caught the child to her. 'Don't be afraid, I won't let them take you away. Open the door, there's a good girl. Open it quickly.'

'*No . . . No,*' cried Linda desperately.

Well, here it is, thought the old woman grimly, no use postponing it. 'Wait just a minute while I put something on!' she called. . . .

'All right, take your time. . . .' came the deep answer.

Gathering all her strength, all her powers of resistance, she got out of bed, slipped on her coat, and opened the door.

CHAPTER X

WHEN THE embarrassed young policeman, after apologising awkwardly to Mrs. Collins, looked round for Linda, she had disappeared. He accepted the chair offered him and his eyes went to the door behind the bed.

'So it's you', said the old woman, sitting herself on the edge of the bed with her coat drawn tightly round her. Good afternoon, officer.' This young Wilson was already known to her through Neil's former escapes. As she spoke to him she suddenly felt a warm little hand grasp her ankle—Linda had dived under the bed.

'Mrs. Collins,' began the young policeman, 'excuse me intruding on you like this, but I saw the little girl climb in through your window. I waited for her to come out, but time's getting on. She hasn't come out, has she?'

'The little girl!' exclaimed Mrs. Collins, as if puzzled. And so she was. Why was he using this preliminary to his real business? Why start his questioning and search by talking about the child? Or was it that, decent fellow as he had always been to them, he was trying to make sure that the child actually had gone before he asked permission to search the place for Neil? But then there were usually two or more of them. Had he left more men outside? She must get the child out. Her heart had begun thumping in a strange frightening way. Funny how the sight of a policeman had that effect on her now. Before Neil had been conscripted and all the trouble had started, she had looked upon the police as friends. Now, like Nonie, she mistrusted and feared them.

She called softly, trying to steady her voice so that she did not reveal her fear, 'Come out, Linda. No one's going to hurt you. Mr. Wilson here is an old friend.' But Linda did not come out, instead a mournful wail began under the bed.

'I'm sorry, ma'am. I followed her here. There's been so many complaints, you see. We must do something to stop it.

Of course children will do these things—in a way it's only natural—but what can we do when the Authorities insist that something is done about it?'

The old woman was terribly agitated. What *was* all this? Hadn't he come about Neil after all? She must guard herself against any betrayal. Calm . . . keep absolutely calm, that was always safest.

'She's only a mite—only nine,' she said entreatingly, and all the time she was wondering frantically, What *is* it? What? Why was Linda grey-faced and shaking at the word 'Police'? Why had she dived under the bed just as Neil had done? Had he involved the child in some way?

'She was warned,' said the policeman. 'Are those the flowers she brought you today, Mrs. Collins?' He was looking at the wilted carnations in the pink swan. 'Do you know where she gets them?'

'From her friend with the barrow,' said Mrs. Collins, more and more puzzled now.

'Hasn't it ever struck you that they are all very short flowers and that they are usually white ones?' asked the policeman, watching her very closely.

'Yes, it has struck me. But they are not *always* short or white. Children like short flowers. Haven't you seen them breaking them all off to make into a short posy?'

'She didn't break those off short,' said the policeman meaningly. 'They were short when she took them. I saw her take them.'

'*Took* them? Took them?' Light began to dawn on Mrs. Collins. The child had stolen the flowers—that was the trouble.

'Linda,' she coaxed gently. 'Come out, my darling. Come along, there's no need to be frightened—is there, officer?'

'None whatsoever. Come out, Linda, there's a good girl.'

Very slowly a foot appeared from under the bed; then the inadequate knickers and long legs of a little girl pushed themselves out from under the bed. She rolled over, dusting herself down, and stood up sheepishly. Then, at the sight of the policeman, she stared wildly and gripped the old woman tightly round the neck.

'Did you steal the flowers for me?' asked Mrs. Collins gently. Linda nodded and hid her face in the old woman's neck. 'Where from? From your old friend with the barrow?' The curly head was shaken violently but she did not speak. 'I'm afraid you're going to get a shock,' said the policeman in his slow deliberate way. 'Think. What place has plenty of short white flowers which wilt easily from lack of water?'

Then, as comprehension dawned in the old woman's face, he said with a twinkle in his eyes. 'Yes. Off the graves, weren't they, Linda?'

'I'm so sorry for the poor flowers all stuck through with wire and nothing to drink,' said the child, looking at him with her great eyes, tragic now and swimming with tears. 'It's wicked. They're much happier in that pink swan here with Gran Collins.'

'Well, that may be so,' said the policeman smiling. 'But you see, people paid money for those flowers to be put on the graves of their dead.'

'The dead can't see them,' said the child passionately. 'And Gran Collins can. There's heaps of flowers in heaven . . . why do they want them on their graves when they've gone away from them?'

Why indeed, thought young Wilson. She's got something there, as children always have. 'It's stealing to take them off the graves,' he said sternly. 'You know that quite well, don't you, Linda?'

She was mute now, her great eyes regarding him obliquely.

'What time does your mother get home?' he asked her, taking out his notebook. 'She's not your grandchild, is she, Mrs. Collins?'

'No,' said the old woman reluctantly.

'I know your granddaughter, young Nona. I thought you hadn't one as young as this.'

He carefully avoided mentioning Neil, although he knew him best in the family. This avoidance of Neil's name alarmed the old woman. Was all this really leading up to Neil? If so, why didn't the man get on with it? Was he playing cat and mouse with her? Neil must have heard his voice. It was absolutely still in there now. Supposing he sneezed or coughed? He must have recognised Wilson's voice. Wouldn't anyone recognise the voice of the man who had twice arrested you? He must be terrified—just as this child had been—and still was. The lovely pink bloom of her cheeks was gone and she was white and there was a curious ashen look about her—just like Neil. She held the child close to her. She could feel the beating of the frightened little heart—like a small bird in one's hand.

'Her mother gets in about half-past six,' she said bluntly. 'But I hope you won't go worrying her. Linda'll give me her word not to take any more flowers. She took them for me. I guarantee that she won't do it again.'

'Will you promise, Linda?' asked Wilson sternly, but his eyes were warm and kind.

'You're not going to take me away to one of those Homes where you took Anita?'

'No. Not if you promise never to take flowers again. You must keep away from the cemetery, Linda. What makes you go there?'

'I like to play there,' said the child simply. 'And if they can't see they can't mind, can they?'

'I've told you,' said the policeman carefully. 'It's the people who've bought the flowers who mind. It's *stealing*. And if you do it again you'll get into trouble.'

The sternness of his voice unnerved Linda, already upset by the man hiding in the ruins. She burst into loud sobs again, and clung to the old woman.

'Now . . . now,' soothed Mrs. Collins. 'It's all right. The officer isn't going to hurt you. You promise to leave the flowers alone and we won't mention it again. Promise me you'll keep away from the cemetery, Linda. Will you?' The little girl nodded violently, sobbing in great gulps. Then, stopping as suddenly as she had begun, she said shakily. 'I'm very sorry. I didn't think it was stealing. Shall I take the flowers back?'

The man looked from the miserable carnations in the dingy room to the tear-stained child clinging to the old woman. 'No. We won't take these back,' he said, getting up. Will you let me out, Linda. Goodbye, Mrs. Collins. I'm very sorry in-

deed to have had to upset you like this—but something had
to be done.'

'Better me than her mother. She has worry enough and to
spare,' said the old woman acidly. 'Thank you, officer. I promise
you it won't happen again.'

'It's because I know you have such a strong sense of duty
that I feel it won't,' said the policeman quietly.

She watched the child show him out and saw him shake
the small hand ceremoniously and pat Linda's shoulder. Then
she leaned back against the bedrail. Her heart was thumping
as wildly as the child's had. A strong sense of duty . . . a strong
sense of duty. . . . *Had* she? *Had* she? With Neil in there behind
the bed, hiding in his sister's clothes?

He had said nothing about Neil. *Nothing.* He had only
come about Linda. She thought of all the flowers the child
had brought her. They had all come from the cemetery. She'd
stolen them all from the graves. Something died in her.

'Come here, Linda,' she said gently when the little girl returned to the room. Linda approached the bed. She was still
sniffling and wiping her eyes on the corner of her cotton
frock. 'Do you mind very much that they came off the graves?'
she wailed. 'It's so dingy down here—you can't see the sky or
the trees—only little bits of them. But the dead ones under the
grass can't see the flowers either.' She watched the old woman's face anxiously.

'No. It's not that they came off the graves that I mind. I
shall be there soon enough myself and I'd be glad for anyone to have flowers off my grave. But it's *stealing*, Linda. Like
the policeman said. Did *all* the flowers you brought me come
from the cemetery?'

'Yes. I had no money to buy any.'

'You made that all up about the old barrow man who gave
you flowers?'

'No.' She shook her head vehemently. 'There *is* an old barrow man with lovely flowers. Only he doesn't give me any.
He's mean and grumpy. Once when I asked him for some for
you he told me to beat it or he'd make me. I pretended he

gave them to me. It's what I'd like him to do. If he were nice he would. . . .'

'You'd better be getting along home now, Linda,' said Mrs. Collins rather sadly. 'Your mother will soon be home.'

For the first time in their friendship she wanted the child gone. She knew that Neil was listening behind the door and the strain of wondering whether he would make a noise which this inquisitive little girl would hear was becoming unbearable. 'Run along now, darling,' she said. 'And mind,' she ended sharply. *'Keep away from the cemetery.* You've promised. And don't you go over on that bombed-site where you saw that soldier.'

'I ought to have told the policeman about him,' said Linda, thoughtfully. 'He frightened me.' Then she said, dismayed. 'But if I can't play in the cemetery or over there—where am I to play?'

'You run along home and help your mother to make the meal. Girls should help in the kitchen. You're getting a big girl now.' Then seeing the child's surprised and disconcerted face she patted her dirty hand, and kissed her affectionately.

'Don't mind me, darling. I'm a tired old woman . . . perhaps I worry too much. . . . Your mother's away so long.'

'I'll see you tomorrow,' called the child. The door slammed, she was gone, turning as always to blow a kiss as she ran up the steps.

I must tell her mother to get her some larger more substantial knickers, thought the old woman worriedly. When Linda crawled out from under the bed that young Wilson must have seen even more than I did. There was no more than an inch covered—and that not the right inch either. She had a vision of the soldier watching the house, the one who had been watching Linda and Cissie. Linda had been quite frightened of him—but now it was she herself who was uneasy. Watching the house was he? The child had been positive that it was this house he was watching. Was he out there now? And if so, why? He was a soldier Linda had said. He wore a uniform like Neil's. Suddenly the old woman sat bolt upright.

'Neil,' she called imperiously, 'Neil.'

The door behind the bed opened softly and she heard her grandson's voice. . . . 'Is it all clear? . . . Can I come in now?'

'It's all clear. Come in.' she said grimly.

CHAPTER XI

'WHO WAS IT? *Who?*' demanded Neil as he came in answer to her call. He was trembling with excitement and strain.

'Didn't you recognise his voice?'

'No. . . . I couldn't lean close enough to the door—that old bedstead creaks. . . .'

'It was that young Wilson who came to arrest you last time. . . .'

Neil became even paler and he swallowed twice before he could speak. . . . 'And? What did you tell him?'

'He never mentioned you. I don't like it. He mentioned Nonie—but not you. Usually he asks Nonie how you're getting on if he meets her. Today he said nothing. I wonder if this business of the child is merely a blind to find out if you are here? The police are wily. Some people think they are stupid—I know better.'

'They can't have missed me yet,' said the boy, stammering a little. 'He can't have known about me.'

'Who's the man watching this house?' demanded the old woman harshly.

'How should I know? I've not seen him. Probably the kid made it up.'

'So you heard what she said? That he wore a uniform exactly like yours and that he threatened her. Who is he?'

Her searching eyes caught the flicker which passed as a small ripple over his white face. He knows, she thought. He knows who it is—or at least he's got a very good idea. But he remained silent, looking at the floor.

His grandmother examined him as one might examine a specimen in a case. He's made of putty—in the image of anyone who likes to mould him she thought. Why haven't I moulded him into something worth-while? *Why?* I've tried hard enough—and so did Len. Someone is doing that now.

Someone has been at work on this weak malleable creature. Someone has taken Nona's place in his life. He's changed—and not for the better. He's not only frightened of others. He's frightened of *himself.* Why? What's going on in that thin-skinned head?

Aloud, she said relentlessly, 'Nona will be here any minute now. Tell me quickly who that man out there is.'

'I tell you—*I don't know.*'

'Look at me,' she insisted. 'You've not looked right at me since you came in at that window early this morning.'

Slowly the boy raised his eyes until they met hers. It was he who looked away first. She was appalled at what she saw in them. 'You're lying,' she said harshly.

Suddenly he broke out. 'Leave me alone . . . can't you? *Leave me alone.*'

'Listen. It was all I could do to stop myself from giving you away to young Wilson just now. I ought to have done so. I don't like this story of the man over there. There's something I don't like about this whole business. I'm sorry I had anything to do with it.'

'You wouldn't go back on me, Gran? *You wouldn't do that?*' She felt sick at the craven fear he was displaying. As she looked at him in his sister's clothes she could scarcely contain her anger. 'If you want Charlie to help in this you'll have to put your cards on the table. *What's happened up there?* Why have you come home? No . . . don't tell me that it was because of Len . . . don't tell me that you couldn't stick it—that's obvious since you've run away—*why?* That's the question. *Why?*'

Neil buried his head in his arms and his slight frame shook. 'I can't tell you. Don't ask me. I *must* get away tonight. As soon as possible. *I must.*'

His grandmother regarded him with a pity which he could not see. She was moved to that terrible flooding compassion again—it had been the undoing of her strongest determinations always. It had ruined Edward. Whenever she had been most angry and most hurt by his blindness and indifference to his family he had always disarmed her with some queer childish uncertainty, some groping after truth which showed her the helplessness and weakness of all human beings, and that flood of pity, of love for all humanity would overcome her. So it was now. She was full of anger at the inability of this lad to face up to his destiny but that anger was flooded by warm compassion for that very weakness in him.

'Pull yourself together, boy,' she said gently.

'Sometimes,' he said wretchedly, 'I begin to wonder if I'm going round the bend.'

'Dangerous way of thinking. We all reach it some time or other. What's eating you especially to make you think that now?'

'Dunno. Sometimes I think I'm the wrong chap in the right skin—and at other times I know I'm the right chap in the wrong skin—but it's never both right. I don't fit in, Gran. I never will.'

'Listen, Neil. You've got to grow to fit your skin—you can't change it. Get that into your head. As to fear—it's nothing but a skin—an empty one. As soon as you realise that the fear will be gone.'

'Not mine. That's real enough. It's no use trying to hide it, the others can smell it—they know. I get such strange ideas at times.'

His grandmother peered intently at him. 'Not violent ones? You're not getting violent are you?'

'No. No. I just wonder why some people should be able to make life wretched for others. Why should the right to do that be given to great red-faced stupid men? *Stupid*. That's what they are. To be afraid of a brainless clot like the sergeant up there. I despise myself—but I'm still terrified when he begins to shout at me . . . I just dissolve into jelly . . . my brain's liquid.'

Oh God, thought the old woman, he's beginning to talk like Edward. It doesn't sound like Neil. It's someone speaking through him. Someone imposing his thoughts and ideas, his actions, perhaps, on to this weakling. She said gently, 'Who's been talking to you? Putting such ideas into your head?'

'No one,' he answered. 'I've had time to think a bit—that's all.' And he relapsed into silence again.

Now I've shut him up again—and I wanted him to talk. If he would go on I might have a chance to learn what sort of person this is who is taking possession of him. Could it be a woman? A girl? Had he met some girl up there?

'Haven't you got a girl near the camp?' she asked suddenly.

The question appeared to disconcert him—he looked astonished. 'No. There's no girl. There was only Mary. It's always been her. I'd have married her some day I suppose. How old was the man she went with?'

'I told you—I never saw him. He's old enough to be her father Nonie said, but you know what girls are—always think anyone over thirty is old.'

'Did you see her before she went away?'

'She came to say goodbye.'

'Did she say anything about me?'

'Yes, she did. She said she didn't care for this new friend of yours.'

'She's never met him.'

'She knew him just the same—through your letters— Mary was smart.'

'How d'you mean?'

'She noticed the change in you—through your letters.'

'It was Mary who changed. This old man must have changed her. . . . She's like all the others. . . .'

'Like what others?' challenged the old woman angrily. 'You've never known any others. There was only Mary ever since you were at school.'

'They won't wait. They want everything at once. Cash down—that's women.'

His grandmother looked at him again. He couldn't have thought that out. Or could he? Had he changed more than she thought he had? Was he becoming a spinner of words like his father?

'What's come over you?' she asked. 'You never used to talk this way.'

'Perhaps I'm growing—to fit my skin as you said I must.'

'Now stop stalling. *Who's that man over there, Neil?*'

'I tell you I don't know,' he said angrily. 'For God's sake quit nagging at me.'

'Ssh! Listen.'

Light steps were approaching the door. 'Nona . . .' breathed the old woman softly. . . . 'Keep out of sight of the door.'

A key was inserted, the door opened very cautiously and Nona came in. Her face was flushed with hurrying, little beads of perspiration showed on her short upper lip, and her soft hair was in damp tendrils over her forehead. She flung her coat off her shoulders impatiently as she turned from the door. 'Well?' she said quickly, looking from one to the other. 'What sort of a day have you had?'

'Interrupted,' said her grandmother. 'Five visitors in all—that's including Mrs. Danvers and old Evans wanting to come in—they're most curious and suspicious. They've been told you're home with a cold.'

'Who were the others?' Nona's anxiety gave a pinched look to her small face, so like her brother's.

'Miss Rhodes came.'

'*She* came in the shop.'

'She saw Neil. The idiot fell through the door—that's what comes of eavesdropping.'

'So she said.'

'She told you about it—*in the shop?*'

'Yes. She warned me. I think she means to make trouble. We'll have to get moving quickly.'

'That cop Wilson was here,' said Neil, frantically.

Nona's eyes widened. . . . 'Then they *know?* What did you say? *Did you lie? Did you say he wasn't here?*' She turned excitedly to her grandmother.

'He didn't come about Neil. He came about Linda. He never mentioned Neil at all. He usually asks you how he's getting on, doesn't he?'

'Yes—but I seldom see him.'

'I had the strangest feeling all the time he was here that he was playing with me—that he knew all the time that Neil was behind that door there.'

'He couldn't have known. He came about that kid,' said Neil, decidedly. 'I sweated the whole time he was here. It was terrible holding my breath and not daring to stir . . . I *must* get away, Nonie. I can't stick it much longer.'

'How d'you think I felt? Don't you think I was sweating too?' asked the old woman. 'And the child was terrified and hid under the bed. I had a job to coax her out.'

'The child? Linda? What did he want with her? And why should he come *here* for her?'

'She's been taking flowers off the graves in the cemetery and bringing them to me. Those,' she pointed to the carnations in the pink swan, 'came from the grave of a newly-buried according to Wilson.'

'Ugh! How revolting. Let's throw them out. How can you keep them . . . what a horrible child!'

'Leave them alone. Don't touch them,' said the old woman fiercely. 'The child took them for *me*. She offered to take them back but Wilson said to leave them here.'

'But why did he come *here*?' Nona was bewildered.

'He followed her from the cemetery. She'd been warned previously. They were watching her.'

'Don't waste time talking of the kid. We've no time to lose. Nonie's right. That Miss Rhodes means trouble. I must get going. What did Charlie say, Nonie? Will he help me?' Neil's anxiety communicated itself quickly to his twin. She put a hand restrainingly on his arm. 'Don't worry so much. I spoke to Charlie at lunch-time.'

'Will he do it? *Will* he?' Neil, in his impatience, was almost screaming.

'Quiet,' warned his sister. 'I don't know, Neil. He was difficult. I'm going to work on him when he gets home.'

'He must. He *must*. You must make him, Nonie. I've got to get away—and in his lorry. You can make him do it, Nonie. You know you can.'

'Charlie's not all that easy,' said the old woman quietly. 'Nonie doesn't get it all her way. Oh yes . . . I can still see . . . I've got good eyes in my head—and good ears.'

Nona flushed a dark ugly red. 'You can hear right across the hall?'

'The whole street can hear when Charlie gets going.'

Neil looked at his sister's distressed face. 'If he treats you roughly I'll have something to say to him,' he said, in a bragging, bombastic voice.

'Charlie *is* rough,' said his sister simply. 'I know that.'

'He's not good enough for you,' said Neil angrily.

'But he's good enough to help *you*?'

'Sorry, Nonie. I shouldn't have said that.'

Nona got up wearily. Her legs ached from eight hours' standing at the counter. 'I'd better see about some food, I'll bring it in here tonight, Gran. I want to talk to Charlie before we come in. I'll cook in our room. If you're going to talk Neil, put the radio on. That Mrs. Danvers is upstairs now.'

'If the radio is on we can't hear anyone coming,' objected Neil.

'Take your choice. Keep quiet—or put it on.'

She went out dispiritedly.

'Nona's properly upset by all this,' observed her grandmother. Nona had not offered to make her bed, to help her wash, or to tidy up the room as she invariably did as soon as she got home. She said shortly to Neil. 'Get into the room behind there. I'm going to tidy up the room—open the window wide for a while, will you?'

'I'll help you. I'll sweep up a bit,' he said quickly.

'No. You go in there. I can manage. I'll call you when the window must be shut.'

He picked up a journal which Nona had dropped on the bed, and went through the door into the little closet-room and sat himself down again on the bed. It's not much larger than the cells are, he thought. And somehow it seems even more like prison than it did there. And that was bad enough. He tried to read, but he could not concentrate on women's interests. He was burning with fear and the impatient urgency to get away—to start on the journey to freedom. In the bedroom his grandmother was slowly and laboriously getting herself out of bed. She was acutely worried. Charlie was going to be difficult. She had seen that on Nona's face. What sort of mess had she let them all in for? She felt ill and unable to face one of those family scenes. She was old . . . they forgot that—as she did usually.

CHAPTER XII

ALISON RHODES, the neat suit hung over a chair, was dressing to go out with Rodney White. She was tired and depressed. Her day's visits had left a taste of dust in her mouth. That boy Collins had thoroughly upset her. She suddenly felt the utter uselessness of the work she was doing—and for which she had been trained. One needed something more than training. Few of the people she visited wanted her in their homes. They accepted her offers of help sullenly and grudgingly—her advice they ignored. They would listen to her with a polite smile, eyeing her sceptically—eyeing the expensive neat suit and the neat suitable shoes, the expensive bag and gloves, as much as to say, 'Yes, we know. We know what you think we should do—but do you know what *we* think? What we think of you and your sort? It would surprise you if you did.' In the dull apathetic faces, the meaningless smiles, she read the cynicism of the disillusioned.

Old Mrs. Collins for instance—she was an unusually intelligent woman—would listen to her with such a queer resigned smile on her finely-carved old face that Alison was reminded of the Mona Lisa. There was something so secretive and faintly derisive in it. Once she had said abruptly, 'Where d'you go when you leave here?'

'To the next house on the list,' she had answered, startled.

'No. I mean when all the lot on the list are finished. Where d'you go then?'

'To my flat,' the social worker had replied.

'Tell me about it.'

And Miss Rhodes had found herself telling Mrs. Collins all about the lovely central-heated flat with constant hot water and the very latest decoration, each wall being differently papered or painted. She had also told her about her mother's home in the country, about her sister Janet and the children.

'So you've no need to do this work then?'

'I feel a need to do it. I don't need the *money*—no.'

'I can't imagine anyone wanting to take up work which those you want to work on resent,' the old woman had said, but she had a reluctant respect for this girl who came from a comfortable home and chose to go into the drab, dirty and often unhappy homes of the unfortunate.

Alison Rhodes picked up a cocktail dress and slipped it over her head. It looked awful. She tried another one—but that was worse. As she swung resentfully away from the un-flattering reflection in the mirror she noticed a little fold in her neck. She lifted her head up as high as possible—then scrutinised the reflection again. No, she was not mistaken— there was a fold. A little unwanted piece of flesh was developing under the sharp line of her chin. She would soon be thirty—and she had always looked more than her age. What should she wear? What? Rodney would be here any minute now—and she looked a sight. Even as she rummaged through the wardrobe, hunting for something more flattering, the front door-bell rang imperiously. Rodney hated to be kept waiting. She pulled on a Japanese kimono and hastened to let him in.

There were rain-marks on his light coat.

'Oh,' she said bleakly. 'Is it raining?'

'Just started,' he said abruptly, following her into the sit-ting-room. 'Won't matter to us—I've got the car.'

'I'm sorry, Rodney. I'm not ready. I'll give you a drink—by the time you've finished it I'll be dressed.'

'I like the kimono,' he said, eyeing her speculatively. 'You don't look so prim and aloof in that.'

She handed him a glass. 'Here you are—as you like it. Gin, dry martini and ice.'

He took the glass and placed it on the table. It was a charm-ing room. Alison had taste and took trouble. There were always flowers—the latest books—and everything was perfectly ar-ranged. She had several tight lines between her eyes, and her forehead showed parallel ones of the same tense kind. 'What's the matter?' he asked. 'You look upset.'

'I am worried—and depressed this evening, Rodney.'

'Take this then. I'll mix myself another.' He pushed the glass into her hand. 'Go on, drink it. Do you good. What's the matter?'

She sat down on the divan and he sat beside her. 'It's partly everything—it all seems so futile,' she said despairingly. 'But in particular it's a family I visit. When I got there today the old woman was alone—she hands me the keys out of the window. Later—half an hour later—there was a terrific crash from the wall behind her bed—I had no idea there was a door there; it's papered over—and a boy dressed as a girl simply fell into the room.'

'How d'you mean, a boy dressed as a girl?'

'What I say. He wore jeans, a sweater, plimsolls and pink socks and as he fell a scarf slipped from his head and there was no doubt at all that he was a boy. I knew at once who he was—the twin brother of the granddaughter Nona. The boy there was all that fuss about last time he deserted from the Army.'

'Well?' said Rodney disinterestedly, running his hands through Alison's hair. 'What then?'

'Well—the old woman was very quiet. She sent the boy out of the room and proceeded to talk to me rather unpleasantly. Said I'd seen something I'd no business to see—that if I didn't go poking about into people's homes it couldn't have happened. She said I'd better forget that I'd seen him. He's deserted again.'

'So you had.' Rodney swallowed his drink. 'She's perfectly right. Forget it.' He put his hands on the sash of the kimono tentatively. She pulled herself away abruptly. 'No. No. I'll get dressed now.'

'Alison.' His voice was rough. 'D'you know how long I've been hanging about waiting for you to feel the urge?'

'No,' she said coldly.

'Well, however long it is—it's too long. You're about as exciting as cold potatoes. There's no warmth—no response.'

'I'd rather hoped,' she said carefully, 'that you might want to marry me. It'd be different then.'

'Listen, my good girl. You're all but thirty. I'm not unwilling to marry you—but it all depends on how we make out in bed. If that were all right I'd be willing to marry you. So far it hasn't been any great shakes. You're never willing—you merely oblige. I've had one unhappy marriage because my wife was a cold woman, I'm not anxious to make the same mistake again.'

'You're coarse,' she said, disgustedly.

'You should be used to the facts of life—you've chosen to wallow in them. Isn't trying to patch up broken homes part of your work? How can you understand any of these sexual problems if you've had no experience yourself? It's ludicrous.'

'Not every broken marriage is due to sex.'

'Come off it, Alison. Nine out of ten are.'

'A great deal of my work is not concerned with marital problems at all. Many of the people I visit are old and friendless. Young homes are broken because of their aged relatives having nowhere to go . . . like the old woman I've just been visiting. The problem there is this grandson who keeps on deserting—he's unsuited for army life. But it's not fair on the old woman. It's my duty to inform the police.'

'*What?* Say that again.'

'It's my duty to inform the police about this boy.'

'You'd do that? You'd actually contemplate *that*?' Rodney stopped playing with her hair.

'It's anyone's duty to inform on a deserter.'

'Your duty to whom?' shouted Rodney. 'To your bloody little social workers' world? What's it got to do with you? It's the old grandmother you're concerned with—not the grandson. You saw him accidentally. Forget it. Good luck to the poor devil I say.'

'If everyone shirked their duty to the State it would be a hopeless world.'

Rodney stood up abruptly. 'Alison, you make me vomit with this talk of duty. You talk like a Girl Guide—or a schoolmark. Unless you're very careful you'll wake up one day to find you've grown into a sour old spinster with a straight-

set mouth . . . always interfering with other people's lives because you've none of your own. *It's not love that makes you help
them—it's curiosity.*'

Alison looked at him, horrified, then put her face in her
hands. She thought of that little fold of flesh. The first. She
shivered suddenly. The vision of all those old grey wrinkled
faces lying lonely and neglected in their sordid rooms assailed
her. They came crowding in on her. Soon . . . soon . . . they
seemed to be grinning. Before you've time to think it'll be too
late . . . you'll be like us . . . one of us.

Rodney was remorseful. 'Don't take me literally, Alison,
I'm only trying to make you see that you can't go on with this
stupid life—you must listen to sense.'

Alison stared at him. Strange how she'd never noticed
what a coarse face he had. 'It's a question of principles,' she
said, coldly—'just as that boy's desertion is. We feel differently
about it.'

'If you think it's your duty to give the wretched youth
away to the police then we certainly *do. Keep out of it.* There
are always others to do that.' His voice was bitter.

'Rodney,' she said. 'Did you ever do your National Service?'

'Not I,' he grinned. 'I got out of it. Once had a sort of
hysterical fit as a kid? Got the family doctor to say I'd had
epilepsy.'

'But no doctor would do such a thing.' Alison was shocked.

'Well that one did,' declared Rodney bluntly. 'He was sweet
on my mother and she'd have gone nuts if I'd had to go.'

'And you—you were a party to such a deception?'

'Yes. And I'd do it again. What right have they to force kids
into the Army in peacetime?'

Alison wrapped her kimono closely round her and held her
chin high. 'Now I know exactly what sort of a man you are,'
she said, contemptuously. 'I'm glad I've found it out. Would
you mind going now, please? I want to dress.'

'Oh, go ahead and dress. Why the false modesty—as if I'd
never seen you undressed before?'

'You misunderstand me, Rodney. I asked you to *go.* I'm not
coming out with you.'

He stared at her uncertainly. Had he gone too far telling her she talked like a Girl Guide or a schoolmistress? She was older than he was—several years older—but she had money and brains, and he was fond of her.

'Oh come, Alison. I meant nothing. I was only kidding you. I wanted you to leave that wretched youth alone—that's all.'

He came close and tried to take her in his arms. She withdrew herself coldly. 'I never say things which I don't mean, Rodney, and I meant it when I asked you to go.'

'You're all worked up about this boy. Come on out to dinner and forget it.'

'No,' she said calmly. 'Not tonight or any other night.'

He picked up his hat angrily and took his raincoat from the hall. 'As you like—you've got my telephone number when you climb down to earth.'

She said nothing as he unlatched the door and buttoned his coat. Just as he was about to go he turned, and gripped her roughly by the shoulders. 'You leave that boy alone. D'you hear? *Leave him alone.*' He slammed the door. His face had been hard and ugly. He was gone—gone out of her life. And all because of that Collins boy. She picked up the telephone hesitantly—she knew the police number—then replacing it slowly, burst into a storm of tears.

CHAPTER XIII

As CHARLIE CAME into their room Nona looked up apprehensively. She was cooking at the stove in the corner which served them as kitchen. Not only Miss Rhodes was a danger, but that young Wilson, too. He had come ostensibly about the little girl, but who knew the real reason for his visit? Why hadn't he waited until the child came out of the house? Why had he interviewed her in old Mrs. Collins' room?

And the child herself had told her grandmother some story about a young Serviceman hiding over there on the ground where she played. She said that the man wore a uniform exactly like Neil's and was watching this house. What did Nonie make of that, the old woman had asked.

Nona had immediately questioned her twin. He had insisted that he didn't know who it was, but she knew that he was
lying—that he had a very good idea of who the man was. She
was terribly uneasy, and, like her grandmother, felt that there
was something which Neil was keeping from them. Something which had to do with the reason for his deserting again.
How could she force him to tell her the truth of the matter?
She and Neil had never quarrelled, but they had come dangerously near to it this evening. 'Why should Gran and I help
you if you won't tell us the truth?' she had demanded. Nona
had had to smother down her qualms about her grandmother
being involved in Neil's escape at all. She had left her twin in
a terrible restless state pacing up and down his grandmother's
room imploring her to make Charlie help him. The old woman had become impatient with him. 'If you're in such a tearing
hurry to get off what's to stop you going off now?' she had
demanded; and Nonie had felt an aching pity for his obvious
terror of going alone. He wanted someone to accompany him
out of London, someone to see him safely out of danger. He
simply couldn't face a journey alone knowing that the alert for
him was probably already out.

She had left him, after imploring him to stop panicking.
She would do what she could with Charlie when he came
home—but Charlie was late.

And here was Charlie coming in now. He was tired and
his face dark and uncompromising. He flung his jacket over a
chair and went over to the sink to wash his hands. While he
did this he did not look across at Nona. He had been away on
a long-distance run for three days and was furious at being
greeted on his return with the news of Neil's dilemma. He did
not kiss his wife, although he had not seen her for three days.
When he had dried his hands he ran a comb through his thick
strong hair and flung himself on to the divan. Nona winced—
his boots were dusty and he would crumple the divan cover,
but his face was so withdrawn that she said nothing after her
first greeting had been received with no more than a casual
grunt. He took out a cigarette and began smoking. She hoped
he wouldn't flick the ash on the divan cover; there were al-

ready two holes burned in it from his carelessness. Nona wasn't house-proud in the least, in fact she cared little about domestic chores, but she was fastidious, and she was practical. She hoped to sell the divan, which had been a wedding purchase, before they went to Australia. She knew a young couple who were waiting for it—cover and cushions too. Why should the price be lessened by Charlie's carelessness?

She waited while he smoked in silence, until she could stand it no longer. Swinging round from the stove she asked, 'Have you arranged for the lorry to take Neil?'

He went on smoking deliberately before he said flatly, 'No.'

'Why not?'

'I told you. I won't help the rotten little quitter.'

She turned on him furiously. 'Don't talk of my brother in that way. You'll regret it.'

'How else can one refer to a coward who keeps running back to sister?'

'You beast, Charlie. You're cruel. Just because you're strong physically you despise any form of weakness in those who haven't your strength.'

'I do. Especially when they run whining back to an old sick woman and a young married sister.'

He accentuated the word 'married' in a peculiar way so that she stared at him. What was he going to do now? Start one of his jealous tirades just when she wanted him to help Neil. She felt suddenly furious that some people should be able to look down on others not as strong as themselves, but she controlled her temper. Charlie had got to be *made* to help. Quarrelling would not further her plans for Neil. She turned back to the cooking.

'Why aren't you cooking over the other side tonight?'

'Because I wanted to talk to you—alone.'

'About your clinging ivy of a brother?'

She didn't answer and he contemplated her back at the stove. She was small and slender and her back had a grace which never failed to move him. He felt sorry suddenly for his surliness. . . . 'Come here,' he said, gently.

She looked at him lying on the divan. In the one room in which they ate and slept most of the space was taken up by this divan bed. Nonie had insisted that it should be a divan bed—but it was a bed and Charlie never lost sight of the fact. Nonie had wanted to push it into the recess which they used as a storage space for assembling their things for Australia, but Charlie had been stubborn. He was not going to be pushed away into a cupboard even if it were large enough to take the divan. 'How d'you think we're going to get in and out squeezed in like that? Leap over the end like divers every night? No thanks. Put it in the middle of the room with plenty of space round it.' Nonie, he said, had middle-class notions about it being common to have a bed in the living-room. One had divan-rooms not bedrooms, she said. Her conventional ideas about such things came from the school she had attended where the girls were uppish and genteel. Charlie was proud of her having gained her School Certificate of Education as long as it didn't interfere with his standard of living. He had stuck to his opinion about the divan as a matter of principle. In the end they had compromised and the large divan was in a corner by day and pulled out into the centre of the room at night. Even so, Nona had insisted on putting the pillows into covers of the same material as the divan cover, so that they looked like cushions.

'A pillow's a pillow,' Charlie had grumbled. 'What's the use of hiding the fact? What's wrong with a pillow? Or for that matter a bed? I've got precious little time to sit—except on the driving seat of the lorry. When I lie I like to lie in comfort.'

'Come here, Nonie,' he repeated now. He was stubbing out the cigarette and looking at her in a certain way.

'No, Charlie. I'm late with the meal already.'

'Late for whom? For your grandmother and your cissy-boy brother? You're not late for me—and I'm the one you should be cooking for.'

'I'm hungry myself,' she said quietly. 'I was worried today and gave my lunch to the swans.'

'You're worried over him ... I tell you, Nonie, it makes me savage when I see you worried like this. You're only a girl—

the same age, the same height and of less weight than him—why should he rely on you to help him out of his scrapes?'

'They are not scrapes,' she said defiantly. 'Neil's not a criminal—it's the Army making him like this.'

'Oh stop talking about him, and come over here and be nice to me.'

'I'm late with the meal, I can't leave it now. Wait a minute until I've dished up.'

'Oh you've always an excuse. You haven't seen me for two nights and you haven't even kissed me.'

'Charlie . . . that's not fair. I was ready to kiss you tonight when you came in but you scarcely said a word to me.' She went swiftly over to him and kissed him. He pulled her roughly down on to the divan laughing at her protests that the potatoes would burn. . . . 'Charlie . . . won't you help Neil just to please me? *Won't you?*' she begged, stroking his strong thick hair. He did not answer . . . but began caressing her, and in spite of her struggles he would not desist. She dragged herself away from him and, sitting up, said pleadingly, 'Will you do what I want? Charlie, *will you?*'

'Don't bargain with me—kiss me,' he said angrily, holding her down with the weight of his body, and he began laughing softly as presently under his caresses her struggles became feebler and feebler until they ceased altogether. Outside it was raining in a sudden relentless downpour. On the stove the potatoes boiled dry and the pan began to bum.

Across the passage, Mrs. Collins, sniffing the aroma said, sighing, 'Charlie's home; the potatoes are burning again. You'll have to do some more, Neil.'

Neil, still in his sister's jeans and sweater, was collecting plates and cutlery for the meal, when a rapping at the door was followed by a deep mellow voice, 'Mother. How's my little mother? Can her son come in?'

Mrs. Collins sat up abruptly, startled and alert. Of all the people whom she did not want tonight her son Edward came first on the list. With the predicament they were in she felt that the last thing she wanted was her son's flow of smooth vote-catching talk. Last week, his visit had thoroughly upset Charlie who had no use for his father-in-law. Sometimes they did not see him for months at a time. Why did he want to come *now*? As the rapping continued she said resignedly to Neil, 'Let your father in.'

'Must I? I'll never get away if he gets started. . . .'

'Let him in. It'll cause less trouble in the end.' And with a shrug, Neil went to unlock the door for his father.

'Well, well, this is a nice surprise, Nonie. You're not usually home so early.'

'Look again. It's not Nonie,' said his mother.

Not Nonie? I thought she'd cut her hair short like all these girls are doing now. Well, bless me, if it isn't Neil? What in heaven's name are you doing masquerading in your sister's clothes?'

'Ssh! Not so loud. . . .' said his mother warningly.

A look of understanding came over the father's face.

'*Quit?*'

Neil swallowed hard and turned away. His father kissed his grandmother and laid a brown paper parcel on the table by her bed. She peeped in the opening, then said sharply. 'What are these prickly things? Horse-chestnuts?'

'Those, my dear mother, are lichees now available fresh from the countries of their origin. Under that prickly exterior is a milk-white fruit with a stone—the flavour resembles the grape somewhat.'

'I'd rather *have* grapes, you know how fond I am of them,' said his mother, shortly. 'I expect you paid a lot for these, didn't you, Edward?'

'Three shillings.'

'And there are eight. By the time I've skinned them there won't be much for three shillings. For that you could have got me a nice bunch of grapes.'

'Wait until you try the lichees, Mother. They'll bring you something of the glamour and mystery of the Orient . . . let me peel one for you and then I'll tell you about China . . . they grow in India too, but I told you about India when I brought the mangoes . . . I see you haven't eaten that one. Didn't you like it?'

'Not as much as an apple.'

'Well, mangoes may be an acquired taste—but everyone likes lichees. Do try one. . . .'

'Not now, thank you. We'll be having the meal soon. I'm not in the mood for geography lessons, Edward. The only geography in which I'm interested at the moment is where Neil is to be got to.'

'Neil,' said his father. 'What exactly does this mean? Wearing your sister's clothes?'

And when the boy didn't answer, he said, 'How long have you been here?'

'Since early this morning.'

'When did you leave?'

'Yesterday.'

'So you've assumed your sister's identity. You took me in all right. I thought it was Nonie answering the door.' He eyed Neil critically, then said bitingly. 'You make a pretty girl, Neil. Quite pretty—although not as appealing as Nonie.'

'Nonie's too appealing,' said his mother, thinking of the burned potatoes.

Neil had reddened. 'Nonie made me wear these clothes,' he said sullenly.

'Well, I don't like it,' said his father.

'No one asked *you* what you liked,' snapped his mother. 'Nonie thought it would be safer. You never know who comes knocking and wanting to be let in now that I'm tied to this room.'

'Am I to take it that *you're* a party to this business?'

'What business? If you mean am I going to help hide Neil until he can get away—*Yes.* I am.'

'I must say I'm astounded, Mother. Why, you were the one who always preached duty and obligation to us all. What's come over you?'

'Nothing's come over me. I'm just seeing straight, that's all. You could be useful to Neil over this, Edward. Have you any money on you?'

'Money? Money? No. . . . I brought you a bottle of wine.' He pulled it from the pocket of his raincoat which he now hung up behind the door. Seeing from this that his father intended to stay, Neil felt even more desperate. He looked wretchedly at his grandmother.

'You'd better go and do those extra potatoes as we've got a guest.'

'Oh come, Mother. Don't describe your only son as a guest.'

'Well, and aren't you? This is my home. You're here as a guest—and a rare one at that. What's brought you here?'

'Well now, Mother, that's quite a story. I came here to tell you about someone who has changed my whole world . . . given me faith and the vision to see that wonderful truths are here before our eyes waiting only for us to discover and make use of them. She is a remarkable woman—a wonderful woman.'

'A woman?' said his mother. 'I had a feeling that this time it was religion. Last time you were here I got that impression when you kept saying you'd been shaken over Communism.'

'It *is* a woman—and in a way you could call it religion. For she is the religion—if you can understand. She has founded this new and wonderful faith. . . .'

His mother caught Neil's anguished look. If he's got a new 'ism' in the guise of a woman he can just take her elsewhere . . . I've listened to so many new fads and isms of his . . . and they all boil down to one thing—Edwardism! she thought angrily.

'Here's Nonie coming,' she said, trying to interrupt the volume of speech emerging from him.

Neil was staring at his father in anguish. This was just his luck. His father *would* choose tonight of all nights to come home. Once here there would be no getting him away. Neil and the peril of his situation, the urgency for prompt action, would all be lost in the great spate of words with which his father invariably drowned everyone else. Words . . . words . . . his father, once started, rolled on from a small rippling stream to a great rolling river drunk with its own power. Neil watched, fascinated, his father becoming hypnotised by his own voice, anaesthetised by that wonderful flow of his own oratory. . His eyes would become alight, fanatically alight, his head thrown slightly back in his emotion—while from his mouth there emerged those smooth flowing phrases spoken with a golden tongue.

In despair he escaped into the kitchenette. 'Nonie,' he said urgently. 'What am I to do with Father here?'

It's a nuisance,' she agreed worriedly, still thinking of Charlie.

'Nuisance?' exclaimed Neil. 'It's the end for me. Here we all sit chattering and dallying, wasting time while the Red Caps may be telephoning the police.' His face was twitching . . . his hands shaking.

'Neil, don't get so excited. I'll see to you. I'll get you away somehow. I'll hide you until we can.'

'Can't Charlie get me away *tonight*? Nonie, he *must*.'

'It's a question of the lorry. If you could wait until the night he'll be going in that direction.'

'Nonie. I *can't*. I've got to go tonight. I'll go on my own. I must. I've got my civvies—I'll get through.'

'I don't see what the hurry is, Neil. You're safe enough in my clothes for a few hours more. You said yourself that your pal is covering for you.'

'I lied to you. That man hiding over there *must* be Mike Andersen. I don't know what's happened. He was going to wait twenty-four hours before following on. He can't have waited more than a few hours at most. I've got to escape him somehow. I *must*. I wanted to get away tonight before he caught up with me. It's *him* I must get away from.'

'*Mike Andersen!* I thought he was your friend.'

'He's not. I'm afraid of him. I'm *terrified* of him, Nonie. I've got to get away before he comes over here.'

'But if he's already here, why doesn't he come over? Why is he waiting?'

'How do I know? Mike has his own plans—and they include *me*.'

'*You knew he would be coming?*'

Neil nodded miserably. 'There's nothing I could do. I was forced into this. It's no use asking you to understand. I lied to Gran—I just couldn't tell her.'

'I can understand only too well,' said Nona. 'But why didn't you tell me at once? We've been wasting time. The point is—how to get you away without him seeing you?'

'The backyard. I could climb over the wall if Charlie could wait at the back.'

'I haven't persuaded Charlie yet. But I *will*.' Nona put her arms round her twin protectively. 'I'll get you away. Perhaps it isn't Mike Andersen over there . . . after all there are any amount of other Servicemen on leave now . . . and we've only the child's word. You know what little liars children are—she said he wore a uniform like yours—but did he?'

Neil was somewhat mollified by this. Nonie was usually right. Mike had said he would come in his civvies. He per-suaded himself that he had been imagining things as usual. Why should it be Mike over there? It didn't make sense. If it was Mike, surely he would come straight over and ask for Neil. What object had he in waiting? Or was he waiting until it was dark?

'I'm going back to tell Charlie supper's ready. If I'm some time in there you'll know I'm working on him.'

She left Neil and went quietly back into their room. Char-lie lay asleep on the divan. She stood looking down at him. She loved him . . . *loved* him. That was the trouble, and she hat-ed herself for giving way to him every time. Humiliating, that's what it was. Why did she do it? Did he really love her? She would never know, because Charlie was not the sort of person who would ever tell her so. One arm was doubled under his head. He slept so deeply that he scarcely breathed—as if he were dead. She picked up his jacket flung on the floor with his collar and tie. As she picked it up something fell from it. It was a small glazed photograph. She turned her back on the sleeper and took the photograph over to the light. A pointed elfin face with a wide laughing mouth and huge dark eyes. On the back was written 'From Jackie with love,' and a date. Three months ago. On the bottom of the photograph in the right-hand cor-ner was written in pencil 'Charlie from Jackie.'

She stood staring at the elfin face with unseeing eyes. A very young face—scarcely more than a child. Slim, childish body in a bikini. *Charlie had another girl.* Had had for the last three months at least.

As she turned towards the divan, he awoke. 'Hello,' he said lazily. 'Time to eat?'

'Yes. Time to eat.'

He yawned, showing his splendid teeth, then sat up on one elbow.

'I want to talk to you, Charlie.'

'If it's about that twin of yours I'm not talking.'

'You *will* talk—and quickly. Father's turned up. You know what that means. No one else gets a word in. We must talk now. You've got to help him, Charlie.'

'Why should I? Helping a rotten little shirker to get away from what would do him a world of good. I had to do my bit. No one helped me escape.'

'You liked it. You're always talking about Korea.'

'It wasn't so hot—some of it. And I was no older than your little brother. And I was there in April 1951 . . . call that nothing?'

'Well, Neil's different. He can't stand it. You're tough. You can stick up for yourself. Neil's not strong enough. I can't bear to see him so upset and frightened.'

'It's not your business. Leave him to sort out his own problems. The longer someone does it for him the longer he'll remain a coward.'

'Neil's not a coward. Don't you dare say that.'

'What else is he?'

She looked at him contemptuously. 'You don't understand. You're not a twin.'

'I'm damned glad I'm not his twin.'

'Charlie,' she said slowly. 'Don't push me too far. I love you—but I love Neil too. It's something I can't explain to you. But you're right when you say that it's as if he and I were one person. It's always been like that. He knows when I'm ill—just as I know when he's unhappy.'

'Rats!' said Charlie, rudely, taking a cigarette from a packet by the bed. 'Give me my coat will you—I want a match.'

She handed the jacket to him, and watched him hunt for his matches. The photograph of Jackie was in the pocket of her skirt. She saw him feel carefully in the pocket from which she presumed it had fallen.

'Are you going to take Neil to Southampton tonight?' she asked in a hard voice.

'No,' he said deliberately.

'Well, now we know,' she said, quietly. 'Come and have your food—they're all waiting.'

As she went with the tray through the hall to her grand-mother's room Nona was shaken with jealousy. She was nine-teen to Charlie's twenty-six. He was attractive to women, she knew that from the looks they cast on him. That he had had affairs with women she knew instinctively. She was too young to value his experienced love-making and still young enough to be jealous of those women in his past. Did he ever see them now? He was away so much on those long-distance runs. What did he do all the time he was away from her? Little de-mons of doubt and jealousy assailed her in spite of her desire to be fair to him.

She was passionate in spite of her delicate, rather fragile beauty. Her passion for Charlie was the strongest thing in her life—stronger even than her love for her twin. The old wom-an had watched it grow with delight and relief. The close tie between the twin brother and sister who were so extraordi-narily alike had worried her. Had they been of the same sex all would have been well. But they were not—and she had feared that when the question of marriage for them both arose there would be trouble. And so there had been.

Nona could think now of nothing but the girl in the pho-tograph. Neil and his predicament were thrust out of her mind by the laughing girl in the bikini. Why hadn't *she* got a bikini? If she had she would never have time to sunbathe in it. She had never had time—that was it. There had never been time for her to do the things which other girls did. She had always had to do things in the house, and for her brothers, because her grandmother had gone out to work. She had always con-soled herself with the bright thought of Australia and of her future life out there. She would get plenty of swimming and sun, her Aunt Dorothy had written her. And now? With Len dead and Neil in the Army, who was going to look after their grandmother? With each month now, as she watched the old woman grow more and more helpless, that bright vision became more and more a mirage—a mirage which would disappear before she could catch at its fleeting beauty.

Charlie wouldn't wait to emigrate. He was impatient to be off—and it might be that he would go on ahead leaving her to follow when she could. The thought of that was frightening— but the idea of leaving her grandmother who had been both mother and father to them never entered her head. Nona had never been able to put herself first; it was only recently that she was beginning to regret not having waited to marry Charlie. But who could have foreseen that Len, who had urged the marriage, would be killed?

As she entered her grandmother's room her father had just noticed the large envelope with the Royal crest on the mantelpiece. He got up and picked it up.

'So it's true,' he said, looking with unwilling pride at the letter. 'Quite an interesting experience to go to one of these. My friend now, she'd like to see that. I see there is a form enclosed for two tickets for friends or relatives. What are you doing about it, Mother?'

'What d'you mean, what am I doing? I'm going, of course, and Nona and Charlie will use those tickets.'

'Oh, I shouldn't have thought that Charlie would care for this type of thing. Now my friend would appreciate it.'

'What type of thing?' asked Charlie, coming in and kissing the old woman for whom he had brought back a bottle of whisky.

'Charlie! You good boy. Never forget me do you? Just what I need when I'm depressed. Edward's talking of the Investiture, when Len's medal will be given. He doesn't think it will interest you.'

Charlie picked up the letter, examined it carefully and then kissed the old woman again. 'I'm glad, Gran,' he said quietly. 'Yes, of course I'd like to go. I'd like to be there as a tribute to

Len. I'll take you there. Leave it to me. I'll get the boss's car. He's decent about this sort of thing.'

Then, swinging round, he caught sight of Neil in his sister's clothes. He was about to make a scene, had started roughly, 'What the hell d'you mean by wearing those. . .?' when the old woman put her fingers imploringly to her lips and, as he desisted, merely relapsing into a disapproving glare at Neil, she gave him a grateful smile which had such sweetness in it that Charlie was touched. Edward saw the smile and understood its meaning. He resented his mother's fondness for Charlie.

CHAPTER XIV

NONA CAUGHT the smile and the glance which passed between them and misunderstood it. That's it, she thought angrily, as she doled out the liver and bacon carefully. Her father's unexpected arrival meant easing a little from everyone's helping. That's it. Gran likes him. She always did—she likes him because he's big and masculine and strong . . . what would she think if I told her that he can't stand a toothache or a poisoned finger? That he behaves like a child? She thinks Neil is soft and weak . . . but he can bear any amount of physical pain—it's the mental kind he can't take. As she carried a plate over to her grandmother she felt her heart hardening against Charlie. . . . Jackie . . . Jackie . . . with those huge eyes and the small pointed face.

'Hurry up, Nonie, I'm starving,' complained Charlie.

'Go and see to him,' said her grandmother taking the plate from her. 'A man who works as Charlie does needs his food—and plenty of it.' She looked meaningly at her son as she said this, but the remark was lost on him. He and Neil were regarding the division of the last piece of liver with avid interest. Edward finished filling the glasses. The wine, as he said, was a heavy one.

'Goes well with liver,' he said approvingly, raising his glass to his mother.

'Last time you came here you drank wine—and it was Len's death which brought you,' said his mother ominously.

You'd better drink to mine.' Her son did not reply to this but attacked his liver. There was silence for a moment while everyone gave attention to the food, then Edward began again. 'Yes, as I was saying . . . this question of who we are. Now you, Neil, who are you? Number . . . ?'

Neil swallowing his food ravenously looked up, startled. '01278650. . . .' he said automatically.

His father clapped his hands delightedly. 'Perfect! Couldn't have a better illustration. I ask him who he is. What does he reply? Not "your son Neil Edward Collins" . . . No, he answers off pat, "I'm 01278650." Now, Neil, how long have you been 01278650?'

'Eleven months,' mumbled Neil disagreeably. Here was his father getting at him now. It was bad enough to have all his fellow men and the blasted N.C.O.'s always at him. Wasn't that what he'd run away from?

'Exactly. Neil has been 01278650 less than eleven months, yet in that time, that new identity has been so impacted on him, so forcefully imprinted on his mind, that when his own father asks him who he is, what does he answer? Not, "I am Neil Collins, your son"—but "01278650" . . . .'

'Well, what about it?' demanded Nonie, defiantly. 'He's had that number burned into him day and night . . . no wonder he answers to it.'

'I suppose now he's assumed his sister's identity he'll answer to Nona Mary Kent,' drawled Charlie, his eyes full of malice as he again noticed his wife's sweater and scarf on Neil. He had with difficulty prevented himself from tearing the things off him when he had first caught sight of his brother-in-law dressed in his sister's clothes. It was only the pleading looks of the old woman which had kept him from a violent quarrel.

Neil flushed hotly and was about to retort when his grandmother said slyly, 'Neil said today that he did not really know who he was. The right fellow in the wrong skin or the wrong fellow in the right skin. . . .'

Edward leaned forward excitedly to his son. 'But that's quite extraordinary. That you should be thinking in that way at this time. Really, I'm beginning to have some hope for you yet.'

'Why?' asked Neil, glumly. 'If you had to become an automaton at everybody's beck and call, obeying everyone's voice but your own you'd begin to wonder who you were.'

'Edward's never heard any other voice but his own,' said his mother. Her son ignored this and turned again to Neil. 'But I do, my dear boy. That's just it. I do. Now, I think that I am Edward Collins. Why? Because my mother there, Jane Mary Collins, says that I'm her son.'

'And so you are, more's the pity,' sighed his mother. 'This liver's tough, Nonie. Where'd you get it?'

'At the corner shop.'

'Well, it's tough. And the peas are old. I wish I could go shopping again.'

'I wish you could,' said Nona. 'I loathe it.'

'As I was saying,' continued her son, inexorably determined to talk, 'I have been brought up to believe that I am Edward Collins—but am I? If I were to have a sham drowning accident tomorrow, leaving all my clothes and personal belongings on some beach and disappear—what's to stop me from becoming someone else? Jeremiah Jobson . . . for instance.'

'If you go on in that way you'll be locked up—and they'll soon tell you who you are,' said his mother, drily. 'There are people in lunatic asylums who think they are Queen Victoria or Napoleon. I don't care for this wine, Edward. It's sour.'

'It's fine. I like it,' said Charlie.

'Have mine then, I've only sipped this side.' She held out the glass. Nonie took it and tipped the wine into Charlie's. He raised the now brimming glass mockingly to her. 'Here's to your bright eyes,' he said, giving her one of the intimate looks she normally loved but which at this moment she resented. She raised her own. 'To those which are brighter!' she said calmly. Charlie looked at her, puzzled. 'Here, what are you getting at? Trying to be funny like your Pa?'

'Not funny,' she said, looking straight at him, 'Thinking of Jackie.'

Charlie gulped his wine, choked, put down the glass. 'Just what do you mean by that?'

'Don't you understand plain English? Thinking of Jackie.'

Charlie's face was ugly. 'You've been looking in my pockets. I should have thought it was beneath you—with all your ideas of culture.'

'I did not go looking in your pockets!' Nonie sprang up from the table, her lips set, her eyes blazing.

'Here. What's all this? Surely you two can keep your quarrels for the bedroom.' Edward was angry at having the limelight diverted from him like this.

'That's just it. Which bedroom—hers or mine?'

'Nonie . . . Nonie . . . Be careful, child . . . think what you're saying. You'll regret it later.'

'No. I know what I'm saying.'

'Well, stop it now. Get on with it later. Let's eat now. You and Charlie can finish this in private.'

'We'd eat in private if I had my way,' said Charlie, furiously. 'All this walking about with cook-pots and trays—it's too much for anyone to stand.'

Nona sat down again. 'Sorry, everybody,' she said, briefly.

Neil, his face taut with anxiety, put a hand on his twin's arm. 'Don't take on so, Nonie,' he pleaded.

'And you shut up,' said Charlie, even more angrily. 'You don't make it any easier for any of us . . . coming back like this. It's Nonie who gets all the worry of you. I'd be ashamed to skulk in my sister's clothes. . . .'

'Neil's got nothing whatsoever to do with what is riling you,' said Nona. 'What's mine is Neil's. What's Neil's is mine. It's always been so.'

'Then I suppose you're 01278650 too?' said Charlie sarcastically.

'Yes,' her answer was calm, 'I *am*. And it's not only Neil who's going to get away—it's me too.'

'Listen! Are you starting this dreary nonsense like your father? If so I'm not listening. I'm sane. But I soon won't be if I have to listen to any more of this moonshine. . . .'

'Would anyone like to try a lichee?' said Mrs. Collins, soothingly. 'They're most misleading. . . .' She held the bag out invitingly but as there was no response she continued to eat them herself.

'I think it's time we behaved like civilised people,' said Edward. 'All this brawling is so out of date. Everything is settled nowadays by arbitration.'

'You mean your genius for inciting strikes is of no further use?'

'I never thought that strikes were of any use—but they have served a purpose . . . the result is arbitration.'

'There are five strikes on at the moment,' said Charlie, flatly. 'How do you account for them? Lack of arbitration, I suppose?'

'Edward's very clever. He's created himself a second job. First to incite the strike—then be called in to assist with the arbitration. . . .' said his mother acidly.

'Now, Mother . . . that's not quite fair. It's true that I have been employed by both sides after insistent demand . . . but it's a position requiring considerable tact . . . considerable courage . . . and the gift of words. . . .'

Suddenly Neil could stand this no longer. Jumping up, he flung his arms dramatically above his head. . . . 'You're all quarrelling and talking . . . *talking*. . . . Why don't you do something about me? I sit here waiting for the cops. Why can't you help me? *Why? Why?*' he almost screamed in excitement.

'Don't be theatrical,' said his father. 'It won't bring the cops any quicker or keep them away any longer. I think I'll have a lichee after all, Mother. Now, Nonie, can you tell me on what sort of a bush a lichee grows?'

'It grows on a tree,' said Charlie, sourly. 'I saw them in Korea—plenty of them.'

If Neil collapsed like a bubble at his father's words, Edward was disconcerted by Charlie. He always forgot that his son-in-law had travelled widely during his Army service. It was this which had given him the desire to emigrate, to make for the other side of the world. Edward, beyond a few trips with labour rebels to France and Belgium, knew nothing of the world outside his own country.

'Neil's right. What are we going to do? He's got to get away,' said Nonie, urgently. She was rapidly becoming as frantic as her twin.

'Have a cigarette, it's said to be calming.' Her father held out a packet of an American brand.

Charlie was surprised. 'I thought you wouldn't have anything to do with American goods or Americans? Too capitalist for your taste.'

'That was so,' said Edward, portentously. 'That was so. But for a long time I've had doubts. Serious doubts. And now this new friend—the one who gave me these cigarettes, has made me see differently. She has shown me the way to the truth. . . .'

'She?' His mother looked up sharply, remembering what he had said before the meal.

'Yes. She. Through her I have been led to discover great truths and philosophies of which I have never even dreamed. Great things are possible . . . are going to happen. The future holds out its golden path and all I have to do is to tread it to such heights, such dizzying heights of fame and power as this simple man has never even visualised.'

'You've never been simple,' said his mother. 'Sounds like religion. I had an inkling that it would be.'

'It's a woman,' said Nona, and she looked at Charlie.

'Yes, a woman. But what a woman! A pearl, Mother. A pearl.'

'You don't know how to appreciate a pearl. You had one before . . . I knew you had some new "ism" when you came here tonight. Are you thinking of marrying this pearl?'

'She comes from across the Atlantic . . . she's a cultured travelled lady . . . I have not yet summoned the temerity to ask her. I want you to meet her, Mother. I want her to come here and see you. . . .'

'She can't come here, Gran. Tell him she can't come!' Neil shouted.

'She's not coming,' said his grandmother quietly. 'Don't get so excited, boy.'

'Now you, Neil, are the very one who could most benefit by the marvellous truths which have been revealed to me through this lady from across the Atlantic. To you, young, disorientated and mixed up, everything will straighten out and become possible. Her theory is that everything is possible *if* you will make it possible. You can't afford to miss this chance of talking to her. It may change your whole life. . . .'

'Father, you won't see. I've got to get away. I *must*. Oh, God! Why do I have to come home just as you choose this new craze? Why?'

'No one asked you to come here,' said Charlie, angrily.

'I must get away tonight. *Soon*. Are you going to help me, Charlie? Are you?'

Neil, in his mind the picture of Mike hiding over there watching the house, was becoming more and more strung up as time went on and his family appeared to him to be indulging in a normal evening scrap such as they often had. He simply couldn't understand why they refused to see the peril he was in. The last times he had come home *they* had been the tense strung-up ones—he had been calm. He had been calm because it had been such heaven just to get home—to get away from the chivvying and hustling of the camp. He looked at his brother-in-law now with desperation. Charlie was about to reply in an abrupt negative when he caught a look on Nonie's face. It was an expression he had never seen there before. A threat? Or a warning? Which? Or was it both? He hesitated. 'We'll have to talk it out,' he said, roughly. 'I can't take you tonight—it's impossible. If you want to go tonight you'll have to get off by yourself. . . .' His tone indicated his scorn that Neil was not doing this but relying on others to assist his getaway. 'If you lay quiet until tomorrow night I might be able to make Southampton.'

'You'll take Neil tonight—or not at all,' interposed Nona carefully. 'Tomorrow will be too late.'

'Then why is he dressed in your clothes? Why is he hanging about here at all? Why didn't the young fool get straight off to Ireland?'

'He had to have clothes,' said Nonie.

'But not yours!' shouted Charlie. 'I loathe seeing him masquerading as you! I hate to see a double—a weak double of my wife. . . . Go and take those things off and I might do something.'

'He has to go tonight,' said Nonie, inexorably.

'Do *you* approve of this business? Aiding and abetting a deserter?' demanded Charlie of his father-in-law.

'Of course he does. Hasn't he been advocating it for years?' said Nona, contemptuously.

'And you, Gran. Do you approve?'

The old woman was silent.

'I persuaded her,' said Nona, defiantly. 'Of course she didn't want to help. She wanted to send him back—as she did before—*as she does now.*'

'If you take my advice that's what you'll do now.' Charlie got up from the table noisily. 'You won't persuade *me.* I'm not so easy.'

'If you won't help Neil to get away tonight I intend to go with him.'

The old woman looked up sharply. 'Careful . . . Nonie. . . .'

'You don't understand. Charlie's got a woman. He's keeping another woman.'

'Oh, for Chrissake!' shouted Charlie.

'You can't deny it.'

'So what? Yes. I've got a girl up there. What d'you expect me to do three nights of the week? Lie on old Ma Tanner's hard bed and dream of you and your twin brother?'

'You admit it then?'

'Of course. It doesn't mean anything. If you'd let me explain.'

'Charlie's right,' said Edward. 'I'm surprised at your attitude, Nona. You're back in the dark ages.'

Nona went up to Charlie and said urgently. 'Does she know about me? *Does she?*'

'Of course,' said Charlie, disinterestedly. He seemed almost bored by the subject.

Nona began clearing up the plates and dishes and stacking them on a tray. 'That's enough. I'm going with Neil.'

'What about Gran?' demanded Neil, nervously. 'No one cares about her but me. She can't be left.'

'Then stay and look after her yourself—in your sister's clothes,' snapped Charlie. 'Come in our room, Nonie.'

'No. I'm washing up in here.' She carried the laden tray through to the kitchenette. Charlie followed her and shut the door. The sound of their angry voices rose above the clatter of crockery.

'I don't think I'll offer to dry,' said Edward.

'I will.' Neil got up. His face was contorted.

'Leave them alone. . . .'

'But it's horrible . . . Charlie having a girl like that. . . .'

'Oh wake up, Neil. There are always other girls—the sooner Nonie learns that the better. Hasn't it occurred to you that *you're* the main cause of the trouble?'

'Me?' Neil was startled.

'*Yes. You.* Nonie's always worrying and fidgeting about you . . . no man likes that. He likes to be first. . . .' his grandmother said quietly. 'It was just beginning to get easier when you came home, Neil.'

'How could it have been easier if he has this other girl?' Neil asked, angrily.

'It's because Charlie's jealous of you that he fools with this girl.'

'Of me? But I'm her twin . . . how can he be jealous of me?' Neil was bewildered.

'Oh don't be dumb,' said his grandmother. 'Husbands are often jealous of anyone who takes their wife's attention and affection.'

'Neil, my boy, I seldom give you advice but I give you this piece of advice now. Go back. Now. *Quickly.* You're causing more havoc than you think.'

'You tell me that? *You?* Why, you've always raved at Len and me for accepting our National Service at all. Why, what's come over you? The one person I thought would approve was you, Father.' The boy's bewilderment at his father's attitude was obvious.

'Neil's right. You're a nice one to tell him to go back,' said his mother, sarcastically.

'I've changed. I'm beginning to see that we are put here to work out a destiny and that we must accept it whatever it may be.' Edward was pompous, sickeningly so.

'But just now you said that anything is possible if we make it possible. I want to get away. I want to be free. Free. I tell you.'

'There's no such thing. It's just a lovely word—and the sooner you realise that the better,' said his grandmother. 'As for you, Edward, I suppose your changed views are due to this pearl beyond price with whom you've taken up. What is she? One of these Rock 'n Roll hot-gospellers?'

'Not exactly,' said her son, laughing. 'But you're not so far off the mark. You've an uncanny way of sensing things, Mother. She is the founder of a new faith.'

'Is she a friend of that great negro, Josh?'

'Yes. He introduced her to me.'

'Now *he's* got something. He's genuine. You can't tell me he's a Rock 'n Roll preacher. . . .'

'No. He plays jazz in some club and uses the money he earns for helping down-and-outs.'

Above the clatter in the kitchen they could hear Charlie and Nona arguing. Neil began walking up and down between the door and the bed.

'Sit down, do. You make me nervous.'

'Why do they have to tear each other's guts the night I'm home?'

'It's *because* you're home that they're tearing each other. Can't you see that?'

'Yes. I've had it rubbed into me enough. I'm going. I'll find some old clothes and clear off.'

'You'll walk straight into the cops,' said his grandmother. 'You're the sort who never gets away with anything. Just sit down and relax, can't you?'

'I don't think you should dissuade him from doing what he knows to be right,' said Edward, unctuously.

'Don't you say things of that sort in my presence, Edward. I've got a good memory and I can think of too many occasions when you have deliberately been blind to right and wrong.'

Neil sat down. He was shivering and his face still had small beads of perspiration on it.

'Have you got a fever?' asked his grandmother. 'It's warm enough for it.'

A violent crash brought Neil to his feet as he was about to reply in the negative to this. They heard Nona screaming. Something was thrown and hit the door with a thud—then there was silence.

'Sit down,' repeated his grandmother. 'They're almost through.'

'Pleasant evening's entertainment,' remarked Edward, smiling.

Almost immediately they came through the door, Charlie hot and furious-looking, Nona white and tense.

'Well, well,' said Edward, looking from one angry face to another. 'You make a lot of noise settling your problems.'

'At least we settle them ourselves,' said Charlie, pointedly. 'We don't expect other people to do it for us.' He turned angrily to Neil. 'This is all *your* fault. Just because you're yellow and can't stand on your own miserable feet.'

'I'm going now. I've just said so,' said Neil, getting up. He was still shivering and his eyes were desperate.

'Charlie. Are you going to help him? It's your last chance. *Are* you?'

'No. What's wrong with the train? Take off your sister's clobber and put on your own—and go and buy a ticket like a man. I'll give you the money—anything to get rid of you.'

'I'm coming with you, Neil. Charlie and I are washed up.'

'Think what you're doing. You're a married woman, Nona. Your husband comes first—your brother afterwards.'

'I'm going with Neil. I'll go right over with him on the boat and come back on the return one. I'll get Mrs. Danvers to see to you. It won't be long.'

'Nonie....' Neil looked miserably from his sister to Charlie. '*No.* I don't want to make trouble between you two.'

'You've made it!' shouted Charlie.

'A girl called Jackie made it,' said Nona, calmly. 'It's nothing to do with Neil.'

'Oh, stop quarrelling,' said Edward, plaintively. 'It's so stupid and gets us nowhere. Sit down and let's talk this out like sensible people.'

'Settle it by arbitration,' said his mother, drily.

'Listen . . . listen. . . .' whispered Neil, frantically. 'Someone is coming up the steps.'

They were suddenly all silent. Neil, edging towards the door behind his grandmother's bed, had the terrified air of the fugitive again.

The front door was evidently open, for whoever it was came down the passage.

'Mrs. Collins . . . Mrs. Collins. . . .' called a plaintive female voice. 'Can I come in?'

The old woman looked quickly from one agitated face to another. 'Who is it?'

'Linda's mother.'

With two waves of her hand Mrs. Collins motioned Neil into the closet-room and Nonie to open the door.

The woman who entered was tall and striking. She would have been attractive had it not been for the deep lines of discontent and the acute anxiety on her face. She stood in the doorway looking from Nonie to Mrs. Collins in the bed. Ignoring the two men, she said tersely. 'It's Linda. It's after ten—and she's not come home.'

CHAPTER XV

THERE WAS a silence after the woman's words and then Nonie quickly shut the door behind her.

'Sit down, Mrs. Sanderson,' said her grandmother quietly, 'and tell me about it.'

'I came home at half-past six as usual,' said the woman. 'Linda is always waiting for me at the end of the road. She comes to meet the bus. She wasn't there tonight. If she's late she always waits for me outside the house. Tonight she wasn't there. I've waited and waited. No one has seen her. I thought perhaps she was here, Mrs. Collins. I know she often comes to you. . . .'

'She *was* here,' said Mrs. Collins. 'There was a bit of trouble. Linda's been taking the flowers off the graves in the cemetery and bringing them to me. It seems that people have complained, and today a policeman followed her and came here. It

was that young Wilson. He warned her—but he was very nice.
She went off earlier than usual—about half-past four.'

All the time the old woman was talking she was thinking.
That man the child said was hiding over there in the ruins
and whom she said was watching this house. *Ought I to tell
her about that?* Ought I? And if I do, what about Neil? What if
Linda had gone there again? She was an inquisitive child and
her curiosity had been aroused. 'It was just like a film, Gran,'
she had said, 'him lying there and threatening Cissie and me
like that.'

'Can your daughter get into the house—has she a key?'
asked Edward, breaking the silence.

'My son,' said Gran briefly, glancing in Edward's direction
and then back to Linda's mother. 'And this is my granddaughter Nonie and her husband.'

'Linda always has a key. She wears it on a ribbon round her
neck.'

'A very dangerous habit, madam, and one which I observe
is becoming more and more prevalent amongst women who
go out to work.'

'That's enough, Edward,' his mother said shortly. Hadn't
she herself had to do the same thing when Edward's children
had been at school?

'Do you think that perhaps she lost her key and couldn't
get in?' asked Nonie.

'More likely she was thoroughly upset by the policeman . . . and afraid to go home,' said Edward. 'Fear is the cause
of most crime.'

'Young Wilson was very decent,' repeated his mother. 'I saw
him shaking her hand and patting her shoulder. They parted
very good friends.' But was it the man on the waste ground
over there that frightened her? And has she gone there again?
worried the old woman.

'Charlie,' she said coaxingly. 'Go out and have a look round
for Linda will you? She plays over there on that waste ground
a lot. Have a look round. There are deep holes over there. She
might have fallen down or twisted her ankle or something.'

'Then she'd cry out—we'd have heard her—or someone would have heard her,' said her mother, worriedly. 'Do you think I'd better tell the police?' There was acute anxiety now on her face.

'Not yet,' said Mrs. Collins. 'You go home in case she should come back—she'd be upset at finding no one there. Charlie and Nonie'll go and hunt round for her.'

'She's never been late before, that's why it worries me so—all these assaults on young children lately—but Linda's a good child—she's never stayed out before.'

And that's partly because I send her home early, thought the old woman but she did not say so.

'Thank you, I'm grateful, Mrs. Collins. . . . Linda's so fond of you I thought you wouldn't mind my coming here to ask . . . I'm sorry if I've interrupted your evening. . . .' She looked from Edward to Nona and Charlie, nodded to the old woman, and hurried out.

'I'll come with you and look for her,' said Charlie, gruffly. He gave Nonie an angry resigned look and followed the woman.

'It *would* happen now when we're trying to get Neil away,' said Nonie, hopelessly. The door behind the bed was cautiously opened and her brother came into the room. . . . 'Blessed kid! She's causing a lot of trouble for me,' he said. 'Nonie, what *am* I going to do? Can't you get Charlie to change his mind and take me?'

'No,' said Nonie in a hard voice. 'I told you. It's all washed up between Charlie and me.'

'Nonie,' Neil pleaded, 'can't you forgive Charlie and make him help me? He's really awfully fond of you.'

'He's got another girl,' said Nona, flatly. 'D'you want me to condone that just so you can get a lift on his lorry?'

'No, Nonie, I don't mean that. I mean can't you just string him along until I've got away?'

'You saw for yourself how it is.'

'But you could tide it over until I'm away. You *could*, couldn't you, Nonie?'

'Why don't you put on your uniform and go back?' asked his grandmother, suddenly. 'You say you may not be missed until tomorrow morning. *Why don't you go back again?*'

'No, I can't, I can't.' The panic in his voice shocked all three of them.

'Have you committed some crime that you're so afraid?' asked his father, curiously. 'I'm not speaking of those endless and petty charges by which the Army destroys the soul of a man. I mean something which *matters*. Have you?'

'No,' shouted Neil, violently. 'I haven't. Can't *you* of all people understand that I just can't stick it. *I won't go back.*'

'You realise that if you persist in this it will mean a lot of worry and trouble for your sister and grandmother. The police'll come here again and again questioning them . . . the house will be watched . . . you know all that? You should have pleaded conscientious reasons and refused to join the Army.'

'It isn't *you* who'll have the trouble, Edward—you'll be far away as you always are when there's trouble,' said his mother, drily.

All the time he was talking Neil was watching the door. He had been terrified when his grandmother had suggested that Charlie should search the ruins. He was waiting now . . . listening for his return. Over there waiting, was *Mike. Mike.* He was sure of it.

'Don't keep watching the door like that,' said the old woman. 'It gives me the willies. . . .' But she herself was listening too. Why, she asked herself, had she sent Charlie out to look for the child? And especially told him that she often played on the waste ground? Was it because Charlie was strong, a great hulk of a man, afraid of nothing, and should he come across that fugitive of whom Linda had spoken he would be quite capable of dealing with him?

They sat there again, the four of them, each busy with their own thoughts. Neil, desperate by now, was frantically turning over plans in his mind. Nona sat white and silent thinking of Charlie's face as he had looked at her before he went out. Edward was furious at the turn the evening had taken and resentful of Neil's inopportune arrival. He had come here hoping to interest his mother in his new friend and to prepare her for the idea of his possible remarriage. Now he saw that the reception of such an idea in this atmosphere would be even more charged with suspicion and contempt than was his mother's normal reception of his schemes. He looked purposely at his watch. 'Twenty to eleven . . . have to be getting along . . . well, Neil, what are we going to do about you?' He took his raincoat down.

'Here, look in the paper! It says the call-up'll be ended in 1960.' He held out the evening paper.

The boy sat silent and did not answer.

'Oh, don't be so idiotic. How can that help him? All *you've* got to do is to keep your tongue quiet about this,' said his mother. 'And that's a difficult thing for you to do, Edward.'

'I see no reason why you should imply that I would risk giving away my own son by talking,' said Edward with dignity. 'The Army destroys a man, kills his soul and coarsens his mind and body. It's legalised brutality and murder. I'm the last man to send Neil back there.'

'How d'you know the Army does all you say it does to a man? You've never been in the Army. It didn't hurt Len—he loved it.'

'It murdered him.'

'The Army didn't murder him—one of those Cypriots did,' retorted his mother. 'And Len would be the last boy to have borne them any ill-will. I can't understand your attitude to something you know nothing about.'

'It's not your fault that I never suffered as Neil is doing,' said Edward bitterly. 'You did your best to push me into the war. Your patriotic humbug sickens me. I suppose it's your having been brought up in State homes. I should have thought that having lost Father in the First World War you'd have got over all that and have been glad enough to have kept me out of the second one.'

'Don't let's go into all that again,' said his mother, wearily. 'Here's Charlie back.'

Heavy steps sounded outside. All four watched the door until Charlie's knock sounded on it. 'Can't find the kid anywhere—no one's seen her. The rain'll send her home if she's still out playing.'

'Did you look over there by the ruined flats?' The old woman's voice was tense. She was watching Neil as she spoke. His face, intent on Charlie, showed a desperate anguish which ravaged it, making the thin young outline so taut with strain that the old woman was again overwhelmed with pity.

'I did—it's dark and I had no torch so I couldn't see into the deep bits in the foundations, but I called and called. If she had been down there she'd have heard and cried out. She's not there.'

His grandmother, looking again at Neil's face, saw beads of sweat dripping down it. The tautness sagged suddenly and he looked old—old and lifeless.

'Charlie.' Nona's voice was like a whip. 'Are you going to take Neil in the lorry?'

Charlie looked from his wife to her twin, then at Gran. 'No,' he said, deliberately. 'You can get your twin *sister* away yourself.'

Neil sprang up, his hands clenched. Nona pushed him down, turning a furious look on Charlie.

'Good. Now we know where we are. You can get out of here and go to your Jackie. She can have you seven nights a week and welcome.'

'Nonie. Nonie,' pleaded her grandmother.

'I mean it,' said Nona, angrily. 'And now if you'll kindly get out of here, Charlie, Neil and I can get going.'

'You can't leave your grandmother like that,' said Charlie. 'I don't know what's got into you. You'll smash up your marriage and leave your grandmother without a thought, all for this weakling who can't face up to life.'

'Nor can you,' said Nona. 'You can't face up to the fact that a man can only have one wife in this country. You're just as weak as Neil.'

'Now, now,' said Edward. 'That's enough for tonight, Nonie. Think carefully what you're doing. Let Neil work out his own problems and you stay with your grandmother.' He got up, holding out the evening paper. 'Look!' He pointed to the headlines, 'Call-up to be ended by 1960'.

'Edward,' said his mother, 'stop it. How can that do anything but upset the present conscripts still further?'

Edward looked in his pocket-book and brought out a small card. 'Here,' he said, grandly. 'This is the best I can do. I'm moving about a lot just now—this'll find me if you want me.'

His mother took the card distastefully and read aloud, '"Box 3125, c/o Newton's News Agency". That's about the best you've ever done,' she said, quietly. 'I remember when Connie was having the twins—and desperately ill—the only address we had was care of some tobacconist. I remember what the doctor said too.'

'Now, Mother, there's no use in bringing up old scores. . . .' Edward was putting on his raincoat. 'I've told you that my work is above domestic worries and sentimental ties. . . .' He stopped short as he remembered with dismay that this evening had been meant for the introduction of his new woman friend, just such a possible domestic tie—and heard his mother saying, 'I don't know about that, Edward. It seems to me you've been coming here a good deal more lately than you have in years. Why? Because you're getting on now, Edward. The road becomes even lonelier when you're old. . . . You're almost forty-nine.'

Her son said good-bye hurriedly. His mother's words had taken him aback. He'd always thought the old woman was a witch. Seemed to know a fellow's thoughts in the most uncanny way. Just now . . . why did she have to go on about age like that? How could she know that he'd been uncomfortably conscious of that very fact. At one of his recent meetings the promoters had said, 'You're slipping. Not the same attention tonight. You'd better take stock of yourself, Collins. You can't afford to slip.'

It was typical of him that he took leave of his daughter and son without any further reference to the situation which was tearing at them both. Edward, champion of a multitude of causes, was deliberately blind to those of his own flesh and blood.

'Well,' said Charlie, when the door had closed behind Edward. 'What now?'

'You can take Neil in the lorry. *Now.* He ought to have been away long ago.'

'It's not my lorry. Give a chap a chance, Nonie.'

'You can get it when you need it for others; it's strange that you can't get it now.'

'You can't get out of it that way.' Nona's eyes were hard and did not waver as she looked at Charlie.

'It's easy enough if I've a load for that way, but there's the speedometer—it shows the mileage and it's checked every day.'

'You can fix the speedometer,' said Nona, stonily.

'No,' said her grandmother, sharply. 'Surely you don't want Charlie to start those sort of games.'

'It doesn't matter to me what he does. He can do as he likes.'

'If it doesn't matter, why d'you ask me to take your brother in the lorry?' Charlie shouted angrily. 'Women are always illogical—go off at a tangent and never stick to the point.'

'If you think I'm going to trade in your Jackie for Neil's ride in the lorry you're mistaken.'

'But, Nonie. . . .' Charlie was genuinely bewildered now. 'Look, you haven't got this straight. I'm not that sort . . . surely you know that by now? Let me explain.'

'I know nothing about you—I've just discovered that.'

'Oh, for heaven's sake, let's get going. We've wasted hours just talking, *talking*. . . .' Neil sprang up and started pacing up and down the room.

'Oh shut up!' snapped Charlie. 'All right, Nonie, I'll get the lorry. I'll go along about four. Five is the normal time for the start of the long-distance runs. I must get there before that. I haven't got all the keys. It'll mean picking a lock. I've always gone straight—I don't like doing this—it may get me into a packet of trouble—even lose me my job. But I'll do it. Not for your brother—I don't care if he's caught. If he wants to be on the run he shouldn't ask anyone to share it. I'm doing it for *you*. No one matters to me but you, Nonie.'

'There's still Jackie. What about her?'

'Nonie,' snapped the old woman, 'Charlie has offered to do what you've been worrying him to do all evening. He's doing it against the grain. Be gracious and accept it. You can thrash the other out later—if you must.'

Neil took his sister's arm turning her face to his, and urged, 'You *will* forgive Charlie, won't you? The lorry's the only way that's safe for me.'

Nonie pulled herself away and went over to the window. In some vague way she felt that she was being sold. Sold by these three people. By her grandmother for her peace of mind, by Neil for his freedom, and by Charlie to exonerate himself about Jackie. Something in her resented this violently and something else accepted it as her lot. It seemed to her now that this bargain with Charlie—for as such she saw his proposal to help Neil—was but a foretaste of the renunciation of the whole plan to go to Australia. Her grandmother was too ill to be left alone. And how long would it be? No one knew. It could be months and it could be years. She was a tough old woman with a strong heart and tremendous will power. Charlie would have to go alone—and that might mean more successors to Jackie. He would have to go on ahead and she and Neil would follow later when Gran was gone. But already the picture her aunt had painted and strengthened by the photographs she had sent them of a life in the sun with clean air to breathe, time to play, and space in which to rear children was becoming dim. If she accepted this thing from Charlie she would have to forget Jackie. Could she? She turned round to her grandmother's anxious face and her twin's wretched one.

'All right, Charlie. You win,' she said at last. 'But you must get the lorry *now*.'

'Look, Nonie. Have a heart. I've been driving all day—two hundred miles and more. I must get a few hours' sleep. If we start about five we'll make Southampton by nine. I'll go on to Weymouth where I'll pick up a return load so it'll look all right.'

Neil looked anxiously at the clock by his grandmother's bedside. It was almost eleven.

'Give me till four. Nonie can set the alarm and you can come with me to get the lorry, Neil.'

'No. I'll meet you on the corner somewhere. It's safer.' Neil was thinking again of Mike. He would have to slip out the back way to avoid him. *But suppose Mike should come before then?*

'I'll come with you and see you off,' said Nona.

'Come along and get some sleep,' said Charlie, putting his arms round her.

She said, quickly, 'No. I'll sleep in here a while. I'll curl up on the end of Gran's bed.'

Charlie looked mutinous. 'No. That's not in the bargain. You've been sleeping here long enough. You sleep where you belong.'

Nona looked at the old woman but she got no help from that quarter. Her grandmother stared stolidly at her and in those intelligent old eyes Nonie saw that she realised perfectly well what was going on in her granddaughter's mind. She would have to sleep with Charlie—after she had said that everything between them was washed up because of Jackie. She would have to capitulate—because of Neil and because of her grandmother. Charlie would insist on his pound of flesh. If he were sacrificing his moral scruples by picking locks and taking a lorry without proper authority to please her, then she would have to forget Jackie with the laughing eyes and the bikini. She felt the crumpled photograph now in her pocket as she hesitated. 'I'd rather stay here with Gran, then I can give Neil some food before he goes off. I'll wake you with a cup of tea, Charlie.'

'No,' said Charlie. 'If you don't come in with me now there'll be *no* lorry.'

He stared at her and his look was challenging.

'So that's it,' said Nona, slowly. 'When I suggested that you were trading Neil's lorry ride with me for Jackie just now you denied it.'

'Are you coming or not?' shouted Charlie.

'I'll follow you in one minute. I must have a word with Neil about everything.'

'If you're not in our room in ten minutes the bargain's off,' said Charlie. 'I'm a man of my word. If I say a thing I mean it.'

'I've told you I'm coming,' said Nona, quietly.

When the door was closed she went over to her grandmother. 'He's hateful, hateful!' she said, fiercely.

'Do as he wants now,' soothed her grandmother. 'And get your brother away. You can get your own back afterwards. There's a hundred ways a woman can do that with a man.' She kissed her granddaughter, stroking the pale face and noticing the shadows under her eyes.

'I've lost my job,' said Nona, suddenly. 'I've packed it in a week from today.'

'I thought you liked it there. What's happened?'

'I cheeked the manager; he was unfair. Then he tried to make me take back the notice by bribing me with a tin of salmon for you. I ought to have taken it. I ought. I'm a selfish pig!' She suddenly burst into tears. . . . 'What's the matter with everything, Gran? It's all so dirty . . . the world's horrible.'

'It's how you look at it. Stop crying now, Nonie, and get some sleep. I'll wake Neil. What is he to wear?'

'He'd better wear his slacks and a jersey and that old tweed jacket . . . hadn't he?'

'I'm not going like *this*!' said Neil.

'No one suggested you should,' retorted his grandmother. 'It's a criminal offence for a man to wear women's clothes in the streets. But you'll keep them on until it's time for you to go. There's been so many unexpected callers here today that there's no knowing who'll come in the night. I wouldn't be surprised if Linda's mother didn't come back again. I do hope that child's found.'

Nonie went into the kitchenette and put a tray ready for breakfast. She came in, kissed her grandmother and then put her arms round Neil. . . . 'Don't look so frightened. *Don't*. There's nothing to fear. Nothing. Just do as I tell you and you'll be all right. In Ireland no one will bother you.'

'But it's difficult to get work there,' said Neil, anxiously. 'There's a lot of Irish chaps joined up because they couldn't get work over there.' He was suddenly overcome with fear at the thought of a strange place.

'Your Great-aunt Liz will help you. I'll write a note to her. Give me a piece of paper and a pen, Nonie.' Nonie handed her a small writing block and a ball-point pen.

'You get along next door. I'll wake you at four,' she said to Neil. 'And you too, Nonie. Leave me now, I'm all right for the night.'

Nonie went reluctantly. She had lingered hoping that Charlie would have fallen asleep. 'I'll put the catch down on the door then?' she asked as she was about to close it.

'Yes, lock it. Goodnight, my darling,' said her grandmother, 'don't fret. It'll all come out in the wash . . . you'll see.

'Neil,' she called sharply. 'Come here.' And when he stood at the foot of the bed she said. 'Listen. Don't think that fear is going out of your life. Your life will be one long fear. *Yes! far worse than any you've known up till now.* If you stray over the border into Northern Ireland they can get you, and if you set foot on this soil they can arrest you. Understand? You'll never lose the feeling that you're not safe. Are you willing to feel terror every time you pass a policeman? Every time you come face to face with an army sergeant? *Are you?*'

'Yes. I am.'

'Then you're braver than I thought you were,' said his grandmother, drily. 'I should have thought that it would take far less courage to go back. You know what to expect there— you've no notion what being on the run will be like.'

'You were so decent, Gran, agreeing to let me hide here— and when I came through your window this morning. Why have you changed? Now you're trying to make me go back.'

'Perhaps seeing your father tonight. He's never faced up to reality. You don't want to, either. And perhaps, Nonie. I've never realised until tonight how unselfish Nona is. She loves Charlie—you can't know what that is—you've never loved yet—oh, don't interrupt me, you've that to come. Nonie loves Charlie with a terrible devouring love—and yet she's risking her whole happiness to help you get away. Do you realise that? Do you? Are you worth it?' She took his face between her old hands and looked searchingly at him as if she would penetrate the man behind the mask, '*Are* you, Neil?' They stared at one another, then the boy lowered his head and said wretchedly, 'No. You know damn well I'm not.'

'You could be,' said the old woman, sighing. 'That's what puzzles me so. What's made you so jumpy—like this? You've never been spoiled, never been ill-treated. You were sent away from the bombs in the War. It's a puzzle.'

'I don't see why there has to be a reason,' he muttered, sullenly. 'We can't all be heroes like Len. I was born frightened I suppose. I know I'm a coward and I'm ashamed. But what's the good? It's like some chaps up at the camp being bed-wetters—being ashamed doesn't stop it.'

'Being on the run is a terrible life—don't make any mistake about it. Life's full enough of kicks wherever you are, but desertion invites a double load.'

'I'll be all right,' he said, resentfully, but he said it without conviction, and his grandmother said sighing:

'You're no more cut out for a deserter than you are for a soldier. Both take some kind of character and it seems you've neither. God help you, Neil, I don't know how you'll end up.'

'If I could grow another skin or another body to fit into this one. . . .' he said, smiling ruefully, 'I'd be fine.'

'You make me desperate for you. *If only I could give you some courage—just one burst of it would help.*'

'I'll be all right once I've got away. They make a chap into a drivelling idiot with their bullying. Once they start I go round in circles trying to find out who I am.'

'If you're set on Ireland there's one thing you'd best forget, and that's your army number. I can't get over how you came out with it last night when your father was asking you who you were. I'm going to write a line now to my sister. It must be thirty years or more since I've seen Liz. She was a bonny girl . . . with yellow hair like Nonie's.' She said 'Nonie', but her eyes were on her grandson's as she said it, and her glance went from the sweater and the jeans to Nonie's plimsolls. The boy did not miss the look as he turned to go.

'I'd fight if anyone was to hurt you or Nonie. I'm not all that yellow,' he said, awkwardly. 'But I hate being forced into khaki and being made a fool of just so that some bloody sergeant can raise a laugh.'

'Oh go and sleep,' said his grandmother, impatiently. 'You'll need it. After tonight there'll be no one to watch for you . . . you'll have to sleep with one eye open.'

She heard him moving about in the tiny room behind the bed, heard the cot groan and the springs creak as he lay on it, then he was quiet.

It was silent now in Charlie and Nonie's room too. While she had been talking to Neil she had heard their voices, Charlie's shouting, then a little scream from Nonie. But it was not a serious scream, only one of protest. But now it was silent . . . as it was outside. The rain dripped, making a strangely mournful little tune as the gutters emptied. A little wind rustled the loose papers in the road outside. Someone went by whistling a popular tune. A siren sounded eerily from the river. A girl's voice called, 'Goodnight and thanks ever so. . . .' Young Sally from next door, nice girl, thought the old woman smiling. And now it was quite quiet except for the rain. The old woman heaved herself up on one elbow, took up the pen. 'Liz, my dear sister,' she wrote laboriously. 'It is a long time since we met, and it seems to me that it's doubtful if we will ever meet again, for I am ill with a disease from which one does not get better.' She put down the pen as she wrote this, and her thoughts went back to her childhood. She lay a long time thinking of those early days . . . there had been good people in those Homes, kindness in some and a strict aseptic impartial treatment in all of them. Only one thing had been lacking and that they had never had from their parents and so did not consciously miss. She and Liz had twice been in the same Homes. Little Agnes had been sent to different ones. The two boys had been put into training ships and with them she had completely lost touch. Strange that a State which aimed to take the place of delinquent parents should separate families like that. She had heard that nowadays it tried to keep them together whenever it was possible. But she did not feel strongly about keeping the children of one family together herself. Children grew up and married. They separated naturally and often did not meet again for years—if at all. On the whole she thought that an upbringing with strangers was of more direct use in adult life than one sheltered and cherished in a family. The old woman had no illusions about anything. They had been lost at the age of eight, when she had been put in a Home for the third time and told that this time her parents would never get her back.

A clock struck twelve. She sighed. There were four hours to go. She set the alarm clock beside her very carefully and put a handkerchief under the bell. It might look suspicious if old Mr. Evans or Mrs. Danvers heard it go off at four. She took up the pen again and began to write about Neil. . . . 'I'm afraid he is very like his father must have been,' she wrote. 'For, unlike Len and Nonie, he doesn't seem to have any sense of responsibility to anyone or anything. He seems content that the world shall give him everything he needs without him giving anything at all. And yet he's not a bad boy, Liz. If only they would not try to make a soldier out of him. . . . Help him, please Liz, if it's only for the sake of the old days when we were left so often to fend for ourselves. . . .'

She signed the letter 'Your loving sister, Bunch', smiling a little at her foolishness as she added her childhood nickname. Putting it in an envelope she wrote on it in large letters 'Mrs. Elizabeth Maguire', and laid it with a sigh by the alarm clock. She put out the light by the bedside and lay back on her pillows. She would not take her tablets tonight. She must wake as soon as the clock went off.

No pain. Heavenly to have no pain. Rain, rain . . . it dripped monotonously and continuously. . . . 'Rain, rain, go to Spain . . .' they had sung as children . . . and when it snowed 'Old Mother picking her geese, selling her feathers a penny a piece. . . .' One rhyme after another went through her mind. It must have been signing herself 'Bunch' like that, she thought, brought back all those funny old rhymes and games. . . . What was it they had played in the Home where she and Liz had been together? 'Farmer's wife is dead, farmer's wife is dead' . . . that was it. They all stood in a circle and the farmer had to choose a new wife. Then the wife chose a child, the child a nurse, and the nurse a dog. Then the last round went 'We all pat the dog ... we all pat the dog ...' and the unfortunate child chosen to be the dog got thumps and smacks from everyone in the game. She remembered how they used to play it and arrange that Jean usually got chosen as dog. No one had liked Jean. She snooped and told tales. The children loved to get their own back in the game.

'Farmer's wife is dead. ...' She chuckled as she saw again the concrete playground in front of the Home and the circle of children in their white pinafores with the Housemother standing watching or, if it were pleasant weather, sitting some way off reading a woman's magazine.

She and Liz had always stood next to one another on Empire Days, when they hoisted the Union Jack and saluted it. Liz and she were twins ... like Nona and Neil. Silly names both of them . . . Nona and Neil. Outlandish and pretentious. Her own name, Jane, and her sister's, Elizabeth, were not grand enough for Edward. He had chosen Nona for the girl and, after a long search, Neil for the boy. Why he should have bothered so much about naming these off-spring had puzzled his mother, after showing no further interest whatsoever in his first-born beyond naming him Leonard when his wife had wanted George.

She lay very still now, wondering at her freedom from pain. How warm and comforting and lovely it was to be able to breathe and move one's arms without the Monster attacking. He's gone to sleep himself, she thought drowsily . . . after all, even a Monster must sleep sometimes.

A clock struck one in the distance . . . one deep stroke ...'one for a wish ...one for a wish ...' a wish for her grandson . . . she couldn't hear a sound from the next room. He slept lightly as Nonie did. . . . A wish for him. What? That he should get safely to Ireland? Or that he would somehow as if by a miracle be given the courage to go back and face the hundred and twelve days in a civil gaol, which this third desertion could mean? She was unable to decide . . . the effort tired her more than writing the letter had done. But she knew in her heart the wish for the latter was really a prayer—her prayer. The rain was soothing with its steady regular drip. She sighed gratefully, free from the embrace of the Monster. She knew suddenly that there was most definitely a hereafter. Why, she couldn't tell. I must tell Josh ... get Edward to send him round again, she thought sleepily, and she found herself repeating again and again, '*Let him go back ... let him go back ... let him go back. . . .*' and knew that it was as a prayer which could be answered that she said it. She sighed again, shifted to a more comfortable position and slept.

CHAPTER XVI

ALISON, WALKING BLINDLY and without direction, away from her sister's flat was arrested only by the bright lights of an espresso café and was aware suddenly of an aching ravenous hunger. She had been sitting weeping by the telephone, still in the Japanese kimono, when Janet had called her begging her to come over immediately. Janet had been angry because their mother had ordered her a washing machine for her twenty-fifth birthday and not the fur coat which she craved.

Oblivious to the distress in Alison's voice, she had insisted on her sister dressing and going over to her. The visit had ended disastrously with Alison rushing away from a flood of angry criticism. Janet, in one of her most spiteful moods, had loosed upon Alison a flood of resentment about the dreary monotonous domestic life she led with her penniless composer husband and her two babies. She envied Alison her independence, her set hours of work, her leisure for reading, theatres and music while making fun of what she called Alison's frustrated virginity. Alison's distraught air, so unlike her usual calm competent self, had at last forced itself upon Janet and she had asked her what was wrong.

She had immediately taken Rodney's part in the quarrel, and Alison, caught off guard, had told her about Neil Collins and the moral problem which the situation presented to the welfare worker.

'You're mad to quarrel with Rodney White,' Janet had cried. 'He's got plenty of money—and a car—and you're almost thirty. Come down to earth. There's no such thing as the moonshine mother taught us to recognise as love. There are no romantic dances with programmes and little gold pencils as she had—there's the cooking-stove—sink, the dustbin—and the bed!'

Alison had been disgusted. Janet's home had been, as usual, an untidy uncomfortable muddle with the babies howling and Nigel vainly trying to compose on the hire-purchase piano. Janet's real reason for summoning Alison emerged during the quarrel. She was pregnant again, and wanted Alison to help her to obtain an abortion with which the elder sister had indignantly refused to have anything to do. Janet had furiously called her a prude, and old-fashioned in spite of her training in modern psychology, and had returned to the subject of Rodney White and Neil Collins. '*It's nothing to do with you*' she had insisted, and when Alison had again repeated that it was her duty to report the boy to the police she had fetched and drawn Nigel into the argument. He had been as incredulous as his wife.

'Oh, for Chrissake, Alison, aren't you supposed to be full of the love of humanity? No wonder Rodney was furious. I saw enough misfits when I was in the Army. Who the hell are you to pass judgment on any kid? There's no nationalism or patriotism taught in the schools now. It's all internationalism—how can you reconcile that with conscription?'

'You make me furious!' Janet had shouted, 'Mother wouldn't be such a sadist giving me a washing machine when I want a fur coat if George hadn't been killed like that in the War. You always have moral problems, Alison. Other people just sin—or don't sin. What's the use of forcing all these kids into the Army when the scientists are inventing bombs powerful enough to blow up the whole country?'

Alison had gone into the room where the two babies were howling instead of sleeping, and tried to calm both them and herself. The floor was littered with soiled napkins and dirty garments, and she understood why her mother had decided on a washing machine. Janet was a hopeless manager. When Alison had asked her for a snack because she had missed her dinner with Rodney and had not stopped to get anything on her way, there had been nothing in the flat except some milk for the children and some unappetizing cold spaghetti. Janet had forgotten to buy bread—and there was no butter.

Alison had put the quietened babies one by one back in their cots, powdered her hot agitated face, and, picking up her coat, had been stumbling over her niece's scattered bricks when Nigel had called after her, 'If you see that young deserter give him my blessing! He's given me an idea for a new song. *Boy on the Run! Boy on the Run!*' and he was already picking out a tune and singing the words as Alison ran down the stairs.

She was hungry—terribly hungry. She entered the dim carefully-shaded place, wrinkling her nose distastefully at the thick warm smell. The lighting appeared to be confined to the frontage. Within, against trailing indoor plants, Mexican straw hats and skin water-containers, couples were sitting at low plastic tables. When her eyes became accustomed to the gloom, the reason for the lack of light was obvious. Not only legs and arms were entwined but bodies also, she saw resentfully, as she searched for a vacant table and found one in a corner.

She ordered some coffee and sandwiches and sat there eating them mechanically. What had Rodney said? That she did her welfare work from curiosity—not from love. Was he right? Did she try to find in the lives of others what she herself missed in her own? Life seemed suddenly utterly grey and pointless. It stretched ahead, pathless, monotonously blurred and cobwebby into a drab fungus void such as that in which her widowed mother lived.

What she and Rodney White had had together now seemed altogether arid. The slick cocktail bars, the restaurants where she listened to his near-the-bone jokes, the theatres with his pretence of weighty criticism, and the hour's charade of love afterwards, stretched backwards over two grinning years for what they actually were—a pitiful façade, not only of love but of life. Nothing was felt, nothing cared about, nothing constructed. She clenched her hands in frustrating wretchedness. Was she what he had called her? Sterile, frigid and unresponsive? But she *wasn't*, she *wasn't*, she thought fiercely. She wanted love—a home, children, a home which meant something and in which something strong, warm and enduring would hold not only her but her children to it.

She had seen enough of broken homes, of unwanted children. How could Janet guess that when she was begging her sister to help her with an abortion, she herself lived in constant dread of having to face such an event herself? Janet thought of her as a rapidly ageing spinster—a virgin, as she had said contemptuously. And the strange thing was that in spite of the two years' affair with Rodney she still felt virgin. She was suddenly violently resentful. . . . She wasn't like Janet. Janet would suit Rodney. Janet wanted fun, admiration, excitement, the restless shifting life which her contemporaries lived in their bed-sitters or studios—and yet Janet had two children and was expecting a third.

She put down her empty coffee cup. It was made of plastic—synthetic, like the froth on the coffee, the washable table-top and the misleading romantic cosiness of such places. They hid emptiness, dreariness, just as make-up hid one's true face. Her mother, lolling in bed or on a *chaise-longue*, eating chocolates secretly and reading dirty literature, embarrassing her companion, Miss Pearce, for her own amusement, suddenly appeared to her as pathetic instead of revolting. What did the chocolates and the smutty books hide? Had she, too, since her brother George's death, found that emptiness which ended in utter desert?

She saw clearly now that both she and Rodney had tired of the dreary intrigue because of its sheer destructiveness. Both had entered it without love, expecting in its place escape, pleasure and excitement. She, at any rate, had experienced none of these things. She had been held back from pleasure not only out of fear of conception but also by some clinging relic of religious teaching at school. Chastity, purity, abstinence. These had been taught continuously as those qualities to be admired, aimed at and achieved. She was resentful that they should cling so obstinately to her, while Janet had shed them so lightly. Rodney had never once suggested marriage, and her face burned now as she thought of what she had said to him this evening and of his retort. She remembered his first approach to the sex question and her reluctance to comply. He had called her a prude, old-fashioned, had told her that she would wither quickly without some sex-life.

She thought of him now as she had so often seen him, complacent, stretched out on her satin-hung bed, smoking, after discussing her faults as a lover, her lack of enthusiasm, her failure to excite him, her many shortcomings. And she had suffered under his withering scorn, his biting remarks, had felt inferior and lacking in some essential feminine quality.

'After all, it's what we're made for . . . you can't get away from that . . .' he would grumble. 'Try some drink . . . perhaps that'll warm you up a little. . . . Have a cocktail, a good strong one. . . .' And so on. She could hear his hard matter-of-fact voice 'selling' her the idea much as she imagined he sold a new advertisement scheme. The picture was humiliating and that last vision of him as he strode out of her flat was even more so. She shivered suddenly as the slim pony-tailed girl at the nearest table put up her mouth to the dark-browed skinny boy with her and they kissed across the table—each with their coffee cup still in their hand. They seemed to mock her . . . she hated them, even as she envied them, because the girl's eyes were like stars and the boy had a wondering, newly-awakened look, which was infinitely moving in these tired pseudo-exotic surroundings.

She got up abruptly, paid her bill, and left. Outside in the night it was warm and a little wind stirred the dirt in the gutters and the cardboard boxes and package wrappings piled on the dustbins outside the shops. Cats prowled and one cried loud and challengingly in the quietness. She could hear the clack of her small pointed heels on the pavement and it alarmed her suddenly that she was alone in the street now.

She began to hurry back towards the world which she knew. She had taken a wrong turning in her blind flight from her sister's and this environment was alien to her. Crossing first one main thoroughfare and then another in the direction of the river, she found herself suddenly by a high railed-in piece of ground with trees and strange white shapes. Then she came to higher iron gates showing a long ghostly walk under heavy cypresses, dark and menacing, and she saw from the board on the gates that it was a cemetery. Memories of school again and the German lesson—a story they had had to translate—what was it? About a cemetery and a good knight who was so brave and pure that when escaping from his enemies he had gone bravely through the graveyard and all the skeletons had risen to form a barrier between him and his pursuers. She shook herself angrily at these foolish childish memories. She knew where she was now . . . if she went straight on and then turned left she would soon reach the river and the block of flats where she lived. But she did not like walking by the cemetery. It depressed her. Against her more matter-of-fact sensible judgment she decided to cross and walk on the opposite side of the road. It was just as she was leaving the pavement that she heard a child cry out.

She turned back sharply. She could see nothing. It must have been a cat. But just as she was again starting to cross the road the cry came again and this time there was no doubt. It was the wail of a frightened child.

'Where are you? What's the matter?' she called. She peered distastefully into the cemetery and it seemed to her that something moved against a white tombstone. 'Where are you? Come out. I'm here by the railings,' she called again. There was silence and then very slowly the form of a child appeared crouching down behind a grave. 'Come out,' repeated Alison irritably. 'If you aren't quick I shall go away.'

A child in a pale frock stood up and came cautiously to the railings. She was crying, and her voice was frightened. 'I'm locked in. I can't get out.'

Come here and let me look at you,' Alison coaxed, gently.

The child, a girl with long legs and a mass of curly hair came and pressed herself against the railings. Alison took a small cold hand through the iron bars. 'How on earth did you get here?'

'I lost something. I lost my key,' said the child, 'and I came to look for it. And I looked and looked, and when I gave up looking for it the gates were shut and I couldn't get out.' She began to wail again, but softly now.

There was a small lodge by the gates. The child saw Alison look in its direction. 'It's no good, the keeper's not there, he's gone home and only comes back when it opens in the morning.'

'I'll have to get the police to come and get you out,' said Alison briskly. 'It won't take me a minute to find a policeman.'

But the child cried out in terror, 'No. No. Please. Please. Not the police. Please not *them*, miss.'

It was after ten o'clock, and few people were in the street. A bus came lumbering down and sped by with its flashing red bulk and then came a man on a bicycle. He looked curiously at Alison by the railings and then at the child behind them. 'What's the matter?' he asked, dismounting and wheeling his bicycle on to the pavement. 'Shut in, is she? Well, here's a nice kettle of fish.'

'I want to get the police but she gets alarmed at the mere mention of them,' said Alison.

''Course she does. Don't want the perlice nosing round you, do ye, luv? Pretty high, isn't it?' He stood scratching his head and eyeing the railings. 'Tell yer wot! I could shin up them gates and get over and lift her over to you, if you could climb up on my bike to reach her. Could you try that, miss?'

Alison assented resentfully. She felt that there was no end to the things she was drawn into this evening and that one more would make no difference.

'We'll wait till there's nothing coming by,' said the man. 'After all, it's breaking-in so to speak.'

'Much better let me get the police,' said Alison, sharply. 'If they come along we'll get into trouble for not calling them.'

'Can't leave her there while we hunt for a bleeding copper,' said the man tersely. 'Now then, miss, just hold the bike while I hop over.'

Reluctantly, Alison held the bicycle. Her whole training in welfare had embodied in her a respect for the aid of the law. She did not see it as this man did. To him a frightened child was locked in a rapidly-darkening cemetery. He was all for the obvious way of getting her out. He shared the child's aversion to the police.

'Hold it steady now while I climb on the saddle,' he ordered.

'How are you going to climb up with her on the other side without the bicycle to help you?' Alison said, destructively. 'You'll never do it.'

'That's where you're wrong, Miss Know-all,' he retorted. 'There's the shelf made by that great lock. I can stand on it and hand her over to you.'

It seemed to Alison that this man was very much at home with climbing difficult obstacles. She watched him go up the gate with the ease of a trained burglar and over the top, balancing on the great lock as he had said he would, and vaulting lightly to the ground, where he coaxed and petted the child into getting on to his back. 'Put your arms round my neck and hold tight, luv,' she heard him say, and then he was coming up again easily in spite of his burden.

'Reach up and take her....'

But Alison, balancing on the saddle of the bicycle, lacked the nerve to complete the operation as he had planned it. 'I can't!' she said urgently. 'As soon as I move the bicycle slips—we'll both fall with the double weight.'

'I'll have to drop you, luv,' said the man resignedly. 'The lady can't make it. Think you can drop on your feet safely?'

'Yes,' whispered the child. 'Let me go, mister.'

She landed with knees bent and arms out in the way recommended to athletes after a jump, then stumbled on to her knees on the pavement. The man stood upright on the gate, outlined against the dark cypresses for a moment.

'Quick! mister, there's a lot of people coming,' cried the child, urgently.

'Can you step on to the bicycle if I hold it?' asked Alison.

'No. I'll jump like the kiddy did. Look out!'

He was down almost as lightly as the child and without falling as she had, and before Alison could do so, he had picked her up and was examining her dirty knees.

'Aren't you going to say thank you?' asked Alison. 'It's not everybody who would do all that for a little girl who had no right to be in the cemetery at all. What were you doing there so late at night?'

'It wasn't late when I come,' retorted the child, sullenly. 'I told you I stayed long looking for the latch-key I lost.'

'And did you find it?' asked the man, curiously.

'No.'

'How did you lose it *here*?' asked Alison.

'I lost it this afternoon. Someone frightened me and I for- got it,' she said, beginning to cry.

'Where d'you live?' asked the man. 'It's late for little girls to be out.'

'How late?'

'After ten,' said Alison looking at her watch.

A look of fear crossed the small face.

'You'll cop it,' said the man wheeling his bicycle into the road. 'And so'll I if I don't get on. . . . Don't go getting shut in there again. I may not be coming along next time. And you cut along home double-quick now!'

'Where do you live?' asked Alison again. The child named a road well known to her from her round of visits.

'Come along then, I'll take you there.'

'You won't say where I was, will you?' asked the child anx- iously, hanging back. 'I've been in trouble already over going in the cemetery, but I had to look for the key.'

'What key?' queried Alison, puzzled.

'The door key. I couldn't get in without it. I couldn't find it here, so I was going to Gran's till Mother got home.'

'You have a grandmother?'

'No,' said the child regretfully, 'not a proper one—I've only got Mum. But Mrs. Collins—she's just like my real grand- mother and I call her Gran.'

Collins . . . Collins. . . . Was she never to get away from this family? The boy had made trouble enough already; now this child who had caused her all this delay in getting home was talking of the old woman. The old woman lay in that bed like an old spider watching the world as if from a web.

'Come along,' she said, shortly. 'What's your name?'

'Linda.'

'Well, Linda, I don't know what your mother will have to say to you, but she must be anxious so we'd better hurry. I'm going your way and I'll see you safely back.'

As they were passing the piece of waste ground Linda clung tightly to Alison's hand. 'I wonder if he's still there,' she said fearfully, looking across at the dark murky shadows of the ruins. 'I daren't go and look for the key there; I was too scared. I'm sure it's there.'

'Who?' Alison was scarcely listening. She was tugging the child along quickly and purposefully. 'Scared of whom?'

'The soldier. The one as frightened me. He was watching Mrs. Collins' house. I saw him—so did Cissie. Never took his eyes off it.'

'What soldier? Who are you talking about?'

'The one there all afternoon. Lying in the grass in the ruins he was. Frightened me and Cissie and when we looked at him he told me to beat it and to forget I'd seen him or he'd hurt me.'

'What was he like?' asked Alison, sharply.

'Very dark—I didn't like his eyes.'

'And he was a soldier?'

'Yes. National Serviceman like Mrs. Collins' grandson and Cissie's big brother.'

Alison's eyes went instinctively to the deep shadowed place Linda pointed out as having been the soldier's hiding-place.

'Come on quickly. Let's run!' urged the child pulling now at Alison. 'I don't want him to see me again.'

'We're nearly there,' said Alison. 'One more turning and we're there. I expect your mother will be worried. You're not usually out as late as this, are you?'

'No.'

They had reached the drab, neglected-looking building where Linda lived with her mother.

'Up the stairs, three flights,' said Linda.

Alison toiled up dirtier and narrower stairs than her sister's until they reached the top landing and the child ran to a door and cried, 'Mum! Mum!'

The woman who opened the door caught her swiftly in her arms. 'Thank goodness you're back! Where have you been you naughty girl?' And her pent-up fear found release in action and Linda got a stinging blow across the buttocks. The child gave vent to her own feelings in a loud wail of anguish. Her mother then noticed Alison and said apologetically, 'Excuse me, miss. But she gave me such a fright. All this story Cissie's been telling us of a soldier frightening them on the waste ground this afternoon. You never know with all these toughs around. Why, Linda, the Collins' Charlie is out looking for you. I must run round and tell them you're back.'

'No. No, don't go now. I'm hungry and cold!' wailed Linda.

'I'll be passing Mrs. Collins' on my way home. I visit her regularly. I'll call in and tell them that Linda's found. Goodbye, Linda. I expect I'll see you again one day at Mrs. Collins'. . . .'

'Thank the lady for bringing you home like this. Where did you find her, miss?'

'Linda'll tell you that,' said Alison, making her escape quickly after the child had mumbled something that sounded like thanks.

As she was walking past the bomb-site, dark and silent now, she crossed the road and peered into the depths of the deep shadows cast by the ruined buildings. The child had said that there was a man there—a soldier, that he was watching old Mrs. Collins' house. Long training in the tortuous minds and imaginations of the families she tried to help had made Alison quick in reasoning. The reasoning at which she arrived was not always correct, but she had decided that to reach some definite, if erroneous, conclusion and work from it was the way which most helped in getting the truth.

The soldier had been a Serviceman, Linda had insisted. For what reason should a Serviceman hide all day in such a place? There was only one obvious one—the same one which had made young Collins disguise himself as his sister. Strange that he should be watching the very house in which Neil was hiding. She immediately decided that the man must be a friend of the Collins boy and that he could be up to no good. A man who would threaten a little girl like that was dangerous. Alison Rhodes was accustomed now to going where she was not welcome, to entering homes where she was greeted with hostility and reluctance. The waste ground looked sinister and somehow menacing in the dark, and the heavy rain made it more uninviting, but she was not a person to shirk an unpleasant duty. Children must be protected. She would go and see whether the man was still there and if so she would inform the police. She began picking her way carefully and with difficulty over the blocks of fallen masonry. She came suddenly up against a wall or rather the remains of a wall and, turning sharply to regain her way, she found herself face to face with the man whom she was seeking. She was startled, caught suddenly off guard. None of the things which she had rehearsed in her mind to say to him came to her. She could only stare and then, at his menacing intent look, say faltering. . . . 'So you're still here. . . .'

'What d'you mean—*I'm still here?* How did you know I was here?'

'The child. The child told me. You frightened her.' Then, gathering courage as she saw how young he was, she said more firmly, 'If you go about frightening children you'll soon find yourself in trouble. . . .'

'I don't know what you're talking about. But let me tell you something for your own good, miss. It won't help you any to go around poking about where you're not wanted.'

But what are you *doing* here? You've been here since early afternoon. You can't tell me it's for any good purpose that you're hiding here on a wet night like this. Are you waiting to break in somewhere?' Then, as he did not answer but just continued to stare at her threateningly, she said suddenly, looking at his uniform. . . . 'Of course. I know who you are. . . . You've run away like your friend in that house over there. You're Neil Collins' pal, Mike. . . .' Why hadn't she thought of it before? The old woman had read her bits of Neil's letters when Mike had first taken up with him. . . . What had he written? 'He's got a queer brown face, narrow and with funny eyes, Gran. But he's always laughing so you can't see them properly—they disappear completely when he laughs.' And the child had said much the same . . . 'funny eyes . . . I didn't like them.'

'Have you deserted, too?' she asked, accusingly. But he did not answer. He just went on staring at her so that she said quickly and angrily. 'I was going to leave the boy over there alone. But if there are *two* of you it's different. And you frightened that child. *I warn you now that I intend to go immediately to the police.*'

Then at last he spoke. 'I shouldn't do that if I were you,' was all he said but he advanced a few steps towards her so that his face was very close to hers. The implied threat was a whetstone to her anger, a challenge to her to perform her duty from which she had been deflected by others. She turned sharply to retrace her steps back to the road, and as she began picking her way carefully among the loose bricks and stones something hit her sharply on the neck. She stumbled, putting out her hands frantically trying to find something on which to take a hold: she lost her balance and stepped backwards, crashing into those dark foundations about which she had been hesitating when she had encountered the man. Her head hit the concrete floor, her beret and handbag fell from her as blackness engulfed her.

CHAPTER XVII

ALISON RHODES came to herself on the concrete floor of what had once been the foundations of a large block of flats. She was lying on her back, her beret had fallen off and she was conscious of blackness and wet and acute discomfort. She moved her arms cautiously, and then more cautiously, and then her legs. She could move them both but one hurt quite frighteningly. She sat up slowly and waves of sickness sent her down again. Her head was racking her with a sharp stabbing pain, which was combined with violent nausea.

She was soaking wet and very cold. She groped for her handbag but could not find it. How long had she been here? She felt for her watch; it was still on her wrist but she could not see its small face in the darkness. Looking up at the sky she noticed that the blackness was changing to grey. The dark night clouds were slowly and beautifully giving way to a steel blue vista shot with streaks of bright light. She made another determined effort to get up, but was forced down again by giddiness. Her head and right foot were excruciatingly painful, her back and shoulders felt stiff and strange.

Alison was a determined woman. She realised that even if she called out it was extremely unlikely that anyone would hear her—unless her attacker was still hiding here. She tried to recall the events which had led to her lying unconscious in this horrible place. Her mind v/as clearing but it was still difficult to think. The only thing which was sharp in her memory was the face of the young soldier with whom she had been talking when she fell. Had she fallen or had she been pushed? She put her hands up to her forehead as she tried to re-live that last moment when she had turned to retrace her way back to the road. Why had she been in that road? She lay still, trying to remember. But she could not. All she could see was the face of the young soldier as he stood there on the edge of the deep foundations. Brown skin, strange narrow eyes and a thin mouth. What had she been doing here at all when she encountered him?

The events previous to his face appearing suddenly out of the darkness were blank and she gave it up. She groped again for her handbag, then with a determined effort she began crawling to the wall nearest her. If she could only prop herself against something firm she could pull herself upright, and once up she could try to find a way of getting out. She decided not to call out in case the man was still about. It took her a long time to get to the wall, and when she felt its solid mass behind her she lay still for a while trying to gather her strength. She had the feeling that she must get out quickly or she would relapse again into unconsciousness; the waves of nausea were becoming worse with each movement and she knew instinctively that she should lie still.

Cautiously, like a wounded creature, she began pushing herself up against the wall putting her weight on the uninjured leg until at last she stood upright leaning her body against the wall. All the time it was growing lighter and she would soon be able to see the time by her watch if it was still going. She leaned there for some time. Now she heard the birds chattering and calling one to another and was surprised at the number of them in this oasis from the pavements. There was a tree near her and in its branches there was a noisy activity. She listened astonished at the beauty of the sounds which these small feathered creatures could make.

It seemed to her that she had never noticed birds before, although much of her life had been spent in the country in her mother's Sussex home. And there were trees round the block of flats where she lived, there must be birds there, too. But she had never noticed them. Here, in this waste ground where the grass and fireweed had covered the stones and bricks and only the children came, they seemed to have collected. And as they sang and gossiped one to another the masses of night parted in the hemisphere and with their songs came light, so that it seemed to Alison Rhodes recently returned to consciousness that she was indeed being delivered from darkness and that the birds, harbingers of morning, were welcoming her from the depths of the unknown.

Very slowly she began edging her way round the wall looking for a break in it. And, at last, after what seemed an endless,
agonising journey the wall stopped and in the grey half-light
she could make out the broken staircase which had once led
to the basement of the house. She looked around before putting her good foot on the first step, but she could see no one.
There was nothing on which to lean her weight, or on which
to hold, and she had to drag the injured foot up to the level
of each step. It was a nightmare ascent, she kept swaying and
almost falling backwards again—as she must have done last
night, but she stuck doggedly to it, and at last she was standing
on the level ground above the rectangular pit in which she had
been lying. The birds were now making a veritable chorus and
she thought whimsically that they were congratulating her.
I shall never be oblivious to birds again, she thought. I shall
listen and be grateful to them always. She longed to he down
again, such nausea gripped her; but she staggered as determinedly and blindly as a drunken woman towards the nearest
pavement. Once there, she lifted the barbed wire which failed
to keep the children out, and was in a deserted street.

I have no money and no key, she thought worriedly, and
then she remembered the pound note which for reasons of
prudence she always put folded in the breast pocket of her
suit. Alison Rhodes knew that a handbag could be snatched in
a shop or street and she never risked being stranded without
money. In the same pocket, attached with a safety pin, was a
latch-key. She felt that she was in a dream or a film. This simply
doesn't happen in real life she thought. She had the feeling that
she was a machine, an automaton performing those actions
dictated to it by a brain completely remote from the body, as
she limped slowly and painfully in the empty street. Her foot,
she could now see by the street lamps, was terribly swollen.
A trickle from the back of her head was seeping through the
collar of her grey suit with a dark reddish stain. Horrified, she
put up her hand and it came away red and sticky.

She was now at the corner of the street where it joined a
main one. Her watch was still going. It said half-past three. Towards her came a crawling taxi. She hailed it feebly. The driver

looked hesitantly at her thinking at first that she was drunk. But she spoke clearly and intelligently to him.

'I have been attacked on that piece of ground there. I am soaking wet and must get home at once. Can you kindly take me to Willow Court?'

'You'd better let me take you to the police station, miss,' he said, concernedly. 'They'll see to you there. Look, your head's bleeding all over your collar and your foot's pretty bad by the look of it.'

'No. Take me home first, please. I must change these wet things. I'm feeling as if I may lose consciousness again. I live at 18, Willow Court. It's down by the river.'

'I know it all right,' said the taxi-driver. 'But in case you pass out again, miss, what's the name? I shall have to know it to get you in there. Have you your key?'

'The key's in this pocket with a pound note for the fare. My handbag's been stolen. Fortunately, I always carry a spare pound and a key in this pocket. Could you help me in, please?'

The man lifted her easily into the taxi. She was shivering badly and she looked terrible.

'You'll be home in ten minutes,' he said, consolingly. 'I'll look after you. Anyone at home when you get there?'

'No,' she said, 'I live alone.'

When he pulled up at the entrance to the expensive luxury block and opened the door to help her out, she had slumped down in the corner and was unconscious. The man looked at the closed door of the block of flats and back at the young woman. 'No good taking you up there, lass,' he said. 'It's hospital for you and police station after that for me.'

'Miss Alison Rhodes, 18, Willow Court,' he repeated as he drove to the nearest hospital. 'Shan't take her fare but I'll point out the pound and the key when I give her over to Casualty. Never know. She trusted me to look after her. I'll trust her to pay me later. Poor girl! Now, let me think, exactly where did she come staggering along? The police are devils for details....'

CHAPTER XVIII

IN THE SMALL airless room behind the flower-papered door Neil lay on the old iron cot with his arms folded under his head, staring up at the ceiling. It was dark but he knew exactly when he was looking at the patch of damp, or at the two large cracks in the ceiling. He knew the small area better than any map. He thrust off Nona's scarf irritably. It irked him and degraded him—he would wear it no longer. His hair was damp as was his forehead. He could neither relax nor sleep because he was so afraid. He had failed to get Charlie to help him in time—and he had simply not had the guts to walk out on his own and take the train to Southampton.

Why should he suddenly *know* that the man waiting out there on the waste ground was Mike? Nona had succeeded in lulling his fears so that for a short time at least he had almost forgotten his anguish. Nona could always do that—always influence him, always soothe and heal him. And Charlie was furious and jealous. That's why he had taken up with that girl in the photograph. Neil knew that. He realised now that Charlie loved Nona and that he was the cause of most of the trouble between them. He knew now that he should never have come home. He should have gone straight to Ireland to his aunt and taken the risk. It was unfair to drag them all into it. And it was all Mike's fault. He would never have deserted again unless Mike had forced him to. The thought of Mike was so horrible to him that he could not lie still. Mike loomed ahead like an evil inevitable doom. He tossed and turned and the old springs creaked and groaned so that his grandmother called out. 'Keep quiet, Neil. Try and get some sleep. You'll need it.'

After that he made an effort to He still. Why hadn't Mike come to the house? Was he intending to wait the full twenty-four hours he'd agreed on and then come over? Surely he couldn't wait there all night. And Charlie had gone over there hunting for the child and hadn't seen him. His heart had almost stopped beating when Charlie had come back and Nona had said, 'Well?'

Where could he be all this time? What had happened? Supposing Mike had been arrested himself? Suppose he gave Neil away? He was the sort who might do that if his own plans went wrong. Well, it was only a few hours and he himself would be away. Nonie had promised. Charlie would not go back on his word once he had given it. He would take no risks. He would climb out over the yard wall at the back so that he need not go out in the street at all. Charlie could wait at the corner for him . . . that would be it.

He lay there listening, as did his grandmother, to the chimes of the clock. Each quarter—and then the full hour quarters and then the slow booms of each hour. It had been the very longest day he could remember—and now it seemed the longest night. The door was so frail that he could hear every movement his grandmother made—just as she could hear his. He could even hear the rustle of paper as she wrote to her sister. He watched the line of light go out under her door . . . and then in spite of his determination to stay awake for fear that Mike might come . . . he was suddenly overcome with sheer exhaustion and he slept.

Because she had deliberately omitted to take her tablets, Mrs. Collins awoke constantly. She would sleep a little then wake uneasily, think a while, doze a little and wake again. Occasionally, she would forbear to take the drugs, telling herself whimsically that unless she endured some pain she would no longer be able to appreciate the exquisite pleasure of escaping it. She awoke now just before one o'clock and lay thinking not about Neil and the ordeal which lay ahead of her in helping to get him off, but of the farm where she had spent her girlhood. Shows I'm getting really old, she thought, for she always warned her grandchildren never to think of the past. She longed more and more now to see the farm once more. Not the garden belonging to Miss Rhodes' mother about which she had been told so much, but the farm where she had been sent as a general help when she was old enough to leave the Home.

The farmer and his wife had had five turbulent children. They had been good to her and treated her as one of the family, and she had been happy with them—very happy, although the work was hard and was never finished. After three years she had met Jim. She thought now with tender amusement of their meeting. It had been at a local farmers' ball. She hadn't known how to dance but the two eldest farm children attended a dancing class and they had done their best to teach her what they themselves had been taught. The farmer's wife had given her a dress. It had been of soft blue with a silver sash. She had never possessed anything so beautiful. How shy and awkward she had been—her hands had seemed enormous and red and her feet felt strange in the silver shoes with heels; but friends of the farmer had come up and been kind and she had not missed a dance. Quite early on she had been introduced to Jim and after that it had been wonderful. He and his brother had worked a small farm in the neighbourhood.

In the spring she had married him in the ugly little church where she had worshipped with the farmer's family. The two eldest girls had stood behind her in hideous stiff frocks as bridesmaids. How good they had all been to her. Because her parents had not been heard of by any of their children for more than ten years, her employer himself had given her away and no one could have been kinder or more motherly than his wife. People have changed now, she thought, thinking of Charlie's family and how they made fun of Nona's having been to a good Secondary school and of her love of books and music. They're harder—or maybe times are harder now.

But times now were nowhere like as hard as those which had followed the First World War in which Jim had been killed in France. There had been no work for her in the country which she loved. Jim's brother who had been exempted to care for the farm, had married a young woman with whom she had not been able to get on. In fact there was not enough work for two women in the small farm-house and there was a surplus of women—widows and those who would never marry now. Unable to bring up Dorothy, Edward and Agnes on the tiny widow's pension which the Army allowed her, she was obliged to accept the too small sum of money which her brother-in-law offered her in exchange for Jim's share of the farm. With this she moved with the children to London.

There was a scarcity of work there, too. The same surplus of women and scarcity of men—and yet those who had come back from France with their health ruined or minus a limb were walking the streets offering matches for sale; and outside the unemployment exchanges there were long queues of grey-faced, haunted-looking men waiting hopelessly for the dole which kept them alive but did not pay for sufficient food for a family. No, times were not so hard now . . . people, even foreigners, got not only unemployment money but often the rent of their flats or rooms as well when they were out of work.

She had found work in a tall grey London house which was run as a private hotel. The hours were long and the stairs unending but she had earned enough somehow to keep the children decently fed and clothed. The money from Jim's share of the farm she banked and husbanded carefully, adding to it every few shillings she could spare. She was determined that Edward, who showed signs of promise, should go to a Grammar school.

She had only returned to the farm twice for brief summer visits. She had been shown plainly enough by her sister-in-law that she and the children were not welcome. Except for a few day-outings to the sea or country she had never left London again.

At the hotel she had soon become indispensable, rising to be a head housekeeper; and when it was enlarged and brought up to date she had been offered the post of manageress. She had refused—and never told her reason, which was that she found that the staff, growing more and more difficult, invariably resented the manageress while respecting the housekeeper. She remained as housekeeper all through the Second World War when the hotel was commandeered as a sort of Army hostel for foreign visitors.

All three of her children had been sent to Grammar schools. Dorothy had married well and gone to Australia; Agnes had died of some obscure disease during the Second World War.

After Edward's wife Connie had run away, she had taken his three children and made a home for them, sending them too to good schools. She had made great sacrifices for those six children—three of her own and three of her son's. She had refused two offers of marriage because of them. Had it all been wasted?

Sometimes she thought that it had. Dorothy was in a primitive part of Australia where her education was useless; Edward had used his only to cause strife among men. Agnes was dead—and Len, too. There remained only Neil and Nona now. *And what of Neil?* What future was there for him—even if he managed to get to Ireland? Her sister Liz was an old woman and a poor one. She would send her a sum of money somehow to help until the boy found work. Nona would go to Australia with Charlie. She might quarrel with him but she loved him. She would manage splendidly in Australia. Nona would manage anywhere. She had a man's knack of dealing with machinery, with electricity, with all such things. But she hated domestic chores as so many young women did nowadays. Extraordinary, she thought, how the modern young woman hated having to do household chores. Worse, they even resented their husbands not doing them as well. The old woman could never get used to seeing the husbands with aprons tied round their waists standing at the sinks washing up for their wives.

She hated to see Neil messing about in the kitchen. He loved it—and did many household jobs better than his twin. There was, in fact, decided the old woman, no longer any dividing line between a man's and a woman's work. They merged—and rightly: and she was angry with herself for her conservatism on the subject. Miss Rhodes now, had said that her young sister Janet hated doing anything in the house. A lot of the things she had told her about her sister Janet reminded Mrs. Collins of Nonie. Two determined young women—wanting their own way but not knowing how to make a man give it them.

Miss Rhodes . . . *Miss Rhodes* . . . would she do anything about Neil? Had she done it? If she had gone to the police surely they would have been here by now? Somehow she did not think that Miss Rhodes would give Neil away for all her sense of righteous duty—but one never knew. The clock was striking three now, only an hour or so to go and he would be away. Was she doing something which she would later bitterly regret? She wouldn't be able to go and receive Len's medal. You couldn't dress up in your best and go and receive one grandson's medal for bravery when you had deliberately helped his brother to desert from military service for that same Sovereign. Edward might be able to reconcile the two anomalies—but she could not. Would they accuse her of having a hand in it? And Charlie? He and Nona—and later, Neil too, would be emigrating to Australia. Would it make any difference to that? What if this thing should mar their whole future?

She was suddenly violently agitated at what she had agreed to, terribly perturbed at the stand she had taken. It was all very well to argue that she had already lost her husband and one grandson to the country, other people had done the same. Mrs. Elders down the street had lost three sons in the last war. Edward had never given anything to anyone. Edward was her great failure—was Neil to be, too?

She could no longer keep still or lie in bed so great was her agitation. The anxiety had brought on the Monster again . . . and the pain was becoming too sharp for comfort or repose. She must get up. One thing was sticking out in her mind, that this was the first time in her life that she had deliberately gone against the strong voice of conscience. She was deliberately doing wrong. At my age, she thought grimly, I'm deliberately committing a crime. I ought not to have been persuaded. She had heard that the Emigration Authorities were very strict now about anyone who had been in trouble with the police . . . Nona hadn't thought of it—but *she* should have. Why hadn't she stuck to her guns and refused? Pain was becoming too acute now for clear thinking and she slowly edged herself out of bed, and softly, so as not to wake Neil in the room opening out of hers, padded her way into the kitchen. She would make herself a cup of tea. Perhaps she would take just one tablet—two was the maximum she was supposed to have. One deadened the pain while allowing her to keep awake. Two put her right out.

Strange she thought, as she pottered about filling the kettle and waiting for it to boil, that the mind and the body seldom decayed together. Her own mind was still clear and sharp while her body was slowly rotting. Old Mr. Evans now, was as spry and pink-faced as ever, agile physically and capable of walking long distances still, but his mind rambled and wandered and his sense of time and even of generation was already faulty and he talked nonsense. There ought to be some means of making a bargain with Nature, thought the old woman, as she measured two tea-spoonfuls of tea into the small pot. Those with good minds should be able to exchange sick bodies with those whose minds had decayed. It was useless trying to live with only one of them healthy—the two were too intricately fused to be separated. Maybe there was a way of separating them in the hereafter—if it existed.

She was sitting on the wooden kitchen chair watching the steam slowly grow from the kettle. She picked up a newspaper. *Did the hereafter exist?* Or did we live on only in our children? Then what of those who had none? That was what Josh had said to her. If that was so, he had said, then everyone without exception would surely want to reproduce themselves. Josh believed implicitly in the next world just as he believed in the resurrection of the body. Edward, who thought highly of Josh, and was usually so loquacious, had himself been strangely silent on the subject of the hereafter. Perhaps his pearl would change all that. . . .

The pain was almost unbearable again. The tablets were in an aspirin bottle—they came in small white cardboard boxes and Nonie had put them in an aspirin bottle. Should she take a tablet with her tea? It would deaden the pain but she would risk feeling deadly sleepy when Neil had to be got away. Suppose Nonie failed to hear the alarm? They were depending on her. She would not take the tablet unless she could no longer stand the pain . . . and it was better now, just because she had decided to have a cup of tea. She took the little tray with the teapot and the two cups on it into the bedroom. She was very tired suddenly—she would have the tea in bed. A sudden fresh attack of the Monster made her rest on the edge of the bed.

When the pain eased a little she put the tablets on the tray. They were there if she could not stand it. She poured out a cup of tea and then began the slow tortuous crawl back into the bed.

She stretched out her hand to lift up the cup when she heard a sound. Neil? No . . . it was not from that direction. From the hall? It was a faint scratching sound . . . from where? She listened . . . there it was again . . . It was from the direction of the window. She raised herself up and peered at the dark panes. The window was open in spite of Nonie's protests; the night was so close and airless that she had opened it. There was another sound and now she saw a hand come round the side of the window frame . . . in spite of her courage the old woman felt a stab of acute fear, and regretted her refusal to have netting across the window frame. The whole gap was filled now with the form of a man . . . *he was coming in through the window*. . . . She had not switched on the light . . . the light from a street lamp was sufficient for her needs unless she wanted to read or to see the clock. . . . Should she scream for help? Should she call to Neil?

The figure in the window frame was now leaping lightly down . . . as she began struggling to get herself near enough to the window to shut it. But she was too late . . . the man was in, he had come in exactly as Neil had done. There was light enough for her to see that he wore khaki, that his hair was dark and glistening with rain and she knew without any doubt that this was the man who had been hiding over there on the waste ground. She opened her mouth to scream, but a hand pushed her backwards so that she doubled up with excruciating pain, and while one hand remained clamped down on her mouth, the other one shut the window. The light from the street lamp showed up the face which bent over her. . . .

'Going to be quiet?' asked the intruder, keeping his hand firmly over her mouth. She was in such pain with her legs doubled up under her that she would have agreed to anything so that she could straighten up. She nodded . . . and he removed his hand. 'Sorry . . . Mrs. Collins. . . .' he said. 'If you make a noise I'll have to hurt you—and I wouldn't like to do that to an old woman. Where's Ninny?'

She did not answer as she tried with difficulty to straighten her limbs. When she succeeded, she said quietly, 'Who do you mean?'

'You must be Mrs. Collins, Ninny's grandmother, aren't you? Well, where's your pretty grandson? Ninny we call him up there.'

'Why do you think he's here?' she asked, trying to gain time to think.

'I know damn well he's here—*and* he's expecting me.'

'He's gone,' said the old woman quickly. 'Why should he hang about here? He's gone.'

'The dirty little twister . . . wait until I catch up with him. We had a rendezvous here tonight . . . it was all arranged. Where's he gone?'

He was standing now between the window and the foot of the bed. She put out her hand to switch on the light but he forestalled her. . . . 'No, you don't. Not until the window is covered. Do you think I want the bleeding cop on patrol to look in?'

'I can't move easily—as you see. Do it yourself. There's a piece of blue material on the table there.'

He said threateningly. 'You keep quiet then.'

'I'm not afraid of you. I'm going to drink my tea. . . .' she said, steadily.

He hung up the material and swung round to her. 'Tea? All ready too. I could do with a cup. I've got a bleeding head-ache—from lying about in that damp place. . . .'

She poured out the tea.

'Sugar?'

'Two lumps.'

He noticed the aspirin bottle suddenly. . . . 'I'll have a cou-ple of these—do my headache good. Just what I want—all waiting here for me. Tea and a couple of aspirins! . . . Here they go!' And before the old woman's fascinated eyes he took a drink of tea and washed down the two small white tablets which he had placed on his tongue.

'That's good,' he said gulping the rest of the tea down quickly. . . . 'Any more tea?'

'Help yourself,' she said, indifferently, and picking up her own cup she sipped it, trying in vain to steady the trembling of her hand and lips. Suppose he took more tablets thinking they were aspirins? He might die. She watched fascinated while he poured out more tea. Dark . . . with queer eyes and a straight thin mouth. It was the man Linda had described. She knew immediately who this was. . . . 'You're Mike Andersen,' she said, accusingly.

He nodded. 'Where's Ninny?' he asked, looking closely at her. 'I know he's here—so don't stall—*where is he?*'

She retorted sharply. 'Before I answer you anything, just you tell me something. How did you know that you could get in that window? How did you know that it would be open?'

'I didn't. I was going to get it open—I was struck dumb when I found it all open inviting me in. Ninny gave me all the details . . . I told you he's expecting me. . . .'

Suddenly Mrs. Collins understood. Neil's terror, his insistence on the time, his continual panic as the clocks advanced . . . she had been puzzled by it, because if, as he said, this other lad had covered for him and Nona had disguised him in her clothes there had been no cause for such desperate haste. Looking at this Andersen's tight-lipped, hard look which made even young faces appear old, and his eyes—horrible eyes, gay and smiling but with something like a reptile peeping from them—she began to get a glimpse of Neil's fear of this man. He was tall and strongly built, and he moved easily and quickly.

'Why have you come here? Have you deserted?' she demanded, harshly . . . and all the time she was thinking . . . twenty minutes for the average person . . . thirty minutes or more for me because I'm addicted. I've got twenty minutes before he flops. For that the tablets could not fail to have their effect she knew. They were dependable—inevitable in their action.

'I told you,' he said, impatiently, 'Ninny and I had a rendezvous. It's all planned out. We're going to Ireland. . . .'

'Did *you* persuade my grandson to desert?'

He nodded. 'Didn't take much persuading although he was unwilling. People have a habit of doing what I want them to . . . just my charm I suppose. . . .' And he grinned at her . . . and suddenly he was young, for the first time, so that she thought, He really is only a kid—like Neil. . . . How is it that he appears years older?

'Poor old Ninny's always in the soup. . . .' he continued. 'Can't seem to do anything right. They've got it in for him up there.'

'And you don't help him—of that I'm convinced. My grandson is not going anywhere with you. You'd better get that clear. If you want money I'll find you some. Just take yourself off. If you don't I'll ring this bell here and my grand-daughter's husband will come in. You're big—but he could pick you up as easy as a sack of coal.'

'I wouldn't touch that bell if I were you . . . in fact I think I'd better take care of it.' He put his hand over the little bronze bell with which she summoned Nona, and took it from the bedside. 'That's the gorilla who was out calling for some kid this evening. I'm not scared of him.'

'How d'you know he was calling for a child?'

'Saw him. Came over there in the rain calling out. He never saw that snooping skirt in the foundations over there. . . .'

'In the foundations? Not the child?' she said quickly.

'No. Not the kid. I told you . . . some inquisitive woman dressed classy. I took her handbag so they couldn't identify her. Might make trouble for Ninny and me. . . .'

'What's that?' He whipped round at a slight noise behind the bed, and she thought as she saw him furtive, alert, on the defensive, that he would be a nasty customer if cornered. The door had opened and Neil stood there. He had been asleep and his face was as pink and childish as his sister's was when awakened. When his grandmother saw his expression at the sight of Mike Andersen she knew. Here was the real trouble—the real danger to the lad—the real reason for the desertion. This Mike had a hold over Neil as she had suspected.

'Well, Ninny! Here I am—like I said I'd be. . . .'

Neil's sleep-dazed face had lost its pink tinge. 'I thought you promised to wait until I'd been gone twenty-four hours before you followed me. You promised to cover up for me....' he stammered.

'Things happened up there. I had to get out sooner than I expected. There was a blasted inspection ... bleeding bad luck. Now, with that snooping woman over there we'll have to get away *at once*....'

'What woman?'

'I was just telling your grandmother. . . . The bleeding woman came snooping about over there where I was hiding. She never saw me ... it was dark and wet ... she slipped and fell backwards on the concrete.'

'And,' said Mrs. Collins, 'do you mean to tell me that she's lying there in the rain? Is she hurt?'

'She's dead—that's why I took her handbag. I'm no bloody thief ... I didn't want her cash ... although it will be useful to Ninny and me....'

'Don't look at me like that,' he said roughly as the old woman stared at him in horrified incredulity....'I didn't mean to do her in. I just gave her a little slog—how the hell was I to know that she'd overbalance like that? I only wanted to keep her quiet for a while....'

'Keep her quiet for a while....' the old woman glanced furtively at the clock ... eight minutes since he'd taken the tablets. Another twelve or fifteen before he began to feel their effects.

'She cracked her bloody skull on the concrete....' he was saying.

'How do you know she is dead—she may be unconscious. We must do something about her at once.'

'No, you *don't*. Not until Ninny and I have got away....'

'Give me her handbag,' said the old woman, faintly.

Without a word he handed it over.

The dark expensive leather bag was damp and muddy but Mrs. Collins recognised it ... she had seen it before. In this very room and on this very afternoon.... She couldn't bring herself to handle it.

'Have you looked in it to find out who she is?'

'Yes. A Miss Rhodes . . . some bloody kind of social work-er. . . .'

Miss Rhodes . . . Miss Rhodes. . . . What now? The appalling mess into which this escapade of Neil's was bringing them all seemed to have no end to its repercussions. . . . She heard Neil gasp as he heard the name arid saw that he was so horrified that he was shaking. She knew from the rough way in which he had handled *her* that the blow Andersen had struck Miss Rhodes had been no light tap. He had intended that she be put out of his way—for a time at any rate.

CHAPTER XIX

NEIL HAD NEVER seen Mike agitated and on edge; that he was now visibly, horribly shaken by the occurrence on the bombed-site was apparent.

'You'll have to find me some clobber. I wasn't able to change into civvies . . . no time with that blasted inspection,' he began, threateningly. 'Yours'll be too small but what about your brother-in-law, Charlie . . . his should fit me. . . . Or do you suggest that I get myself up in female things like yours? Hurry up now, you little bastard.'

The sneer in his voice and the look he gave Neil infuriated the old woman. 'Don't talk like that here,' she said. 'I won't have it. You won't frighten me with your blustering.'

'Mike . . . have they missed me yet? *Have* they?'

'Not when I left. They will have by now. We must get moving, Ninny. That bleeding woman has just about done it for us. Have you fixed things for us?'

'I don't want to come with you. . . .' Neil stammered. 'I *won't*. I don't want to be mixed up with your hurting Miss Rhodes. She's been good to my grandmother. . . .'

'Don't want to come with me?' repeated Mike, softly. 'Well, *well*. Fancy that now. I shall have to find a means of making you. You've got an old aunt—and some cousins in Drogheda. They're too useful for me to allow you to go there without me.'

The old woman, listening intently, was thinking as rapidly as she could—and as clearly as her emotions would allow. She realised that Neil had told Andersen every detail of their family life, every detail of the house and which rooms they occupied, of her illness, and all about Aunt Liz in Ireland. It was no use despising the boy for his cowardice, or reproaching him for his stupidity. She knew from the callousness with which he spoke of Miss Rhodes that any appeal to the better feelings of Mike Andersen would be useless.

'We've got to be off in ten minutes . . . *get the clothes* and make your brother-in-law fix the lorry . . . have you got the bloody money you said you'd get?' He stood menacingly over Neil. But Neil, to his grandmother's astonishment, was making some kind of resistance.

'Did you say you *hit* Miss Rhodes?' he demanded.

Yes—but it was only a tap. I tell you she fell backwards.'

'You frightened her.'

'Serve her right. She frightened *me*—coming snooping round like that. Said I'd upset the kid and it was her duty to report me. . . .'

'You did threaten the child . . . *and* she hasn't arrived home,' said Mrs. Collins. 'Charlie was out looking for her—she's been missing all evening.'

'I told the kid off for staring at me—but I never touched her. Honest, I didn't. I haven't seen her since.' Mike Andersen, for all his charm and confidence was looking frightened himself. . . . Was it her imagination or was he looking less alert? Ten minutes . . . surely something must happen in ten minutes. The old woman had no other thought in her mind than that the tablets which this intruder had swallowed, thinking they were aspirins, must shortly take effect . . . she was feeling guilty that she hadn't stopped him. But would he have believed her if she had told him that they were not aspirins? He had swallowed them so quickly that she doubted if she could have stopped him.

'What time is it?' she asked Neil, although she knew.

'Three o'clock. . . .'

'I tell you, Ninny and I have *got* to get away. This business has put the lid on it for us. . . . Where's your brother-in-law, Tarzan? He must fix the lorry. We can't risk the railway.'

'I told you—I'm not coming with you. What you've done has changed everything. . . .'

'Look, you miserable twister. It's my belief that you meant to double-cross me. You've been making plans to get away before I turned up? Haven't you? *Haven't* you?'

Neil, his face grey and sweat on his forehead, stammered, 'Yes, Mike. I changed my mind . . . I don't want you with me . . . let's go our own ways . . . it's safer.'

'Cut it out. Nothing doing. I can't lose my pretty boy, my frightened little nit-wit . . . I'd be bored—bloody bored without you. . . . Hurry up now and find me some clothes. If yours are too small get your brother-in-law's.'

'If you think Charlie will lend you anything of his you're mistaken,' said the old woman, sharply. 'And if you think he'll help you get away after what's happened over there on the bomb-site you're even more mistaken. My grandson's not going anywhere with you. *I forbid it, Neil.* I'd rather give you up to the police and get you taken back than that you should throw in your lot with this worthless creature.'

The two lads began quarrelling and the old woman strove to think what she should do, while keeping an eye on the clock. . . . *Would the tablets work? Would they?* She had a strange feeling that the doctors sometimes put some harmless ones among the real ones . . . they were always afraid of you becoming addicted as they called it. As if it mattered to what an old person like her got addicted. *Supposing they didn't work?* What then? She could detect no signs yet that Andersen was becoming affected by them. She must have imagined it just now. Suppose the effects on a young tough person like him were different? That they had far less effect? It seemed to her that the best thing to do was to summon Charlie and Nona before this Mike had persuaded Neil to fall in with the plan he was now demurring from complying with. That he would succeed in doing so was obvious. When the police had arrived to fetch Neil on both those previous occasions there had been nothing so appalling on his face as the expression on it when he had come through the door and found Mike Andersen in her room. She understood his desperate anxiety to get away before this man arrived. He had intended, as Andersen had said, to double-cross him.

What should she do? How to summon Charlie? The bell had been removed from her reach. *Should she scream?* That surely would be the best. The house was very quiet the only sound the voices of the two arguing at the foot of her bed. Would Charlie and Nonie wake? Nona was a light sleeper, accustomed to listening for the bell. If she were to scream loudly Nonie would hear—*but what would be this creature's reaction to it?* That he would stop at nothing she now knew. His eyes told her that—quite apart from the episode with Miss Rhodes. Always laughing were they? Laughing at what? At the stupidity of those he fooled with his plausibility, laughing at ninnies like Neil who were too scared to resist him. The thought of that poor girl lying over there on the waste ground made her frantic.

The two were still arguing but Neil's protests were becoming weaker. She saw that Andersen had abandoned threats and was now cajoling Neil into agreeing to fall in with his plans. A loathsome kind of bantering cajolery—and she saw those hands on Neil.

Dispassionately she considered what weapons she had. *Nothing*—unless she could get a knife from the kitchen . . . but that was impossible. Although Andersen was intent on his persuasion of Neil they were standing at the foot of her bed between her and the doors to the kitchen and the hall, and those quick-moving eyes of his were constantly on her.

The scissors! The huge strong scissors which she used to cut the thick tough wool for the rugs she made. They were at hand, lying under her pillow where she usually kept them so that she did not lose them. Her fingers curled as she realised that she could lay her hand on them now if she wished. She would scream and if, as he had done before, he tried to smother her cries by clamping his hand over her mouth she would not hesitate to use the scissors.

'Stop arguing,' she said sternly. 'No one is going to stir a finger to help either of you until Miss Rhodes has been attended to.'

'*I've told you,*' said Mike Andersen, fiercely. 'Not until we've got away. After that you can bloody well cover her with cotton wool and lilies if you like.'

'Listen! She was sitting here in this very room this afternoon. Can't you see that whether or not you get away it's bound to come out that you attacked her? She must have seen you ... and that child will have talked. If she told Miss Rhodes that you had frightened her then she'll have told others—as she told me. There's always a witness. ...'

'I knew she was here, I saw her come out, that's why I had to put her out for a while. ...' he said contemptuously. 'And if that bastard Charlie doesn't help me to get away—and quickly, *then I shall swear that Ninny here attacked her.* My word's as good as his.'

Did he mean it? Was he bluffing? If he showed not the slightest anxiety or compunction over what had happened to Miss Rhodes—why should he be bluffing? If he thought her dead, then all that mattered to him was to get away. 'And if Miss Rhodes recovers, Mr. Clever? She must have seen you. *Did she speak to you?*'

His face darkened at the recollection. 'Yes. Interfering busybody. But it was dark—she couldn't have seen me clearly—it could just as well have been Ninny. ... She knew he was here. She told me so. If she was going to give him away he had as good a motive as I had to keep her quiet. ...'

The old woman's hand crept quietly under the pillow and felt the scissors. They were large enough and sharp enough to penetrate anything. Miss Rhodes had given them to her, it would be no more than right that they should be used to avenge her. The trouble was that her wrists and arms were old and weak now. But if she could goad this Mike Andersen sufficiently he might attack her, and then surely fear and the fury of self-preservation would give her the necessary strength for what she had to do. For one thing and one only stuck out in her mind—to get Neil out of this creature's clutches even if it meant sending him back to take his punishment again. She had made a terrible blunder in giving in to Nona. She had been as weak as her grandson and had no right to criticise him.

In the same way as she was accustomed to mustering her strength to resist the onslaughts of the Monster, so now she summoned them to resist this young creature, the spread of whose influence could be compared in her mind to the spread of the Monster in the corruption which followed in his wake. And if she used too much strength? If the scissors should prove fatal? She had plenty of those tablets saved. She would never be a burden on the young people when they were ready to emigrate. She closed her fingers round the scissors firmly keeping her arm still under the bedclothes. She said, loudly:

'If Miss Rhodes is dead, *you* are going to answer for it, Mike Andersen, and I'm warning you now.' Then, gripping the scissors firmly, she screamed as loudly as she was able.

The scream, high and shrill although not strong, shattered the quietness of the brooding tenseness of the house. In a moment Mike had put a hand roughly over her mouth, cursing as he did so, and she lunged upwards at him with the scissors as violently as she could. With his other hand he gripped her wrist as in a vice and began forcing the scissors inwards and backwards until their points were against her own throat. She could not cry out . . . she was almost choking from the vicious clamp of his hand over her nose and mouth. She began feeling herself suffocating as she struggled wildly and valiantly until she could resist his grip on the scissors no longer, and suddenly she felt their sharp points pierce her skin through her thick nightdress and a warm trickle run down her breast. . . . *Well this is it . . . I've been too clever. . . he's turned the tables on me . . .* she thought despairingly, not because she was afraid of death—she was too accustomed to its nearness for that—but because she would have failed to put right the great wrong she had done Neil.

And then she was aware that her grandson had hurled himself on Mike, knocking the scissors from his hand, and that he was hitting savagely at her attacker, forcing him to release his hold on her mouth to protect himself from this unexpected quarter. The two fell to the floor locked in a hold and, summoning her failing breath, she screamed again, twice. The cries were much weaker than the first cry had been. Nevertheless, there were sounds now all over the house and she could not imagine why Nonie did not come.

Neil, in a fury of which she had never suspected him capable, was raining blows on Mike, hitting hard and horribly. She could hear the impact of their respective blows and the quick painful panting breaths from them both as they fought, crashing into the furniture, knocking down things, each hitting the floor only to get up in his turn and begin again.

Was it her imagination or was Neil getting the better of Mike? The boy himself did not know what had come over him. The sight of the blood on his grandmother's nightgown had released something in him. All the insults, miseries, indignities and obscenities he had endured from this youth flooded back to him now and he fought violently and ferociously, rather as a small creature will resist a large one with every weapon at its disposal. Every word of his brother Len teaching him to resist his tormentors both at school and in the *Army* came back to him suddenly. It was as if his brother was in the room at his side, encouraging and counselling him. 'Attack. Attack . . . Neil. Never wait for your adversary. Always try to get the first blow in. Get it in hard and sure . . . *there!* and *there!* and *there! Go on, lad, go on. . . .'* And he heard the voice of the boxing instructor telling him up at the camp that he had all the lightness, quickness, and strength needed for a lightweight fighter if only he could pull himself together and get over his fear of everyone and everything.

Oblivious in his excitement that Mike's blows were becoming less brutal, less direct and deadly in aim, he went on like an automaton hitting out at the face he loathed. He was overwhelmed with hate, not only of Mike, but of himself and everything that had been between them. An urgent violent revulsion demanded the complete obliteration of his enemy, Mike. For *Mike* was the enemy. *Mike.* He had become the enemy which they were always quoting in the Regulations . . . the enemy who had to be killed . . . *to kill the enemy . . . in order to kill the enemy* . . . everything learned in the rifle and sten-gun drill was to achieve one end—the death of the enemy.

Here, at last, was the enemy whose obliteration was vital . . . *kill* . . . *kill* . . . *kill.* . . . Attacking desperately again, he took some appalling punishment; his breath was coming in short agonised gasps, one eye was blinded and blood was pouring from his nose, filling his mouth. Its taste excited him and, unconscious of pain, he saw only the receding and advancing face which mocked and goaded him on. He hit out viciously again, aiming a terrible left at Mike's chin. It was a blow which both Len and the boxing instructor had tried in vain to teach him—he had lacked the guts to deliver it. Now, oblivious that Mike was no longer hitting with any power but was staggering about in a dazed bewildered way he achieved the blow—a hard, horrible crack. Mike began to sag and collapse; and then, as the watching woman screamed again, there came the final crash to the ground. With him fell the pink china swan, so that Linda's carnations were spilled over the fallen body.

And now at last there were sounds across the hall, and Nonie stood there in her dressing-gown. She stared incredulously at the scene; at her twin, leaning panting and gasping over the body of another serviceman, at the turned-over chairs, the broken ornaments, the blood dripping from Neil's nose . . . to her grandmother in the bed. Like Neil, she saw only the bright red stain on her grandmother's nightgown and ran, horrified, to her.

'Only a scratch,' said the old woman fiercely, but the girl saw the dark bruises on her neck and chin and round her mouth and exclaimed at them. . . . 'It's nothing . . . the skin's just pierced, that's all. Get Charlie quickly . . . will you?'

Nonie said, breathlessly, 'He's awake—he's coming. . . . Neil. . . .' she ran to her brother '. . . are you all right? *Are* you?' Then she looked incredulously at the unconscious figure on the floor. 'Mike Andersen?' Her lips formed the name.

He nodded, still gasping.

'You knocked him out? *Really?*' She couldn't believe it.

'Yes,' said her grandmother quietly, looking at the clock. 'He knocked him out—it took a long time—at least it seemed a *long long* time to me—but he did it.' Thirty-five minutes it took! she thought, grimly . . . *but they worked!* I saw their effect . . . I saw his bewildered face when his strength began to fail . . . but Neil shall never know. *Never! . . . never! . . .* It's my private miracle.

In the hall Nonie was screaming to Charlie to hurry. She no longer cared who heard her . . . her brother was repeating incredulously. . . . 'I knocked him out. I knocked him out!' Then he began mopping at his nose at his grandmother's command. 'Are you all right, Gran?' he asked, unsteadily. 'He hasn't really hurt you, has he?'

'Nothing. Just a scratch—but he would have if you hadn't stopped him, boy.'

'If he touches you again, I'll kill him,' he said, savagely. 'He went down like a sack of potatoes . . . to think I was so afraid of him.'

His grandmother thought quietly to herself. . . . He took them himself—snatched them before I could stop him. . . . It was the miracle I prayed for . . . I wonder how long it'll take him to come round?

'Not hurt are you?' she asked Neil.

'No. A bit winded—that's all. My eye's closed up—and my mouth hurts—one tooth seems loose . . . I don't know what came over me, Gran. I wanted to kill him . . . *me . . . wanting to kill.* . . .' He shivered suddenly and went over to look down at Mike. 'Is he all right?' he asked anxiously. 'I don't want him hurt although I hate him. I hate him. . . .'

'Not worth hating,' said the old woman. 'He's a poor misguided creature. There's flaws in everyone—and his got on top of him. Go and wash your face, and pick up that pink swan.'

He was running the cold tap on his head when Charlie burst into the room, sleep still visible on his blank face. . . . 'What's going on? The whole house must be awake. . . .' Then he saw the figure on the floor and Neil come in from the kitchen sink with his hair dripping wet, his eye closing up and his nose still bleeding. 'What the hell? . . . what's going on? . . . Nonie came in screaming that Neil was being killed. . . .'

'Shut the door,' snapped Mrs. Collins. 'I'm in bed—I wish you'd remember that. This room's been like a transit camp all day. We'll have Mrs. Danvers and old Evans down in a moment.'

Charlie bent over Mike with a professional eye. 'Holy smoke! He's out all right.'

'How long will he stay out?' asked Neil, faintly.

'By the look of him, for a very long time,' said Charlie, grimly. 'Perhaps someone will enlighten me. *Who is he?* How'd he get here?'

'Neil's friend, Mike Andersen,' said the old woman. '*He came in my window.* Neil attacked him when he thrust the scissors into me. I had been trying to stick them into him—but the odds were against me. . . .'

'You tried to . . . *what?*' asked Nona, astounded.

'To stick the scissors into that evil young wretch lying there . . . Miss Rhodes gave me those scissors—and he's killed her . . . or so he says.'

'*Killed Miss Rhodes.* . . . Gran, do you know what you're saying?'

'Yes, I do. I'm not under the influence of alcohol or drugs—I never took any last night. He told Neil and me that he'd attacked Miss Rhodes over on the waste ground, and that he thought she had cracked her skull. He brought her handbag here . . . there it is . . . look.'

Nonie looked with fascinated interest at the muddy handbag, then she turned to her twin. 'You knocked him out! Isn't it wonderful! Oh, Neil, I'm so *proud*!' She ran to him and kissed him . . . then said with concern. 'Oh, your poor eye and your nose. . . .'

'Oh, leave the boy alone . . . he's all right,' said Charlie, gruffly. 'This place has become a mad-house. I'm still waiting to know what *he's* doing here.'

'I knew he was coming,' said Neil. 'We planned to escape together. I didn't want to desert—but I was scared of him. He's made my life up there purgatory.'

But why did you come *here*?' demanded Charlie. 'It's the one place they are sure to come looking for you. . . .'

'We planned to meet here. We had to have clothes—my civvies had been confiscated because I'd deserted. We were going on from here together.'

'But why the scrap? What's happened?'

'I discovered that he'd attacked Miss Rhodes . . .' Mrs. Collins answered, 'and he was so callous and indifferent as to whether the poor girl is lying over there injured or dead that I threatened to give him up. He attacked me as soon as I screamed . . . then Neil went for him. . . . See?'The old woman showed Charlie the scratch on her neck, which was bleeding freely.

'I'm going to attend to that. I'll get some warm water. . . .' said Nona. 'Is he all right, Charlie? He won't recover and attack anyone will he?'

'I doubt if he'll be feeling too good when he does come round,' said Charlie, examining Mike again. . . . 'He must have had a terrific knock to go out like this. . . .' He looked in grudging admiration at Neil.

'Charlie, put on some more clothes and go and find Miss Rhodes. She's lying somewhere over there. He said something about her having hit her head on some concrete.'

'That'll be the foundations—looks like an empty swim-ming bath. . . .' said Nona.

'Look, I went over there hunting for that kid early last night. What is this? Hide-and-seek?'

'You do as I ask. *Please*, Charlie. I feel terrible about Miss Rhodes. It seems to me that I've never been nice enough to her.'

Nonie had brought a basin of water and was dabbing with a swab of cotton wool at her grandmother's neck. 'It's a nasty cut . . . the doctor'll have to see it. However are we going to explain it?'

'You don't imagine do you that we can keep this thing hushed up? Miss Rhodes has been injured—perhaps mur-dered. . .'

'But *Neil*!' cried Nonie, 'Neil must get away. He *must*.'

Charlie, now completely dressed, put his head round the door. 'I'm going now. Watch that corpse there, Neil. I can't say I like the idea of going over there. If anyone sees me near they'll imagine that it was I who attacked her.'

'Her attacker's lying unconscious on this floor,' said the old woman, impatiently. 'He confessed to it both to me and Neil.'

'Charlie's right,' said Nonie. 'Let me go. If anyone sees a woman near her they will be less likely to suspect her of an attack than a man.'

'I won't have you wandering about over there,' insisted Charlie, quickly. 'You attend to your grandmother.'

'If you'll keep an eye on Mike I'll go and look for Miss Rhodes,' said Neil.

His grandmother and sister looked at him in astonishment. 'Why not?' he asked. 'I'm still in your clothes, Nonie.' And without further ado he went.

As soon as he had gone, Nonie said. 'Now keep still, Gran, I want to put something on this.'

'Oh, put some disinfectant on it,' said her grandmother, impatiently. 'That's all it needs. The scissors have been cutting wool which is dyed.'

'And what about Neil now?' urged Nonie. 'He's got to get away. He's had nothing whatsoever to do with attacking Miss Rhodes . . . Charlie, you'll stick to your promise and get him away? It's almost four now.'

'And what about *this*?' demanded Charlie.

'Yes,' said Mrs. Collins. 'That's the question. What's to be done with *him*?'

'If he's still out we'll dump him somewhere on the way. I've got no compunction about doing that, after what he's done to you and Miss Rhodes.'

'You'd do that, Charlie? *Would you?*' Nonie was pathetically pleased.

'Yes. We'll dump him somewhere. He can find his own way out of this mess. Whose fault is it but his own?'

'We can't do that without involving Neil. Remember, he threatened to swear that it was Neil who attacked Miss Rhodes.'

'He won't involve Neil unless he's caught. If you dump him near a railway station he'll get away all right . . . he's no fool.'

'Here's Neil back!' cried Nonie, jumping up. . . . 'Well?' she asked tensely as he came in.

'I've searched everywhere. It's quite light now. She isn't there. But she *was*. I know where she was. There's blood on the concrete, and I found this. . . .' He held out a small felt beret.

'That's hers. She was wearing it this afternoon.'

'There's blood on it,' said Nonie in horror. 'That brute leaves blood everywhere.'

'One thing leads to another,' said the old woman. 'He may have told the truth. He said he only hit her lightly and that she overbalanced and hit her head on the concrete. But it won't sound convincing in a Court.'

'What's to be done with him—that's the point,' said Charlie. 'I met Mrs. Danvers coming down the stairs just now. She wanted to know what all the noise was about. I told her that Gran had been having nightmares.'

'And did she swallow that?'

'She looked as if she didn't believe a word of it,' admitted Charlie.

'Neil. *Go and get ready*. Charlie's going to fetch the lorry now, aren't you, Charlie?'

'But, Mike?' Neil was looking again at the youth whom he had knocked out so thoroughly. 'What's to be done with him like this? I hope I haven't hurt him.'

'Serve him right if you have,' said Charlie, callously, 'If you're coming, *get dressed*. I'm not taking you like that. We'll take your friend in the lorry and deposit him somewhere convenient to us—and him.'

Neil hesitated. 'Go on. Hurry up, do,' urged Nona, frantically. 'If he left that place soon after you did, they're bound to be here soon for both of you. Why not just dump him over there on that bombed site he's so fond of?'

'Too risky. You never know with a little runt like that. Might involve you both with the police here if you leave him so near. Me, too, for that matter.'

'We'll be involved anyway by helping Neil get away. You're not going back on that, are you, Charlie?'

'No,' shouted Charlie, violently. 'I'm *not*. I don't go back on people. I wish you'd learn that, Nonie. I'm no saint—but I don't go back on my word. It's not me I'm worrying about—it's you and your grandmother.'

'This has upset everything. I intended to come with you as far as the boat, Neil. I could get Mrs. Danvers to look after you, Gran,' but Neil had gone through to the room behind the bed.

'He doesn't need you,' said her grandmother, quietly. 'This business of having knocked Mike Andersen out is going to make a lot of difference to Neil. He offered to go and look for Miss Rhodes just now—*and he went*. Why, before this he'd never have dared to go over there at this hour and look for an injured or dead woman.'

'I can't think how he ever found the guts to knock Andersen out,' said Charlie.

The old woman smiled to herself. They should never know how it had been accomplished.

'I'm going with Neil—all the same,' said Nonie.

'If you insist on going with your brother, you and I are washed up for good. You're *my wife*. He's chosen a path now which you can't follow. He'll be on the run for years . . . *years* . . . do you realise that? Until he's too old for National Service or it's abolished. A man who can face that can look after himself. I couldn't face it myself. Aren't I right, Gran?'

The old woman looked at the downcast face of her granddaughter. 'Let's see what Neil has to say. . . . Hurry up in there . . . Neil. What on earth are you doing? What's he wearing Nonie?'

'I put out his old clothes for him—they're all in there.'

'Neil? Are you ready?' called Charlie.

There was a silence in the little room behind the bed, and then Neil emerged.

Nonie exclaimed in dismay, staring in disbelief at her twin.

'Neil!' exclaimed his grandmother. 'What are you up to now?'

For he was not dressed in the old tweed jacket and the grey flannel trousers which his sister had put out for him to wear on the journey to Ireland. He was wearing his khaki uniform and he held his cap in his hand. He looked pale and terribly shaken. The events of the last few hours had left their mark on him, in addition to the swollen eye which was rapidly discolouring and the bloody nose. His hair, still wet, was brushed flat and smooth, and his voice as he answered his grandmother was not quite steady—but this time he looked her right in the face.

'It's what you see,' he said, shortly. 'I've decided to go back—that's all.'

'But Charlie's arranged the lorry and everything. Oh Neil, you can't go back to all that . . . to the glass-house—or worse. I *can't* stand it. I *can't.*' Nonie flung her arms round her twin, crying hysterically and unnerving him for a moment. 'It'll be awful. *Awful!* Neil, you *can't.* You *can't.* What does it matter about Miss Rhodes? It's *you* that matters. I can't bear to think of you going back.'

Neil disengaged her arms gently. 'I must,' he said, quietly. But she broke into wild bitter sobs.

'Nonie . . . Nonie . . . *don't, don't.*' Charlie tried awkwardly to comfort her. 'Neil's right. Don't stand in his way.'

But she thrust him away from her and flung herself down on the floor by the bedside and sobbed uncontrollably. Her grandmother stroked her head; then, as she did not stop, she said sharply, 'Control yourself, Nona. You're making a fool of yourself. You should be admiring your brother instead of making such an exhibition. Leave her alone,' she said, fiercely, to Charlie who was trying to lift her from the floor. He desisted, wretchedly looking down at the sobbing girl with a puzzled expression. 'I needn't get the lorry?' he asked Neil, 'You aren't coming?'

'No,' said Neil, his eyes on Nona.

'Hadn't I better dump this former friend of yours somewhere. What are we to do with him?'

'It's no use, Charlie. There's no getting over this business like that. I'm no more use as a deserter than I am as a soldier. *I can't face being on the run.* I'm a coward I suppose. But I knocked Mike out—and I'm going back—there's nothing else to do.'

'No! No!' cried Nona, frantically, '*Don't. Don't.*'

'It's no use taking on like that, Nonie. It's best for us all that I go back.' He picked up his cap again, kissed his grandmother quickly and, hesitating, as Nona cried out protestingly again, he went slowly to the door, 'Could you look after Mike for a bit, Charlie? I'm going to the police station to give myself up. They'll see to everything.'

But Nona screamed frantically at her grandmother, 'You've got your own way! You're making him take Len's place now. Both of them must make up to you for Father . . . you don't care about Neil . . . all you want is to force him to do what you want! Don't go, Neil. Don't go!'

But for the first time in their lives Neil was adamant. Deaf to her pleadings, he turned resolutely to the door, and they watched him in a silence broken only by Nona's sobs. He was not by any standard an impressive figure in the ill-fitting uniform—his shoulders were too narrow, his chest too flat; but somehow, narrow as they were, those shoulders had a new firm lift to them, and when he said good-bye there was a new note in his voice.

The old woman lay silent for a moment. Nona's outburst had shocked her. She watched the girl sobbing, crouched on the floor by the bed, and Charlie's clumsy efforts to console her. Then she said sternly, 'That's enough, Nona. He went himself—of his own free will. No one forced him to go. Go and make some strong black coffee, and Charlie, I want you to try and bring that lad round now. Get some cold water and a towel and slap him briskly. When he begins to stir, try and get some coffee down him. Then you two must walk him about. . . . No, don't argue with me . . . *I know what I'm talking about.*'

Then, as Nona slowly got up to obey her, she held out a hand persuasively to her—but the girl ignored it, and went blindly into the kitchen.

'You've made a lot of trouble for us—and there'll be plenty more to come when the police arrive. As to what you got— you brought it on yourself.' She addressed the still inert figure on the floor.

As both Charlie and Nona bustled about doing as she asked, she turned to the portrait of the Queen. 'He's going back!' she said quietly but triumphantly. . . . 'And I can come and fetch Len's medal.'

She lay back then, utterly exhausted; and wept for her grandsons.

CHAPTER XX

Nona finished sweeping the room and setting it to rights. She fetched a clean bed-jacket for her grandmother. Her eyes were red and swollen and she looked pathetically plain. The old woman looked sideways at her. It would take time and patience to help her over this.

'Has Charlie telephoned the store to say you're not coming back?' she asked.

Nona nodded. Turning her back on her grandmother she surreptitiously wiped her eyes.

'Is it all right now with you and Charlie?' pursued the old woman.

Nona nodded again. 'He's been very decent about Neil— and everything . . . but I can't forget Neil going off like that and coming back with the police. . . .' and she began to cry again . . . 'And that Mike Andersen he was so sullen and beast-ly. . . .'

'The police will look after him. He's got to explain about Miss Rhodes. She's badly hurt; the inspector said that she'll recover all right though, thank heavens. . . .'

'You'd better try and sleep now, you've had a bad night,' said Nona.

'I'm not so sure it was a bad night. I've seldom felt better than I do this morning. I'll have plenty of sleep soon whether I need it or not. . . . Listen, Nonie! There's someone tapping on the window. I shall have to discourage my friends from doing that although it's my only diversion. It's not so pleasant in the night. . . . See who it is. Oh, it's Linda! . . . let her in, will you, Nonie?'

Nona did not seem at all pleased at the sight of the child but her grandmother was delighted to see her favourite.

Nona opened the window unwillingly and the child stuck her bright head in. . . . 'Gran Collins! Gran Collins! can I come in?' She called in the voice of the Three Little Pigs game.

'What d'you want at this time of the morning?' asked Nona, crossly.

'I want to give these to Gran Collins,' said the child importantly. She held out some bright pink daisies. 'I'm on my way to school.'

'You're late, aren't you?' asked Nonie.

'I was late getting to bed—so Mother let me sleep on.'

'Come along in, Linda,' called Mrs. Collins. 'You gave us all a fright last night.'

Nonie helped Linda in at the window and she stood there looking down at the old woman. Nonie's disapproving presence evidently disconcerted her, for she seemed tongue-tied instead of her usual volatile self.

'What's the matter with your neck?' she said looking at the pad of lint showing above the nightgown.

'Scratched, that's all,' said Mrs. Collins, looking with pleasure at the lovely intent little face.

'That Smokey done it?'

'No. Not Smokey.'

'Some strange old cat?'

'Yes. A strange cat, Linda. Where were you last night? Your mother was so worried. Charlie was out looking for you.'

'Miss Rhodes found me. I was locked in the cemetery.'

'Miss Rhodes!' exclaimed both women at once.

'Miss Rhodes—the one that comes to see you. She took me home after she got me out—then she came on to tell you so you shouldn't worry.'

Nonie and her grandmother exchanged looks. They understood now why Miss Rhodes had been in this neighbourhood again last night.

'You told her about the soldier hiding over there?' The child nodded.

'You promised me you wouldn't go in the cemetery again,' said Mrs. Collins, severely.

'I only went to find the key. I lost it there when I was getting the carnations in the afternoon.'

'And you got shut in?'

'Yes. It got awfully dark under those black trees—and so quiet.'

'And you were frightened, darling?'

Linda nodded, and began a long garbled story about Miss Rhodes, a man and a bicycle. . . . 'She's a nice lady, but she looks sad,' she finished. 'Look! I brought you these.' She held out the pink daisies.

The old woman regarded her intently, then looked meaningly from the child to the carnations which had been replaced in the pink swan. Linda shook her head violently. 'No . . . No. . . . Not this time. I told Mother about the policeman and she gave me sixpence to buy you some flowers. But she said not to get white ones, Gran Collins. She said it was a shame to give you what made her think of what you'll be getting soon anyway. I got these from the old barrow man. He smiled today. *He really smiled!*'

'They're lovely, my darling. Thank you *very, very* much,' said Mrs. Collins taking the pink blossoms from her.

'Oh! someone's chipped the swan's beak. Oh, what a shame! Did that strange old cat do that too? Was he after the swan?'

'Yes. I expect so. It got knocked down, Linda.'

'Shall I throw away those old carnations and put these daisies in him? He'll feel better with the pink ones, and they'll hide his broken beak. There! he's much prettier like that! And the white ones are quite, quite dead.'

THE END

The following is a facsimile of the slip included in copies of The
Fledgeling *sent out for review by the publishers in 1958.*

CASSELL AND COMPANY LTD
35 RED LION SQUARE · LONDON WC1

We have pleasure in sending for review a copy of

THE FLEDGLING
by Frances Faviell
15/- net.
8th May, 1958

To be published on

It is particularly requested that no review
appears before that date

A copy of the issue containing the notice
will be much appreciated

AFTERWORD

I THINK I was about 11 when I realised my mother was becoming a writer as well as being a painter. I was home from
my English boarding school for the summer holidays when my
father suggested that I should not disturb my mother in the
mornings as she would be working. ... At the time I was upset
as my mother had never seemed to worry if I disturbed her.

My mother was born and grew up in Plymouth, Devon.
She was the fourth of five surviving children born to Anglo
Scottish parents. Named Olive, she showed her innate independence at an early age by insisting she be called Olivia. She
showed early talent as an artist and in her late teens won a
scholarship to the Slade School of Art, then still under the
direction of Henry Tonks. Her tutor, and later good friend, at
the school was the painter Leon Underwood.

In 1930 she married her first husband, a Hungarian academic, whose work took him to first Holland and then India.
But they separated while there (and later divorced). She then
stayed on for three months in the Ashram of the great Indian thinker and writer Rabindranath Tagore. Travelling on her
own, painting and sketching, she visited other parts of India
including Assam and for a few weeks lived with the Nagas, a
primitive indigenous people in northeast India. On her way
back to England she travelled via Japan and then China – still
painting and sketching – until she had to flee Shanghai when
the Japanese invaded.

On her return to England she lived in Chelsea, then a haven for artists, and earned her living as a portrait painter. She
met my father, who had recently resigned from the Indian
Civil Service, in 1939, and they were married in 1940 after he
had joined the Ministry of Information. Bombed out during
the Blitz, as portrayed in her last book, *A Chelsea Concerto*,
they spent the rest of the war, after I was born, in the Home
Counties before returning to Chelsea in 1945.

When the war ended my father was recruited to the Control Commission of Germany and became a high ranking official in the British administration, first in Berlin, negotiating

with the others of the four powers on the organisation of the city, later in the British zone of West Germany.

We joined him in Berlin in early 1946 and it was here that my mother encountered the Altmann family. It was her experiences with them that inspired her to start writing her first book, *The Dancing Bear*, which movingly describes Berlin in defeat through the eyes of the defeated as well as the victors.

Each of her books, whether non-fiction or fiction, were inspired by an episode in her own life. By 1951 we had moved to Cologne and it was here that her second book, the novel *A House on the Rhine,* was conceived, based around migrant families (from the east of Germany) she had met and helped.

Subsequently, she published another novel, *Thalia,* based on her own experience in France before the War when she was acting as a chaperone to a young teenager for the summer. Her final novel *The Fledgeling*, about a National Service deserter, was also based on an actual incident.

My mother was diagnosed with breast cancer in 1956 though I did not know at the time. At first radiotherapy seemed to have arrested the disease. But then two years later, it reappeared. She fought the disease with courage and humour, exhibiting the same clear sightedness with which she had viewed life around her as a painter and a writer. She died just after *A Chelsea Concerto* was published, in 1959.

In her books as in her life, my mother had an openness to and compassion for others and, when she saw an injustice or need, would not be thwarted by authority of any kind in getting something done. But as she always pursued her causes with charm as well as firmness, few could deny her requests for long.

John Richard Parker, 2016

FURROWED MIDDLEBROW

Printed in Great Britain
by Amazon

38644811R00119